THE REBEL

JENNIFER BERNARD

1

WHEN IT CAME TO BATTLES AND STANDOFFS AND CONFRONTATIONS of all kinds, Kai Rockwell was a pro. Blowouts with his dad happened all the time, but not like this one. He still felt the fury streaking through his system like lightning, practically crackling out of his fingertips.

He was so out of here. *Done. No more.*

Barely seeing what he was doing, he stuffed random items of clothing into his duffel bag. He'd grab the essentials, the cash he'd been saving, his ID, his iPod, and he'd hit the road. In four months he'd be eighteen, a legal adult. Why wait?

He wasn't sure which had come first during their fight—Dad kicking him out or him yelling that he was leaving. Maybe it had all happened in the same moment because on one thing, they completely agreed. Kai and Mad Max Rockwell could no longer live in the same house. No matter how big it was.

He'd be fine on his own. He passed for twenty-one all the time; just ask the bartenders in the towns outside of Rocky Peak. Everyone here knew him as one of the Rockwells of Rocky Peak Lodge, but outside this dot on the map, he rarely even got carded. He'd get a job, maybe travel around. He had friends outside of the

Cascades—guys who came to work at the lodge during ski season. He could couch surf while he figured out what he wanted to do.

This was going to be awesome. No more getting reamed by Dad over every little thing. No more shouting matches freaking out everyone within a half-mile radius.

"Kai? What's going on?"

And...no more brothers and sisters.

His throat closed up tight. He zipped up the duffel and swung around to see all four of his siblings standing in the doorway of his bedroom.

Shit. Fury at his father was one thing. But he and his siblings had stuck together like lost puppies in a storm during the past year and a half. Leaving them—he might as well rip his heart out and feed it to Gracie's pet gerbil.

"Are you going camping?" Gracie, the youngest, stuck her thumb in her mouth, which meant she was stressed. Her other hand tugged at her curls—which she did when she was *really* stressed. For some reason she was wearing swimming goggles propped on her head, even though it was still ski season.

"No, sweetheart. Not this time."

He couldn't quite break it to her that Dad had kicked him out. Or that he'd kicked himself out. Or both.

"You're leaving," said Isabelle accusingly. "Abandoning us."

Trust Izzy to cut right to the heart of things. And to exaggerate. She was both a truth teller and a drama queen, and he could never figure out how she pulled off that combo.

"Lighten up, Izz. It's either me or Dad, and he's kind of got a family to raise here. You don't want me making your salami sandwiches. There was that whole moldy mustard incident, remember?" Using humor to get through crap was a signature Rockwell trait.

But it didn't work on Isabelle. She just folded her arms and glared at him with those emerald eyes of hers. All the Rockwells had some version of green eyes, ranging from hazel-brown to deep smoky heather, in the case of Jake. But Izzy's were the only pure green.

"Come on, I'd be leaving soon anyway, I'm just a little ahead of schedule."

Jake, Isabelle's twin, looked to be fighting back tears. He'd always been the more soft-hearted of the twins. The kind one, while Isabelle was the fierce one. "Come on, Kai. You can work it out, like always. You know how Dad is. He stomps around and swears, kind of like a bull, but it doesn't last."

"If he's the bull, then I'm the black fly on the bull's as—butt."

Kai shifted course just in time. Gracie had a way of picking up on things, like a little satellite dish. Tomorrow she might be prancing around telling everyone about bull's asses.

"I'm done trying to work it out. Last time we tried I thought he'd pop a blood vessel, or my eardrums would burst with all his yelling. Don't you guys want some peace and quiet around here?"

"But why can't you just...*not* fight with him?" Griffin, the next in line after Kai, still wore his outdoor workout gear, black polar fleece with reflective strips. He lived for adrenaline. Nothing else seemed to matter much to him. "Do what I do. Run or ski or do pushups until your arms fall off."

Kai shrugged. "Doesn't work for me. I just get angrier. It's just the way I am."

"Natural-born rebel, that's what Mom always used to say," said Isabelle.

His throat tightened again at the mention of their mother. If he left Rocky Peak, maybe he wouldn't see her everywhere he looked. Maybe he'd no longer think about those last moments with her in the car.

Looking away from his siblings, his glance landed on a framed photo of the five of them posing in front of Rocky Peak Lodge, with the spectacular Cascades outlined behind them.

Every Christmas, Dad brought in a photographer to take a new picture for the next year's brochure.

"You kids are the best advertising I've got," he'd always say. "God, I made some good-looking kids. Smile, baby Rockwells. Smile big."

Kai's smile, in the latest photo, was more of a bloody-murder glare.

He grabbed the photo, frame and all, and stuck it in his messenger bag. His expression would remind him of why he'd left, in case he got homesick.

"Where are you going to go?" asked Griffin, almost casually, as if it didn't matter much to him. Kai didn't buy that for a second. He and Griff were tight, and his leaving was going to hurt Griff the most. If it was the other way around, Kai would feel the same way. But he wouldn't stop him. A guy had to do what a guy had to do.

"Somewhere warm, for now. Those snow shovels can kiss my as—butt."

"What's an as-butt?" asked Gracie through her thumb. "You keep saying as-butt."

Jake snorted and bent down to snuggle with Gracie. He was her favorite. "Don't listen to him. He's clearly lost his mind. Who doesn't love shoveling snow?"

"What about college?" Isabelle asked. "What about taking over the lodge when Dad gets too old?"

"Yeah, that is *never* happening. No way in hell am I ever doing that. This place can die in an avalanche for all I care." His heart twisted at his own words. Leaving Rocky Peak Lodge—creaky, quirky, historic, beloved—was like cutting off a body part. He couldn't feel it, he had to just do it.

"I'll be fine. I don't want you guys to worry."

"And Dad?" Griffin's jaw worked. He and Kai were different in so many ways. Kai was more fiery on the surface, while Griff kept his emotions banked deep inside. "What do we tell him?"

Tell Dad—" He broke off, unable to finish the sentence. He didn't *know* what to say to his father. All he knew was he had to get out. "Tell him I'm sorry, I guess," he finally said.

He was sorry for a lot of things. For the accident. For his out-of-control emotions. For his rebel-ness.

"Yeah, well, he's never going to believe *that*." Isabelle's flat statement broke the tension of the moment, and they all laughed.

Kai looked around at his siblings, memorizing their faces. The Rockwell kids were a pack of goofy, stubborn, fun, crazy survivors. God, he was going to miss them.

Impulsively, he gathered them all into a kind of group hug. Gracie clung to his legs. Isabelle was sniffing back tears. Jake got very quiet and Griffin squeezed Kai's shoulder. For a moment they all stood like that, like pieces of a kaleidoscope about to be scattered into a new pattern.

"We'll be together soon," he assured them—or maybe himself. "And if any of you ever need anything, you know I'll be back in a flash, no matter what Dad says."

"Don't worry about us," Griffin said. He sounded more mature than he had even a minute ago. As if he were already assuming the role of oldest and most responsible.

"And don't you guys worry about me. I saw this coming a long time ago. I got this."

Kai stepped back from the circle of his siblings. Gracie was sniffling, on the verge of bursting into tears. Her goggles had gotten knocked askew by the hug, so he straightened them.

"Come on, don't be sad, guys. We're Rockwells. What do we do when everything sucks?"

"I'm gonna go with *punch someone*," said Isabelle, going for sassy. "Preferably you, Kai, but I guess I'll have to find a replacement."

"Don't look at me," Jake told her. "Remember our twin armistice agreement?"

"Yeah, we might have to renegotiate that one."

"What's renegoshate?" asked Gracie. Griffin grinned and picked her up so she sat in the crook of his arm. Gracie had always been small for her age.

"It means lots of twin arguments," he told her. "You know how long those last. Long enough for the two of us to get an ice cream cone, or five."

Gracie clapped her hands at the mention of her favorite thing in the world.

At the sight of her delighted pixie face, Kai fisted his hands to hold back the pain. Taking Gracie to the lodge's restaurant for a double scoop of Rocky Peak Nugget was *his* favorite thing.

When would he get the chance to do that again?

This would have been so much easier if his siblings hadn't nabbed him before he slipped out of the lodge. Goodbyes *sucked*.

"Gotta hit the road," he told them in a breezy tone. "This family meeting is officially adjourned. And since none of you got the right answer, I'll say it myself. When life sucks, Rockwells laugh their as—" He broke off with a glance at Gracie. "We laugh our as-butts off. Don't forget it."

They all stared at him, reality sinking in. Not a single hint of laughter to be heard.

So he had to dig deep. Slinging the duffel over his shoulder, he duck-walked toward the door. He made it as goofy and ridiculous as possible.

Gracie giggled, then Isabelle. A half smile tugged at Griffin's mouth, while Jake chuckled. Kai ducked around the doorjamb, then poked his head back to make a face at his brothers and sisters. They were all smiling now, and Isabelle broke out in another giggle. She'd get them all laughing soon. Jake would help, because the two of them always backed each other up. Griffin would step into the big brother part, in his own distracted way. And Gracie —*don't think about Gracie. Don't think about how much I'm going to miss my baby sister.*

He'd made his choice, and he wasn't going to change his mind now. He had to leave Rocky Peak. Had to leave the lodge, these mountains, the only home he'd ever known. Most of all, he had to get the hell away from his father before someone got hurt.

He'd just have to paper over the hole he was ripping in his heart. Follow the Rockwell family motto, the one passed down through generations just like the lodge. The one that he and his siblings lived by. Laugh your ass off, so you don't cry.

2

FIFTEEN YEARS LATER

TWO DAYS of trudging across the Chugach backcountry in a downpour had put Kai in a lousy mood. Now, finally, by some miracle, he'd stumbled across the two teenage girls who'd gotten separated from their outdoor education group. The girls he'd been searching for with barely a break.

Chelsea and Heather, both sixteen, city girls on their own in the Alaska wilderness. They were huddled together in the shelter of a fallen spruce, staring at him with big eyes.

"I'm Kai, I'm here to rescue you," he said, absurdly, to his mind. Why else would he have trekked through alders and across glacial creeks? The two girls clung even closer together, as if he was Yeti come to life.

Oh, right. He touched his jaw and the two-day growth of beard there. He probably looked like a crazed mountain man. Even though he was sore and wet and exhausted, he forced a smile onto his face.

"Look, I'm Kai Rockwell, I'm a mountain guide and paramedic working with a local rescue team. Are you Heather and Chelsea? Are either of you injured?"

Finally the girls relaxed their guard. They scrambled to their feet and exchanged a high-five with each other. "A-plus survival skills," said the one who must be Chelsea. who'd been described to Kai as Asian-American.

Kai dug out his handheld radio and spoke into it. "Victims located. Both appear to be in good condition."

The crew leader answered in a crackle of static. "Good work, Rockwell. Can they hike out or should we send the bird?"

He glanced around at the terrain. No obvious place to land a helicopter. "You girls okay to hike a bit?" he asked them.

The other girl, Heather, groaned. "Seriously, we have to walk some *more*?"

"If you complain about your blisters again, I'm going to scream." Chelsea turned to Kai. "Yes, we can hike. Just get us out of this pinecone hellhole."

At least they were acting like normal teens now. No big damage done during two nights in the wilderness. He had to give them credit for that.

"No on the chopper," Kai told the coordinator. "We'll be back to base in an hour, tops." He switched off the radio and spoke to the girls again. "Do you two still have water? Are you hungry?"

"We rationed our water and our trail mix," said Chelsea proudly.

"One M&M an hour is not rationing, it's torture." Heather made a face at her friend.

Fighting a laugh, Kai grabbed their packs and added them to his load, which was already heavy with first aid and rescue gear.

These girls reminded him of the twins. They used to bicker like that. It used to drive him nuts, until Max kicked him out. Then he missed it.

"You both did good. Two days lost in the mountains can be pretty scary."

"Thanks, Hottie Mountain Guide."

He snorted. Apparently they'd gotten used to the beard. He led the way down the path he'd bushwhacked. The girls had managed to go in circles, so they weren't actually very far from base. He could set a nice slow pace and they'd still get back before dark.

His cell phone buzzed, surprising him. Generally he had no service in these mountains, but occasionally a signal slipped through a line of sight in the terrain.

"Wait. You have *cell service*?" Chelsea gasped.

Kai dug out his phone from his pack. The text was from his brother Griffin.

What's going on with Dad? I got a weird call from Jake, something about some chick changing things up at the lodge. Know anything?

He frowned. Did he even care what happened at the lodge? It wasn't part of his life anymore. All his brothers and sisters had scattered in different directions. He hadn't been back to Rocky Peak since the age of seventeen. He texted back. *Nope. I'd be the last to know. What's up?*

"Can we call our parents?" Heather asked.

"Of course. But don't worry, the crew's in touch with them. By now they know you're safe." He handed over his phone. She dialed, but the call didn't go through. Her lip quivered as if she might burst into tears. "Try texting. There may not be enough service for a call."

But before she could tap out a text, the phone buzzed again. She handed it back to him.

This text was from Jake. Jake owned a pub in the town of Rocky Peak, close enough to the lodge to keep an eye on things.

Sounding the alarm here. Dad's acting strange. Not sure what's up. Maybe it's because of his new nurse.

NEW NURSE? He fired back. *Who? Why?*

Heart disease. Nicole Davidson. Didn't you get his email?

Yes, he'd gotten Max's email but he must have minimized the

danger. He hadn't mentioned anything about hiring a nurse. *What does she have to do with the lodge?*

He likes her ideas. Spa treatments, retreats, stuff like that. Talks like he's ready to dump the place on someone else.

Wow. Max Rockwell had devoted his entire life to the lodge. Not once had he mentioned turning it into a spa. And "dump" it? That sounded so unlike him.

What's the nurse like?

Young. Cute. Never comes to my bar because she doesn't drink. Always at the lodge.

"Excuse me, Mr. Hottie Mountain Guide, you said we could use your phone."

He handed it to Chelsea, who tapped out a text message while Heather looked on.

Kai barely paid attention as he processed the news from Jake. Some non-drinking nurse-type was going to waltz into Rocky Peak and take over the lodge? The historic place his great-grandfather had started as a remote ski cabin over a hundred years ago? That Kai's parents had built into a destination for skiers, families, rock-climbers, hunters, anyone who wanted to breathe fresh mountain air?

Hell, it even doubled as a volunteer fire station, with an engine and rescue gear stored on the property. Kai had helped out there as a volunteer fireman and with the ski patrol from the age of fourteen onwards.

And then there was the cozy, lantern-lit restaurant with its legendary venison chili and scoops of Rocky Peak Nugget ice cream. Guests used to drive miles up that winding mountain road just for a glass of wine by the fireplace.

Of course that was in the old days. A lot had changed since Kai had left. He really had no idea how much.

"You're getting another text," Chelsea called to him, rolling her eyes. "From Isabelle. Is that your girlfriend?"

"Sister." He reached for the phone, but the teenager kept her grip on it.

She read the text out loud. "She says, 'Someone has to check on Dad. I nominate you and everyone else seconds that.'"

"That's ridiculous," Kai said, as if his siblings were actually in front of him. "I'm the last person who should check on him."

"Relax, mountain dude. I'm just reading the message." Chelsea squinted at another text message coming in. "Isabelle sounds really worried, though."

"What else did she say?" God, now he was sounding like a middle school kid himself. Also, this was getting ridiculous. "You about done with my phone yet?"

Another text buzzed.

"If we didn't keep getting *interrupted*..." This time Heather read the text out loud. "It's Isabelle again. She says 'why are you ignoring my texts? You can't just bury your head in the sand.' She's right, Hottie Mountain Guide. Burying your head in the sand doesn't work. When my so-called boyfriend was cheating on—"

Kai threw up a hand to stop her. "Don't need to know. Just wrap it up and give me back my phone." He scrubbed a hand through his hair and took a long swallow from his water bottle. Some rescues—many—were literally life and death. This one was more like a wilderness version of *Clueless*. At least his two rescues were in good shape, already back to their sassy teenage selves.

"You got another text from Jake," called Chelsea. "He says to stop ignoring Isabelle's texts. Want me to answer?"

"Please don't—"

"Too late, I told him you don't appreciate his attitude."

Kai called on his 'first responder' voice, the one that issued commands that people generally followed. "Phone, please."

The girl meekly handed over his phone. Another text had just come in. This one came from Gracie, the only sibling who still lived at the lodge.

Is it true you're coming home? Yay!!!! And then a string of happy-looking emojis.

At that point, the two girls needed his attention—all the blisters and bickering were getting to them.

Later, after he'd delivered Chelsea and Heather to their group leader, he changed out of his wet gear, sat in his truck in the trailhead parking lot and blasted the heater. What he wanted most right now was a giant cheeseburger with extra pickles and a beer, a hot shower and a good night's sleep—in whatever order he could get them.

But first he had to find out more about this Max situation.

He initiated a group text with all of his siblings. *Correcting rumors. Not coming back. If Max wants to pass the torch, that's his right. He wouldn't listen to me anyway. He'd probably do the opposite of what I say. He'd probably GIVE the lodge away just to spite me.*

From Gracie: *How can Dad give the lodge away? It's the Rockwell legacy!*

He's supposed to avoid stress, Jake texted. *No more coffee or alcohol.*

Good argument for me to stay away, Kai tapped out. *If I showed up his blood pressure would go crazy.*

Isabelle joined in for the first time. *He'll have to have surgery unless he can change his lifestyle.*

Lifestyle or anger level? Kai texted.

He could imagine each of them, in their various far-flung locations, wincing at that comment.

That's why Nicole is here, Gracie chimed in. *She's helping him work on his stress. He's a lot calmer than he used to be.*

Griffin texted, *I'd go back but I have the Lucas Pro coming up. Biggest race of my career. Then I can take a break.*

Wow. Maybe this really was serious, if Griff was considering a break from racing. He *lived* for motocross.

I have a few weeks left on this contract, but I'm due for a vacation after that.

Isabelle, take a vacation? Kai's worry deepened. Isabelle was a fiercely dedicated workaholic surgeon who worked with Doctors Without Borders. If she was that concerned about Max, there must be good reason.

What if this Nicole chick is a con artist going after the lodge? Maybe that sounded paranoid, but someone had to say it. Gracie was too naive. Jake too kind. Griffin and Isabelle too absent. Kai would have to take on the role of cynic. Hell, he was used to it.

He waited for someone to tell him that was a dick thing to say, but none of them did.

The next text came from Gracie. *That's silly. She's very nice. But you can find out for yourself when you get here! Squeee!!!*

He'd walked right into that one.

He gazed out his windshield—cracked from a rockfall—at the breathtaking view of Turnagain Pass. Snow still glistened in the cornices of the mountains. Alders and spruce blanketed the lower slopes. God, he loved the Chugach.

But not as much as he loved the Cascades.

The summer guiding season in Alaska would be over in a month or so. A ski patrol team in Montana was trying to recruit him for the winter. He hadn't said 'yes' yet, and he wasn't entirely sure why. He loved rescue work, it was incredibly satisfying. Last winter he'd helped save a high school ski group from an avalanche. He'd rescued skiers who'd broken bones, snow-boarders who'd sprained their wrists, multiple concussion victims, kids who'd gotten lost on the cross-country trails.

On the other hand, he was thirty-two now, and he'd spent his entire adult life roaming from one job to another. Short-term leases, short-term jobs, short-term relationships. Since the age of seventeen, he'd known exactly how to kick the dust off. He knew how to track, how to rescue, how to fight.

One thing he *didn't* know was how to go back. How many

times had he thought about it? Wanted to? Longed to breathe Rocky Peak air again?

Maybe this was the perfect opportunity. It would be short-term, of course. A check-in. A drop-in. No strings. No demands. No obligation.

Geez, now it sounded like a credit card application.

If he could handle an eighty mile per hour avalanche, he could handle a visit to Rocky Peak Lodge. To Mad Max Rockwell, who had a *heart condition.*

A stab of real fear shot through him. He imagined his giant volcano of a father grabbing his chest. In pain. He imagined not seeing him again, ever. Fuck. He *had* to go back.

There's a Rocky Peak Nugget double scoop in it for me, right? he texted.

Squeeeeeeeeeeee!!!!!!!!! wrote Gracie.

Double shot at the Last Chance too, texted Jake.

Griffin said simply, *Good.*

And Isabelle added, *Don't forget—no stress for Dad. No fights. No yelling. No arguments. Promise.*

Oh.

Hell.

3

NICOLE FASTENED THE BLOOD PRESSURE CUFF AROUND MAX Rockwell's arm and pumped it until it was tight. As always, he grumbled at her. Max was nothing if not a grumbler.

"All those brilliant doctor minds, they can't invent a way to measure blood pressure that doesn't pinch?"

"Don't you know that everyone in the medical profession is a sadist?" She winked at him. "Especially us home health aides. We live to torment."

In her experience, teasing Max was the best way to stop him from getting riled up.

She watched the gauge. "Looking good. I think the new diet is working."

"Yeah, working to drive me nuts."

"Oh, come on. You loved the vegetarian chili I made last night."

"It was an insult to beans, that chili. If you were just more honest and called it Flavorless Bean Mush, it might not be so bad."

Nicole rolled her eyes as she stowed the blood pressure cuff back in her bag. "Call it whatever you want, I don't care. As long as you try it."

Max rolled down the sleeve of his flannel shirt so she could button the cuff for him. Max was a big bear of a man with a lion's mane of pure white hair. With his wide barrel chest and booming voice, his hulking stature and charismatic presence, he was a dominating figure, even now that he was battling heart disease and arthritis.

At first she'd found him intimidating. But she'd quickly figured out that Max was all bluster and thunderstorms. There was actually a soft heart behind all that grumbling. Well, soft-ish.

"Are you ready for your visualization?" she asked him. It sounded goofy to some, but she liked trying out different methods of stress-relief. As soon as she'd arrived at Rocky Peak Lodge, she'd started fantasizing about things like healing retreats and spa days.

Which totally wasn't her job here.

Either of her jobs.

"If I threaten to rip my eyeballs out, will that get me out of it?"

"You don't need eyeballs for visualization, you big whiner."

He groaned and lumbered to his feet. "Give me a minute. Even torturers need a break." He wandered over to the sky-high picture window that dominated the "great room," as he called it.

Nicole followed his gaze. Admiring the incredible scenery here at Rocky Peak was never a hardship. It was early August, and people were already talking about the change in seasons. She kept looking for signs of autumn, but Max had explained that evergreen forests didn't change much from one season to the next.

As a city girl, this was all news to her. Maybe she was imagining it, but she sensed the approach of fall in the air. The sky was a deeper blue, the night temperatures dipped lower, and visitors wore more bulky sweaters. She couldn't wait for the snow to start falling. She'd never experienced winter in the mountains. Her hope was that the entire lodge would be blanketed with snowdrifts and she'd forget all the worries and stress of her regular life.

She'd never fallen in love with a place as quickly and thoroughly as she had with Rocky Peak Lodge. It was almost a chemical thing. As soon as she'd driven her red Jetta into the wide gravel lot and laid eyes on the main lodge, with its steeply peaked roofs, rough-hewn log construction, and chalet-style trim, she'd exhaled a deep breath, as if something had settled into place inside her.

It wasn't just the crystal fresh air, or the deep peace of the surrounding forests, or the homey atmosphere of the lodge. She felt a sense of possibility here. If she did her job right, she'd walk away from here with enough money to take care of her sister for years.

Not her Max job. Her *other* job.

"All right, Nurse Nicole. What do you have for me today?" Max turned away from the window and settled his big body into his favorite leather armchair. "White light? Ocean waves? Shark attack?"

"Ha ha." She dug out her notebook in which she'd scribbled some ideas for visualizations. "How about a magic carpet?"

"Ooh, that one sounds fun." Gracie Rockwell skipped into the room, and as always, Max's weathered face lit up. She came over to kiss him on the cheek. "I have big news, Daddy. Do you want it now or after the magic carpet ride?"

Gracie was another reason Nicole had fallen in love with Rocky Peak Lodge. Max's daughter was such a sweetheart of a girl. With her wispy light hair and luminous eyes, her perpetual quirky dimple and petite figure, she was the type of adorable that made boys fall in love with her at a glance.

But she seemed mostly oblivious to that. Gracie rarely left the lodge, except to join friends for hikes on the lodge's trails, or see a movie in town. Nicole would have worried about her, except that she always seemed happy as a bluebird. She kept plenty busy at the lodge, mostly with the restaurant. She scooped ice cream, took reservations, handled the website. On her off hours, she read, or filled sketchbook after sketchbook with her drawings. Maybe she had everything she wanted here at the lodge.

"Sorry to interrupt, Nicole," Gracie added, tossing a smile her way. No one could resist that smile, and Nicole didn't even try.

"No worries, we haven't started yet. This is perfect timing. Max, do you want to chat with Gracie first? I can come back later."

He gave her a "stay here" gesture. "Let's hear the big news, but you don't have to leave for that. You know all about my bodily functions. Might as well know the rest."

"I agree, you should stay, Nicole. If Dad has a heart attack, I'll need help."

"Sweet hell on a cracker, Gracie. What's going on here? Are you pregnant?" Max asked.

Gracie flushed a deep rose. "Of course not. How can you say such a thing?"

Nicole knew the answer to that. Because Max had no sense of tact or delicacy. It wouldn't surprise her if Gracie was still a virgin, judging by her shyness about that sort of thing.

"Oh, don't get your panties in a bunch," Max grumbled. "It was just a joke. Why are people so sensitive?"

"For heaven's sake, Max. Just apologize and move on," Nicole told him. "He's sorry, Gracie. It was a rude comment and he knows it. He just can't admit it."

Max muttered something that might have been agreement.

"As a side note, that's the best way to keep your blood pressure down," she added. "Think of an apology as a pill. They're scientifically proven to reduce stress."

"Is that true?" Gracie asked.

"I think so." In her experience, you could dig up a study to prove just about anything. Besides, preventing an argument was definitely good for Max's blood pressure. "Anyway, back to your news, Gracie."

"Right." She drew in a long breath and faced her father. She was wearing a summer outfit of cutoffs and a baby doll top and was barefoot. Gracie only wore shoes when she had to for health department reasons. "This is big, Dad. Brace yourself."

Nicole braced herself too, mentally running through the steps she should take in case of a heart attack.

"Kai is coming home."

Max went still, as if those words had turned him into a statue during freeze tag. He stared at Gracie for a long, long time, while Nicole summoned every bit of knowledge she had about Kai.

It wasn't much. She knew he was the oldest son, that he'd left Rocky Peak as a teenager and never come back. She'd seen him in the old brochure photos. Tall, fit, stormy-eyed. He was the rebel who'd defied his father over everything, big and small. These days, he was a mountain guide, sometimes. Ski patrol, sometimes. He'd spent some time in the Army, even earned a medal. The closest thing he had to a home was a condo in Colorado, but he traveled a lot.

She also knew the story of his name. Kai meant "ocean," which was odd for a family that lived in the mountains. His mother had named him Kai as a link to the Pacific Ocean because she'd grown up on a sailboat. Marrying Max had meant leaving behind the open seas and embracing the mountains.

Gracie didn't say much about her deceased mother. Apparently she'd died when Gracie was small. Nicole didn't like to pry, but she'd seen a few photos of her on the walls of the family wing of the lodge. There were photos of Griffin winning races, a photo of Isabelle graduating from medical school, Jake at the Last Chance.

But not a single photo of Kai, other than in the old brochures.

"When?" Max finally asked. "Why?"

"Dad, don't be rude. He probably wants to see us, that's why. He's coming soon. Today, actually."

"*Today*?"

Max jerked forward.

Nicole put a soothing hand on Max's arm and shot Gracie a scolding look. "A little more notice would probably be helpful."

"Well, I'm sorry, but I didn't want to say anything until I was absolutely sure it was happening. That would be like Christmas getting canceled. But he's really coming!" She gave a little skip of excitement. "Dad, don't worry. Isabelle made him promise not to get into any fights with you."

Max's arm trembled under Nicole's hand. She squeezed it lightly and checked his color. A little heightened, but not too bad. She checked his pulse and found it slightly thready.

He shook her off. "Good God, woman, can't a man find out his prodigal son is coming home without a doctor's exam?"

"I don't know, can he?" she answered tartly. "Are you okay?"

"Yes, I'm O.K." He dragged out the word sarcastically. "But if Kai is coming back for one of those damn apologies, he can turn right around."

"Dad, it's nothing like that. He's not looking for anything, especially not an apology. And you can't get into a fight with him. Nicole, you'll help, right? *No fighting.* Promise?"

"Me? Why would I get into a fight with Kai? I don't even know him."

She fiddled with her friendship bracelet. "Not you. I'm talking about Dad. You're always so calm, I can't even imagine you getting into a fight."

Calm? Try 'careful.' Nicole had to watch every word she said here at the lodge.

Gracie clapped her hands, eyes gleaming. "Actually, that's perfect. Maybe you can stay closer than usual to Dad just in case they start getting on each other's nerves. Dad's always more mellow when you're around."

"*Mellow*?" Max snorted. Nicole could practically see the steam coming out of his nostrils. "If I'm ever 'mellow,' take me out and run me over with a four-wheeler."

Gracie pointedly ignored him and kept her gaze fixed on Nicole.

"I don't know, Gracie..." Nicole's job here was essentially a grownup babysitter. Gracie sometimes called her the "Max-Whisperer," although that seemed overboard to Nicole. "I wouldn't want to intrude on a family reunion."

"Kai won't mind. He's cool, you'll like him. Kai's like...hmmm, what's the best way to describe Kai? He's like...that feeling when a cold front comes through and suddenly the wind is all brisk and blustery and you feel wide awake."

Max snorted again. "Not bad, Gracie. Not bad. Sounds like Kai in a nutshell. He's half tornado, that kid."

"You're saying your brother's like a weather disaster?" Nicole had never heard someone described in quite those terms.

Gracie screwed up her face, searching for the right words. "He's...exciting. Maybe that's a better way to put it. He's kind of wild and adventurous. But not in a scary way, because he's also really knowledgeable about survival skills. If I was lost in the wilderness, he's the one person I'd pick first to be stranded with. He's rescued so many people from avalanches and accidents."

Nicole shuddered at the very thought. She had no intention of getting lost in the wilderness. Admiring it from the safety of the lodge was good enough for her. And Kai Rockwell didn't sound *at all* like the kind of person she'd like. She wanted peace and harmony, not storm fronts. Life held enough turmoil already.

But for Max's sake, she'd do her best to be nice to Kai—and to keep things on an even keel. That was her job here, after all.

Or at least the job Max had hired her for.

He didn't know about her *other* job. She tried not to think about that one, because she was a terrible liar and stood a good chance of giving everything away.

"I look forward to meeting him," she said, faking a smile. Truthfully, she planned to avoid Kai Rockwell as much as possible. Unless she got lost in the wilderness, of course.

4

AFTER GETTING MAX SETTLED INTO THE MEDIA ROOM FOR HIS afternoon nap in front of the TV, Nicole escaped to her own room, which was in the dorm area set aside for seasonal workers. Since these days the lodge was operating with a skeleton staff, mostly comprised of locals, she'd scored her choice of rooms. She'd chosen a cozy room nestled under the steep slant of the peaked roof. Its round window looked out over the wilderness behind the lodge, where hiking and cross-county trails wound through spruce and birch forests. She absolutely loved her little room.

She ought to call Felicity and report in about Kai's impending arrival. That was her mission here, after all. Instead, she called Birdie. Birdie was the reason she'd taken this job and right now she needed to hear her sister's voice.

Birdie picked up on the fifth ring. That meant she was distracted and it would be a short conversation.

"Hi Birdie, it's your favorite sister."

"*Only* sister."

Their standard conversation opener. "How are ya, kid?"

"Bad."

"Oh yeah? What's the matter?"

"Lulu's a thief."

Lulu was her roommate and definitely not a thief. She was paralyzed from the waist down and nearly always in her bed. She hated using wheelchairs, unlike Birdie, who loved hers.

"What did she steal?"

"My name. She told nurse, call me Birdie."

"Oh man. Sorry about that, Birdie. She must really look up to you." She went to the window and gazed out at the front lawn. A strange man stood in the midst of a small knot of staff members gathered around him. He was tall and very fit, though she couldn't get a good look at his face. It must be Kai Rockwell.

"Look up?" asked Birdie.

"Admire."

"Oh. That's nice then."

She couldn't pull her eyes away from the oldest Rockwell son. One of her problems—according to Felicity—was that she didn't get out much. Making sure Birdie had all the care she needed took a lot of work. She didn't have the bandwidth to get involved with men.

The one time she'd taken a chance, it had been a disaster. Roger, her fiancé, had promised that Birdie could live with them, but a month before the wedding he'd changed his mind. The house didn't have wheelchair access, they weren't properly equipped, it would be too expensive, so on and so forth, until he finally ran out of excuses and admitted the truth.

He was embarrassed by Birdie and didn't want a disabled sister-in-law in plain sight.

That was the end of that relationship. Birdie came first.

She dragged her gaze away from the much-too-attractive Kai Rockwell and wandered over to her bed. "I miss you, Birdie. I'm going to try to visit really soon."

"Okay."

Nicole recognized the uplift in her voice and knew she was

grinning like sunshine. The damage to her brain hadn't quenched her spirit.

"Time for basketball! Goodbye."

"Bye!" Birdie had already hung up. Not much for etiquette, her sister.

Nicole yawned, realizing that she was exhausted. She should probably call Felicity next.

Instead she lay back on her bed with a sigh. "Sorry, Felicity. Even spies have to take naps," she murmured as her eyes drifted shut, and her mind wandered back to that fateful day when she'd taken this crazy job.

TWO MONTHS AGO, *in Seattle, at the high school track where Felicity liked to jog before work.*

The list of things Nicole preferred to do instead of jogging was basically endless. It started with bed and ended with "really anything else."

But her quest to lose ten pounds was ongoing, and early mornings were the only free time Felicity had. In two hours, Felicity would be in her office working on million dollar deals, while Nicole would be with Birdie, playing their traditional game of "Go Fish" over breakfast.

Yawning widely, Nicole tied her shoelaces while Felicity jogged in place, checking her morning emails. "I'm so close to making partner, I could cry," her friend said. "One more big deal and I'm in."

She and Felicity had been best friends in high school, but their lives had gone in radically different directions since then. Felicity worked as a hotshot real estate investor and drove a Jaguar convertible. Nicole worked mostly as a home health aide, which came naturally since she'd grown up with a disabled sister. But that didn't pay much, so she usually doubled up on jobs.

"That's cool. I lost my Uber gig." Nicole yanked her last shoelace tight and stood up. "They banned me for life after that run-in with a fire hydrant. I really think that thing was faulty." Her passenger had gotten drenched and six firefighters had shown up to fix the hydrant. Which wasn't all bad...

"You have bad car karma, that's all," said Felicity loyally.

They set off down the track, Nicole straining to keep up with Felicity. "Any other prospects? You can't stay unemployed forever, girl."

"Believe me, I know." Her heart rate was already rising and her words came in a pant. "I had a phone interview...the other day...for a job at a lodge in the mountains."

"A mountain lodge? How romantic! Except for that mountain part. Ew." Felicity wasn't at all out of breath yet.

"Not romantic...seventy-year old man with a heart condition. Room and board included, low pay. Not an option. Besides...it's too far...from Birdie."

A group of football players jogged past them as if they were standing still. Sometimes it seemed that everyone went faster than her, farther than her. All she wanted...never mind. It didn't matter what she *wanted*, all she needed was to take care of Birdie.

"Shootskies," said Felicity. "It would be fun to take the Jag on all those hairpin mountain roads. Where is this lodge?"

A stitch developed in her side and she slowed down, causing Felicity to shoot her an impatient look. "Here in Washington State. In the Cascades."

"Wait a second...what's it called, this lodge?"

Nicole searched her memory. She'd already written off the whole idea, for all the reasons she'd just told Felicity. At first her imagination had been fired by images of mountain peaks and wildflower meadows. Then reality had sunk in. "Rocky Peak Lodge."

"Oh my God." Felicity stopped dead. "*Rocky Peak Lodge?* Are you serious? You'd be working for Mad Max Rockwell?"

Nicole seized on the chance to stop moving. "Max Rockwell, yes. Why is he 'Mad' Max?"

"Because he's got a wild temper. He threatened a realtor with a shotgun once. We've been eyeing that property for two years, but he won't sell. A hundred acres of pristine forests and trails, practically the last substantial chunk of available real estate in that area. Prime investment opportunity. And he's sitting on it like a dragon guarding his hoard. Oooh, my evil genius mastermind brain is having a moment here." She jogged in a little circle around Nicole.

Nicole rested her hands on her knees and heaved in a few breaths. "I looked up the lodge. It's historic but kind of decrepit."

"Exactly. It needs major capital investment, which makes it a perfect target for the Summit Group. Buy it for a song, sell it for a freaking fortune. With all that acreage..." Felicity looked like she might spontaneously orgasm on the spot. She flipped her inky black ponytail over her shoulder. "Here's the plan."

"You have a plan already?" Nicole started jogging again, Felicity keeping pace next to her.

"That's what makes me so good." Felicity gave her a smug smile, legs pumping. "The plan is that you take that job."

"I can't. Birdie."

"I'll watch out for Birdie. I'll visit her twice a week. You know she loves me. And this will *help* Birdie in the long run."

"Keep talking." Anything that would help Birdie was worth considering.

"I...and by I, of course I mean the Summit Group, will double your salary. Whatever Max Rockwell pays you, we'll twice that, on top of what he's paying you."

"For what?"

"Oh, just a little light espionage." Felicity ran ahead of her, then turned and jogged backwards, facing Nicole. "Geez, can't you kick it up a gear?"

"Don't ... have...another...*gear*," Nicole gritted out, lungs heaving. "And I'm not going to spy on a patient. That would be completely unethical."

"No, of course you don't have to spy on *him*. You're not going to do Max Rockwell any harm, in fact you'll be helping him."

"I still have no idea what you're talking about."

"You'll be our eyes and ears on the inside. It'll be like, I don't know, *Ocean's 8*. Except you won't be doing anything wrong, it's not like that. If Mad Max sells us the lodge, he'll make millions. And if you help that sale happen, you'll get a huge bonus. I'll guarantee it. Enough to take care of Birdie for *years*. This is brilliant." She gave an "evil genius" laugh that made Nicole wonder just when her friend had changed into such a shark.

"How long...would I...be there?"

"It's up to you. You can fly back and visit Birdie whenever you want. Think of it as a mountain vacation with lots of benefits."

The football players jogged past again, inspiring a low whistle from Felicity. "Oh! Word of warning, though. Mountain men. I heard they don't even shave up there in the mountains. I recommend temporary celibacy."

Nicole gave up and stopped jogging, planting her hands on her knees and panting through the stitch in her side. "That's so not even on the radar. But Felicity...I can't be a spy! I'd be terrible at it."

"But think about the *bonus*." Felicity drew the word out. "You can also think about my partnership if you want, but mostly...*booonnnusss*. Bonus for Birdie. Nice ring, right?"

Nicole looked away from her friend, at the dreary sky, with the typical spring in Seattle overcast. At certain times in her life, she'd spent more time away from Birdie. When she was taking her nurse aide certification class, for instance, and when she'd nearly married Roger. Her little sister had managed without her during those times. And now Birdie had a roommate at Sunny Grove—a friend, Lulu.

And Sunny Grove was so, *so* expensive. Birdie's disability

payments didn't come close to covering it. It was on Nicole, always had been.

Slowly she nodded. "I'll do it. I've never been a spy before, so that's something new for my resumé."

Felicity laughed, then gave her a quick high-five. "I'm going to do one more lap!" She whisked off down the track. Nicole started after her, then gave up and flopped onto the grass next to the track. She lay back on the ground, lungs still heaving. Mad Max Rockwell. Mountain men. Decrepit lodge. *Espionage.* How the heck did she get into this kind of situation?

Bonus for Birdie. That was how.

BONUS FOR BIRDIE. *Bonus for Birdie.* Nicole came back awake, those same words running through her mind. If she wanted that bonus, she had to get her act together.

Over the past two months, she'd picked up lots of details that she'd reported back to Felicity. The lodge needed major renovations. Roofs leaked, plumbing got stopped up. Max kept scaring away new workers—even the guests sometimes. Also, the lodge was running at a loss.

She'd come to believe that Max's best option was to sell. She'd also come up with about a hundred ideas to improve the lodge. Why not hold special retreats for nature photographers? What about yoga training? People would pay big bucks for a dose of peace and quiet.

At first she'd only shared her ideas with Felicity.

"That's good, that's good, Nico," her friend had said. "You know what? Tell your great ideas to Max. Make him see the possibilities. Make him want the lodge to be amazing again. Make him see that it will take big bucks and lots of energy to make that happen. None of his children are interested, right?"

"I don't think so. Only Gracie still lives here, and she does her own thing most of the time."

"Perfect. Then the only way to revive the lodge is for Rockwell to sell."

Ever since that conversation, Nicole had let her imagination run free and shared every fun idea with Max. And it was working.

But now?

She rolled out of bed and walked to the window again. No sign of Kai anymore. With a sigh, she dialed Felicity and delivered the news that the prodigal oldest Rockwell son had returned.

Felicity peppered her with questions. "Why? For how long? What's his purpose?"

Nicole answered as best she could. "I don't know. Gracie didn't say."

"Do you think he's moving back? That he wants to be involved with the lodge again?"

Nicole shrugged, gazing out at the thickly forested slopes that encircled the lodge. Why wouldn't Kai want that? It was so beautiful here. "I haven't even met him yet. I just saw him out the window."

"Okay, here's what you do, then. Be a spy. Spend time with... what's his name, Kai?"

"Yes, Kai."

"Sounds hot. Is he hot? I mean, for a mountain man?"

Nicole set her teeth, unwilling to say something so positive about the "storm front" arriving at the lodge. "He's attractive enough from a hundred yards away out a window."

"Well, either way, try to find out what he's thinking. Who knows, maybe he can be an ally. If Rockwell sells, they'll all get millions."

"I was thinking that I should take a break and visit Birdie. He might be gone when I get back. I think he's the free-wheeling type, comes and goes."

"Absolutely not. This could be a great opportunity. No time for retreat. You're doing great. Keep it up!"

"I'll think about it."

Nicole ended the call, tension running through her. Spying was stressful enough, but now with Kai around? She sighed. Best to get this over with and go meet the prodigal son.

5

JUST AS KAI FINISHED CHATTING WITH THE STAFFERS HE HADN'T seen in fifteen years, Gracie came flying across the lawn and launched herself into his arms. He staggered a little as she hit him full in the chest.

"I can't believe you're here!!!!" she kept saying. He hadn't seen her since last summer, when he'd flown her to Yellowstone for a camping trip. He made sure to see Gracie at least once a year, and according to Jake, those trips were her only real exposure to the outside world.

With her baby-duckling hair and crooked smile, Gracie was made of pure delight, in his biased big brother opinion.

He couldn't stop grinning at her. "Crazy, huh? I must be nuts. Does Dad know I'm here?"

"He's taking his mandatory afternoon nap right now. *Not* to be disturbed."

"Good. That'll give us a chance to catch up." He ruffled her hair, the blond wisps catching static and clinging to his hand. She swatted him away as they headed for the entrance.

"You're not allowed to mess with the hair of anyone over twenty," she scolded. "But I'll give you a pass just this once."

"Appreciate it. Because I just can't help myself. You'll have to send me to hair dungeon."

She giggled as he pulled open the big oak front door to the lodge. It swung open with a squeak; the ironwork hinges needed some WD-40.

Not that he was going to mention that around his father. Max took all criticism of the lodge as if it was directed at him personally. Or at least he used to. After fifteen years, who knew?

"The place seems so empty," he said as he dropped his bag next to the front door in the reception area. They walked into the lounge, with its high rafters and stonework fireplace. It used to buzz with guests helping themselves to coffee, or snuggling up with a book. Now it practically echoed, it was so deserted.

The parking lot had been the same way, come to think of it.

"Ten percent occupancy, by choice. Dad's trying to avoid stress, remember?"

"Right. But what about the bills?"

"Every time I ask, he says we're fine. Fewer guests means lower costs, I suppose. I can't tell if he's just not worried about it, or if he's too proud to admit he's worried." She flopped onto one of the long comfy couches arranged around the fireplace.

Which was a mess, he noticed. Ashes everywhere, kindling in a disorganized pile. "Who's been taking care of the fires in here?"

"Joint effort. Whoever remembers."

Did anyone remember? It didn't look like it. He grabbed the whisk broom from the stand of fireplace tools and crouched down to sweep up the mess.

Gracie propped a pillow behind her back and snuggled her bare feet into the couch cushions. "Well? Tell me everything! How are all the ladies in your life?"

"My love life is about as cold and dead as this fireplace."

"Really? Things didn't work out with Meg the Leg?"

"Stop it." Meg was a dancer who liked to show off her toned and perfect legs. She'd come to Yellowstone with them and

Gracie kept walking in ballerina posture behind her back. "That's an off-limits topic."

The smell of the old fireplace ash mingled with a hint of smooth tobacco from someone's cigar butt and the cold air from the chimney. Such an achingly familiar scent, and suddenly he was fourteen again, cleaning out the fireplace as instructed by the captain of the volunteer fire brigade. Mom was sitting right where Gracie was now. She kept laughing at the ash drifting into the room, and Kai's efforts to corral it.

"You need a butterfly net," she'd joked.

He shook off the memory as he swept the pile of ash into a dustpan. It looked as if no one had paid any attention to this fireplace recently. Big oversight in a remote place like this. Old Mad Max must be really distracted.

Probably by his new "stress-reducer."

"So fill me in on this nurse chick who's working for Max. What's she like?"

"Are you talking about Nicole? That's not a very nice way to refer to her."

"Three words. Meg the Leg."

Gracie laughed and crossed one leg over the other. "Fine. But Nicole's different. I don't know a lot about her, but she's good for Dad. I call her the Max-Whisperer."

His hackles rose. What exactly was she whispering into Max's ears? "Why don't you know a lot about her? Didn't he vet her before he hired her?"

"He did. His heart doctor put the word out with a network of home health aides. He interviewed several on the phone but Nicole was the only one he could stand. She was also the only one under fifty. So she came up for an interview and hit it off with Dad right away. You know that never happens. Dad doesn't like anyone."

"Jake says she's young and cute. I suppose that's why."

"I think it's that she doesn't take him too seriously. She jokes with him, and he likes that. He doesn't scare her. He's a lot more calm when she's around. She has this way of heading him off before he gets that steam pressure going."

An ashfall of cinder cascaded onto his head, making him cough. He shook it off. "So she knows how to handle Max, which makes her one up on me. But why don't you know much about her?"

"She's mostly with Dad, not me, and she doesn't talk about herself a lot."

"Have you asked?"

"Isn't that why *you're* here, Mr. Suspicious?" She pushed his shoulder with her big toe. "What's the worst case scenario? There's no way Dad will give the lodge away, if that's what you're worried about."

"Worst case scenario...hm...well, she could be a manipulative, secretive, money-grubbing, legacy-stealing gold-digger who found a lonely old man to latch onto."

"Kai," Gracie said in a warning tone. "That's not—"

But Kai was on a roll now. "I mean—the Max-Whisperer, seriously?" He switched to a high, breathy whisper of a voice. 'Oh Max, I'd really love to reduce your stress, whatever it takes. Oh Max, does this outfit make your heart race? Let me just take it off for you. Oh Maxidoodle, this lodge is soooo much work, why don't you let me take it off your hands—"

"Kai!" Gracie yelled.

He startled, bumping his head on the stonework of the fireplace. Pain lanced through his skull, which didn't improve his mood as he rose to his feet, still holding the whisk broom and dustpan.

Scowling, he turned and found himself face to face with a woman. An unfamiliar woman with indignant blue eyes and a heart-shaped face and a goddamn dimple in her cheek. Who looked like she wanted to tear him to shreds. *Shit.*

"I'm guessing you're Nicole Davidson."

Nicole had never experienced quite this level of fury in her life. Not even when her ex-fiancé had double-crossed her. How dare this stranger assume such horrible things about her and Max? It was unfair, outrageous, absurd. He hadn't even met her and he was thinking the worst.

Of course, she was guilty of something else, but not *that*. She wasn't a gold-digger trying to scam an elderly man. She would never hurt Max.

It didn't help that despite the ash in his thick hair and soot smudging his face, this man was outrageously attractive. Even holding a whisk broom, he was pure rugged testosterone. And with those stormy green eyes, he was clearly a Rockwell.

She clenched her trembling hands into fists. Just because he was a jerk didn't mean she had to respond the same way. She could rise above.

"That's right. You must be Kai Rockwell. Welcome back." She even managed a sweet, if sketchy, smile. "That must have hurt when you bumped your head. Would you like me to take a look at it?"

One dark eyebrow lifted. "No, that's okay. I deserved that whack on the head. Just to be clear, I wasn't saying that you *were* those things. I was…aw hell. Can I just rewind and start again?"

She clenched her jaw tight to hold back the hot response she wanted to fling at him. "So you *don't* think I'm a money-grubbing gold-digger?"

"Of course not. How could I, when I don't even know you yet?" He offered her a ridiculously charming smile, then dumped the dustpan full of ashes in a hammered metal box that usually held the kindling—which was now stacked in an orderly pile. "Luckily, that's about to change."

She swallowed back her automatic response, which was something along the lines of "think again, buster."

Gracie was looking from one to the other with alarm. "Let's start over here. Kai, this is the very kind and wonderful Nicole Davidson. Nicole, this is my very loving and protective oldest brother Kai Rockwell."

Protective? That was one word for it.

Kai hung the whisk broom on its hook and wiped his hands on his jeans. He stepped forward to shake Nicole's hand. "It's nice to meet you. I'm sorry for before, I really am. I was way out of line. It's a Rockwell thing, we make bad jokes out of everything."

His hand enveloped hers, rough and warm. She wanted to take a step back, to flee back to her room, but there was no way she was going to let him scare her away. Whenever she felt unnerved, her invisible armor went on lightning-fast, like a superhero's high-tech costume. She stood her ground against his nearly overwhelming charisma. Storm front? She'd probably say "volcano."

"It's nice to meet you too, Kai. Welcome back to Rocky Peak."

Their handshake ended, his hand dropping away. Her palm still tingled and she resisted the impulse to wipe it against her skirt. That would reveal how much he affected her, and she refused to do that.

"Where are you from, Nicole?" His tone was friendly enough, but she could hear the suspicion behind it perfectly well.

"I don't have a permanent address at the moment." Oops, that sounded fishy, even though it was the truth. She'd let her Seattle apartment go when she came to Rocky Peak, to save on expenses. "But I've mostly lived in the Pacific Northwest," she added quickly.

"That covers a lot of territory."

"You want my birth certificate?"

His eyebrows lifted again. "Driver's license would be fine."

"Kai!" Gracie shoved him again. "Why are you being like this?"

"I'm just asking basic 'get to know you' questions." He gave her another of those charming smiles of his. She noticed a dimple forming, then realized it was a scar. "How do you like Rocky Peak so far?"

"It's been wonderful." Carefully chosen words.

He grimaced ruefully. "Until today, is that what I'm picking up?"

"I didn't say that. Every day is beautiful here. The trees, the sky, the mountains." She left out "the people."

A pause while they assessed each other. It felt like that moment in the boxing ring when the combatants circle each other, looking for weaknesses.

Gracie gnawed on her thumbnail.

"It seems wise to know as much as possible about anyone working for Max. Are you married?" Kai asked. "Divorced? Engaged?"

She bristled again. "None of the above. I mean, I was."

"So you're divorced now?"

"No." Why were they even talking about this? He was throwing her off balance. "I was engaged, but that ended. And it has nothing to do with me working here."

"No family then? No one waiting for you back in...?"

"Seattle. No. I mean, yes."

He cocked his head, catching *yet another* suspicious answer. What was wrong with her? If Kai started digging, he might find out too much. And from the look in his eyes, he intended to dig all the way through to China. She should just walk out of here right now and maintain her dignity.

But Kai brought out her stubborn side. She decided to give him a taste of his own medicine. "You must have missed it here all these years. It's been what, fifteen years since you've been back?"

His jaw flexed, and she knew she'd hit a sore spot.

"Roughly. Where did you work before you came here?"

She set her teeth. "I already interviewed for this position."

"Yes, I heard. Sounds like Max picked you out of a crowd of older candidates."

He said it mildly enough, but there was something in his tone that rubbed her wrong. "I'm twenty-eight. That's not exactly young."

"Younger than him."

"It's not about age, it's about experience." That didn't strike the right note, somehow, but it was too late to take it back.

"And here we are, right back where we started. Got that resumé handy?"

Resentment rushed through her again. She'd faced this same kind of attitude during her engagement to Roger, as if she was some kind of fortune-hunter. Which was just weird. If she actually was one, she would have married Roger and his hedge fund and she wouldn't be here today.

She marched toward him until she was only a few inches away. And those few inches were filled with pulsating, sizzling energy. "I'll show you my resume after you show me one solid reason why you haven't been back here in fifteen years."

His eyes narrowed, their color intensifying. "None of your business, and nothing to do with this."

"Why not? You claim you're looking out for Max. Then where have you been? Maybe I ought to be giving *you* the third degree!"

A muscle tensed in his jaw. She'd landed a clear shot. *Yes!* Victory!

Then she remembered that antagonizing Max's oldest son probably wasn't the smartest move to make. Like stirring a hornet's nest. Or poking a bear. Or one of those other wildlife things she'd read about but never experienced.

He stepped closer, eyes narrowing.

"You know something, Nurse Nicole? On the way here, I kept telling myself to keep an open mind about you. Maybe she's good for him, I thought. Maybe she's exactly what he needs. Give her a chance, I thought. Well, that ship has sailed."

"Oh, now there's a cliche that has me shaking in my shoes," she snapped back. All her usual restraints had disappeared into vapor. Now it was no holds barred.

"You're critiquing my word choice? *With another cliche?*"

She stared at him blankly.

"'Shaking in your shoes' *is* kind of a cliche," Gracie interjected. She was hovering near them, watching like a guest at a tennis match. Nicole had literally forgotten that she was in the room.

"Oh my God, I'm losing my mind here." She clutched at her head, which had started to pound. "We're arguing about cliches? Freaking *cliches?*"

The almost-F bomb? Seriously? Appalled at herself, she clapped her hand over her mouth.Where had that come from? She didn't use that kind of language, at least not here, in the serene setting of Rocky Peak Lodge.

"Don't hold back," Kai said. His eyes blazed. "Not on my account. I'm guessing you never swear around Max. You're a perfect angel around him, a sweet hovering angel whispering words of healing and calm—"

"Shut *up!*" she snapped. God, he was maddening. He was lucky she was hanging onto her control by a thread, lucky she didn't kick him in the—

"Nicole? *Kai?*"

She whirled toward the sound of Max's rumbling voice. Sure enough, her patient was standing a few feet away, mouth ajar in an expression of pure shock.

"Max. I...uh...was just getting introduced to Kai."

"Yeah, I heard. All the way in the family wing. Bet they can hear it in the souvenir shop. Pretty sure a flock of waxwings just fled in terror."

She pressed her hands to her burning cheeks. "I'm so sorry. I...he..." She couldn't blame this on Kai. That would be immature. "I don't know what got into me. I apologize."

"No need." Max's whiskered mouth quirked up. "Reminds me of old times. Welcome back, Kai."

Nicole was so mortified that she could barely look at Kai. But when she did, his shamefaced expression made her feel marginally better. He'd lost his cool too. After fifteen years away, this probably wasn't the first impression he wanted his father to get.

He scrubbed a hand through his hair and squared his broad shoulders. Why did he have to be so mouthwatering? "Max, Nicole, I apologize to you both. This is all my fault. Max, don't blame her for this. You know me, I can rub people wrong without even trying."

She blinked at Kai in surprise. Nice of him to say so, but unexpected.

"You *should* apologize, Kai," Gracie burst out. "You promised you wouldn't fight. Dad's not supposed to have any stress at all. You can't come here and make things worse."

"I know. And I'm sorry." Kai hauled in a long breath. "I did make that promise, though technically I meant that I wouldn't fight with Max."

Max let out one of his booming laughs. "Is that right?"

"Yes. I didn't come here to fight. And that includes with you, Nurse Nicole." Kai turned back to face her, and sketched a funny little bow. "I hope you can forgive me. I promise to behave better from now on."

She had to behave better from now on too, or she was going to blow this whole opportunity. "I'm sorry we got off on the wrong foot. Maybe we can start over. Not right this second," she added quickly. "You and your father probably have a lot to talk about now."

"I'd appreciate the chance," he said, almost formally. A short silence fell, during which she wondered how quickly she could make her escape. From under his bushy eyebrows, Max was looking at Kai with a kind of hooded eagerness.

What must it be like to see your son for the first time as an adult? Especially when he'd grown up to be such a magnificent specimen of a man? Was Max noticing his strength, his hard muscles, his lean and striking face, the air of power and charisma that clung to him? Was he seeing someone who made him proud? Or someone who'd been gone too long?

"Why are you covered in soot, kid?" Max asked Kai gruffly. "Did you come in through the chimney, like a thief in the night?"

Gracie drew in a quick gasp. For a moment, tension reigned in the nearly empty lounge. Then Kai threw his head back and let out a howl of laughter.

"It's good to be back," he said. He strode toward his father and the two of them embraced, almost as if they'd surprised themselves by the gesture. Gracie clapped her hands together with a delighted hop.

Nicole seized the opportunity and slipped from the room.

Breathe in, breathe out. Inhale, exhale. This was a total disaster. She'd pissed off Kai, she'd embarrassed herself in front of Max and Gracie. She had to fix this or she was going to ruin everything.

6

K<small>AI</small> GRABBED ONE OF THE FOUR-WHEELERS AND TOOK M<small>AX</small> FOR A ride out on the trails. The lodge offered access to a network of trails through the backcountry surrounding Rocky Peak. Most were cross-country trails, but a few offered some decent downhill runs in the winter. For the hardcore skiing, guests drove a few miles to Majestic Lodge, which had ski lifts going up Majestic Mountain and a famous black diamond trail.

Like everything else here at the lodge, the trails were no longer up to their former level of maintenance. Kai had to keep steering around overhanging branches so his father didn't get sideswiped. He'd have to come out here with a machete and a chainsaw and do some clearing.

It would release some tension too. The encounter with Nicole had left him all riled up and restless. He hadn't intended to antagonize her right off the bat.

"Not to be critical, but these trails could use some work," he said lightly as he navigated around a tree root.

"Have at it." Max gestured at the expanse of forest surrounding them. He wore a battered leather cowboy hat with a feather in the band and chewed on a long stalk of grass as they rode. "No one does trail work as good as you. I'll even pay you."

The compliment was so unexpected, Kai almost said yes. "That's all right, I have a job. But I'm happy to lend a hand. Volunteer only."

"Jake says you've been working in Alaska."

"Yeah, but that ended. I guess it's more accurate to say that I'm between jobs. But I *will* have a job. There's a crew in Montana that needs a supervisor. Good guys, I've worked there before. I told them I'd let them know soon."

Max grunted. "Pretty country, Montana."

Kai filled in the rest of that thought. *Not as pretty as Rocky Peak.* No place compared to Rocky Peak, in Max's eyes.

He wasn't wrong, either. The majestic wooded hills and valleys, with their sudden waterfalls and hidden cliff faces, made Kai's heart sing. Not even Alaska could compare—not to a Rockwell, anyway. This place was woven into his blood and bones. Being back here was already having a powerful effect on him. Not just the lodge itself, and the wilderness around it, but seeing the staff again. He'd known Loner Douglas, the gardener and Renata Drake, the cook, his whole life.

"I shouldn't have stayed away so long," he said, more to himself than anything else. "I don't know how it happened. Time just goes, you know?"

"I do know." Those heartfelt words, in his dad's gruff voice, felt like an arrow straight to the heart. "Gotta wonder what took you so long, and what's different now."

Now *that* was another kind of arrow—more like a poison dart. His entire body tensed and a knot formed in his gut. "Maybe we shouldn't rehash all that yet. I made a promise, did you catch that? No battles."

Max rumbled with laughter. Kai had to admit that he seemed a lot more mellow now. Maybe Nicole did deserve some credit.

He couldn't shake the memory of that indignant look in her

eyes when she'd caught him mocking the "Max-Whisperer." He was such a jackass. Maybe he'd spent too much time in the backcountry to behave right.

"No battles," Max agreed. "Doctor said no stress, but that's a helluva prescription for a guy like me. I tried ramping down. Skeleton staff, minimal bookings. I don't want to burden Gracie with too much. If she had to run this place, she'd never leave. She'd be buried here forever."

Kai ducked to avoid a sweeping spruce branch. "We agree there. I've tried to get her out to see other places in the world."

"And I'm glad for it. I worry about her."

Max had definitely mellowed; he'd never spoken this honestly with Kai before. Either that, or he was really worried about the future. "There's something else, Kai. A while ago some real estate type came sniffing around and I scared him off. But now I'm thinking different. Something's gotta change or the lodge won't survive."

"Real estate type?" Kai's stomach roiled, and not just from the bouncy ride of the four-wheeler. Was Max thinking about *selling*?

"Worth thinking about, no?"

No. Or was it? Kai took a turn onto one of his favorite trails, the one that looped through a meadow that filled with lupines in the spring.

"Look, Max. I know I don't have the right to get in the middle of this. It's your decision to make. I just want to make sure you know what you're doing."

Max bristled at his phrasing.

"Scratch that," Kai said quickly. "I just want to make sure you've done your due diligence. This lodge has been in our family since great-grandad."

"It's your legacy. I'm aware." Max shot him an ironic sidelong glance. "Didn't think you were. You want to come back and run things? Is that it?"

"No," Kai said quickly. "No, I'm just watching out for you."

They'd reached a juncture between two trails, one that headed uphill onto a ridge, the other back toward the lodge. A glance at his father told him that he'd probably had enough jostling. Carefully, he maneuvered the four-wheeler so it pointed back toward Rocky Peak.

Max spat out the blade of grass he'd been chewing. "Ever since Nicole showed up, all full of ideas, I've been thinking maybe the lodge is due for a change."

"But you barely know her."

"Not the point. She's got good ideas. Fresh-air camps for city kids in the summer, foreign exchange student interns, weddings in the spring. She made me see all the possibilities. She's good people, Kai. Good energy. You should give her a chance."

His hands tightened on the steering wheel. A chance to what? Tell him all the ways she wanted to overhaul his childhood home? And where would the money for all that come from?

Don't fight with Max.

"Sure," he managed. "Sounds good. I'd like to get to know her." A plan of attack occurred to him. "How about if I stay for a month. I'll get to know Nicole, listen to her ideas, and we'll leave things status quo for now. No big decisions about anything for the next month."

"Deal," said Max, so promptly that Kai wondered if he'd played right into his father's hands. "We'll give it one month."

The four-wheeler rattled down the trail, bouncing over roots and rocks. As he navigated obstacles, Kai had a quick memory flash of Griffin, who'd first driven a four-wheeler at the age of five. Then he'd moved onto dirt bikes at the age of ten. A speed demon on a mission from day one. Instead of lashing out at their dad, Griffin had kept his head down and lost himself in the joy of going fast.

Speaking of which ...

"One month without fighting," Kai said. "Think we can do it?"

Max grunted and grabbed onto his leather cowboy hat as they

hit another bump. "I doubt we can last a day. But that's okay. No one has to know." He grinned over at Kai, who laughed and held out his hand for a high-five.

How come he never used to *laugh* with Max, instead of fighting?

As they left the forest into the cleared expanse of lawn that surrounded the lodge, they caught a glimpse of a small figure jogging out from the entrance of the ridge trail. A woman in leggings and sports bra, her hair held back in a ponytail.

Nicole. Looking sexier than Kai was comfortable with. She was still the enemy, after all, or at least a *potential* enemy.

Their paths converged near the barn where the four-wheelers and other vehicles were housed. Nicole waved at them, slowing to a light cool-down jog. Her skin glowed with perspiration and a touch of pink from the sun.

Kai slowed the four-wheeler as they approached her. She bent over, hands on knees, panting to catch her breath. "Good run?"

"No, I hate jogging, it was torture," she managed, with a rueful grimace. "The only good part was the scenery."

"I know what you mean."

Realizing that his comment could be taken wrong—as if she was the scenery—he added quickly, "I used to cross-train on those trails. Running in the summer, skiing in the winter."

"There's a box of trophies somewhere," Max rumbled.

Kai gave him a sideways look—when he left, those trophies had been proudly displayed on the shelf where Mom had put them. "Did you mothball my trophies?"

"Sorry," Max muttered. "I was ticked off."

Kai shook his head and turned back to Nicole. "Well, Nurse Nicole, I'd offer you a ride to the front door, but you'd have to sit on Max's lap, and—" Oh hell, that sounded bad too. As if he was making the same kind of insinuation as before. "I mean, there's no room."

Her lips twitched as if she was trying to hold back the laughter. And why was he looking at her lips, exactly? Face it, he liked this version of Nurse Nicole. Sweaty and relaxed, not righteously angry at him.

"Did you guys have a nice ride?" she asked them.

"Nope," said Max. "With this guy at the wheel, every joint in my body got shook up. Might have dislodged a vertebra or two. Or maybe that shrapnel's finally working its way out. Who taught you to drive, son?"

"You don't have shrapnel." Kai shook his head at his dad, who'd been telling that tall tale all his life. "He got in the path of an exploding car once. Not exactly a war zone injury."

"A wound's a wound. Don't fact-check your father," Max grumbled.

Kai gritted his teeth and reminded himself of his promise.

"Kai and I came to an understanding about the future of the lodge," Max told Nicole.

"About that—" Nicole said. Still breathing fast, she put her hands on her hips, which drew his gaze to the waist, and the tempting curve of her damp flesh there.

He pulled his attention away. Attraction was not on the agenda. Not one little bit.

"I was giving it a lot of thought during my run," she continued. "I know what a big deal it is to have your son home again, Max. I'd never want to make any kind of trouble with a family reunion like that. I think I should leave, at least for a little while. I can train Gracie how to take your blood—"

"No," Kai cut her off. "There's no need for that."

If she left, he wouldn't be able to properly check up on her. Also, Max definitely was mellower than in the past, and if she had anything to do with that, she needed to stay.

"You're taking good care of Max and that's the most important thing. Just because we got off on the wrong foot doesn't mean we have to stay that way. We're adults. We can work around it."

"The wrong foot?" She tucked a damp strand of hair behind her ear. "Is that another of those cliches you like throwing around?"

He laughed, finding her funny this time instead of irritating. Maybe the sports bra had something to do with that. Those things were hazardous to a man's health. "I'm going to stay for one month. That's it. I'm going to work on trail clearing, chimney cleaning, maintenance, whatever else needs doing."

"Nurse monitoring?" she said wryly.

"Future discussing," he corrected. "No monitoring. I promise not to interfere with your work. Max needs you. Think you can handle a month with me around?"

She gazed at him thoughtfully with those clear blue eyes. He remembered the offended expression they'd held in the lounge, when he'd been such a jackass.

"In case it needs to be said again, I'm sorry about the way I behaved earlier."

She waved him off. "No no, please don't apologize any more. That's over and done with. I said some things I regret too. I'm here to reduce Max's stress, not the opposite. I take that very seriously, I hope you both know that. I promise to behave like a proper adult for the next month." She tossed them both a vague, embarrassed smile, then shivered, rubbing her bare arms. "I'd better go take a shower before I turn into a sweat-sicle."

She set off at a slow jog toward the lodge entrance.

Kai touched the accelerator and the four-wheeler rumbled toward the barn. In a month, he could find out everything he needed to know about Nicole Davidson.

Also, maybe it was the rebel in him, but he intended to take that "behave like a proper adult" thing as a personal challenge.

7

ONE MONTH.

It didn't sound like a long time, but it was all relative. A month with a selfish jerk like Roger could last forever. Whereas a month of summer vacation in high school could go in a flash. Where would a month with Kai wind up in the spectrum?

Not *with* Kai, Nicole reminded herself. They'd simply be inhabiting the same lodge—which was enormous.

Felicity wanted her to play spy, but first she needed to do some reconnaissance—away from the disturbingly attractive oldest Rockwell son.

Luckily, Kai plunged right into trail clearing, which kept him out in the woods. Each morning, he headed out early with a chainsaw and a four-wheeler and didn't come back until dinnertime. For a few days, Nicole barely saw him.

The cook's assistant had recently quit, so Nicole jumped at the chance to help Renata in the restaurant kitchen. She loved the old family-style restaurant, even though now it only served lodge guests, of whom there were very few. Nicole could easily imagine the old days when every table was filled with diners ravenous from their day's adventures. That little piano in the corner must have played so many dance tunes. How many couples had gotten engaged in the soft glow of the gas lanterns?

Renata, the gray-haired chainsmoker from the Bronx who'd been cooking for the lodge for thirty years, loved to chat. A session of chopping venison and vegetables for chili was the perfect opportunity to find out more about Max's rebellious oldest son.

Renata didn't disappoint.

"Kai was in the car with Amanda when she died, you know. He got airlifted out and had emergency surgery on his spleen. They said he was screaming the whole time, out of his mind to get to his mother. Had to sedate him."

"That's terrible." From what she'd seen of Kai's intensity, she could easily imagine a scene like that. Poor guy.

"Kai was always a force of nature, just like Amanda. She was a real free spirit, wonderful photographer. He's the one most like her, if you ask me. Max went into a black funk after she died. He's better now, but damn, it took some time."

Nicole dumped a bowlful of green pepper chunks in the soup pot. "And, um, Kai?"

"A mess. Started getting into trouble everywhere he went. And the battles he had with Max, hoo-boy." She whistled. "A year and a half later he left. It's good to see him back, I'll say that. No one appreciated my chili like Kai. He could eat five servings and ask for more. He's a good kid. Lotta heart."

"Is that what it takes to get on your good side, Renata?" Nicole teased her. "Eat up all your food?"

"Yes, and you've been slacking." Renata shoved a cloverleaf roll her way. "Eat that. Plenty of butter."

"I'm not exactly underweight," Nicole pointed out. Hence all the jogging, which still wasn't really working. She took the roll anyway, since she was never one to say no to carbs.

"This is the mountains, and it's almost fall. You need a good fat layer."

Nicole nibbled on the roll, torn between sadness and bliss. The bliss was because Renata's homemade rolls tasted so incredibly good. The sadness came from the fact that if she did her job, she wouldn't be here for the fall. Back home, fat layers were more problematic.

"Why hasn't he come back before now?" Nicole asked through her mouthful of buttery roll. She set herself to her next task, peeling carrots.

"Stubborn," Renata said. "Pig-headed. Obstinate."

"Sounds like a peach."

"I always told Max to lighten up on him. He was so hard on Kai after the accident. No one could understand why. I sure wasn't surprised when Kai left." She sighed as she grabbed the cleaver and set a big cutting board on the counter to cut up slabs of venison. "I wish you could have seen this place when Amanda ran it. It was alive, you know? It had life. It had people. It had *fun*."

Nicole nodded, long strips of carrot furling off her peeler. Renata was a goldmine of information, but she wished they could get back to talking about Kai.

"Amanda put on dances and brought in musicians to play at the restaurant. We had a May Day dance one year. There was always a huge party on New Year's Eve, with all the town invited. She really knew how to make sure people had fun." Renata stuck an unlit cigarette in her mouth, which was her way of preparing for a smoke.

"She sounds like an amazing woman."

"Like I said, she was a free spirit. After she died, I thought we'd shut down for sure, the way Max acted. Like he wanted to die along with her. But then he threw himself into keeping the lodge going. It was like an escape for him. Ignored his kids in the process, but at least he kept a roof over their heads. You can add those carrots now. Be right back." She whisked herself out back for a smoke.

From her apron pocket, Nicole's phone buzzed.

Damn it. Felicity was calling.

She dumped the carrots in the big cast iron stewpot and turned the burner to low. The kitchen was huge and old-fashioned, with deep enamel sinks and a big six-burner Wolf cast iron stove that must weigh half a ton.

A screen door led to a kitchen garden out back. Renata grew green beans and herbs and a mesclun mix for side salads out there. Peering out, Nicole saw that she was busy talking to the kid who came up to mow every week, gesturing with her cigarette.

She extracted the phone.

"Nicole, where've you been?"

"Where do you think? I haven't left this place in weeks." Irritated, Nicole took the cutting board to the sink to rinse it off.

"I get nervous when I don't hear anything from you." Felicity's tone relaxed. "Spying is dangerous work. Also, my bosses are getting antsy."

"Sorry. Nothing new to report, really. What's up?"

"We have a problem. There's interest from a potential buyer. He and his fifth wife are looking for a property to turn into a high-end spa, but his wife's a vegan. I was flipping through all the photos you've sent me, and half of them have dead animals in them."

Nicole's gaze flew to the big chili pot filled with chopped venison. "What are you talking about?"

"Those freaky-ass deer heads. Who wants to come to a spa where Rudolf the Reindeer's beheaded ghost is staring you down? Vegan Trophy Wife might have a panic attack if she saw that."

Nicole had gotten used to the stuffed and mounted deer heads displayed in the lounge, but she could see why a vegan might not be crazy about them. "Tell her it's called ambiance. Those deer are long dead. She doesn't have to eat them."

"No. Ambiance is jasmine room fragrance, not the remains of

a butchered animal. They have to go. I need some pictures without deer heads. Can you do it?"

Nicole checked again on Renata. The cook was now kneeling next to the bed of oregano, weeding. Past her, the craggy cliffs of Wolf Peak reflected tangerine light from the afternoon sun. The sheer beauty took Nicole's breath away.

"I don't know, Felicity. It's the decor they chose. I can't just change it for no reason."

"Then find a reason. Or do it quickly, take the shot, and put them back up. One photo, that's all I need."

"Are you adding onto my bonus for this?"

"Sure. Mark it down. Birdie will thank you."

"I wish you wouldn't do that." A movement from outside caught her attention. Renata was coming back in. "I have to go. But don't talk about Birdie like that, it makes me feel emotionally manipulated."

"That's because you are, Nico." She blew a kiss over the phone. "Just kidding. Talk later."

8

NICOLE DECIDED HER BEST WINDOW OF OPPORTUNITY WAS AT NIGHT, after everyone had gone to bed. She set up a ladder next to a perfectly preserved, bright-eyed red-tailed deer head. Blocking out the creature, she focused on the polished plaque on which it was mounted. Six screws fastened it to the wall. She gripped her screw gun and got to work.

"Sorry," she murmured to the head as she brushed against it. "You're actually quite beautiful, and I hope you had a wonderful life dashing through the snow and the forests. But I'm afraid I have to put you away for a while."

The first screw came out easily.

"I hope you're not too heavy. How much does a deer head weigh, anyway? Maybe I should have googled it before I climbed up here." She shifted to the other side of the head for the next screw. Best to keep it even. "I promise this won't hurt a bit," she joked as she inserted the bit into the groove on the screw.

"Owww!" said a loud voice as the screw came loose. She jumped, causing the ladder to wobble, only realizing in the next second that the voice didn't come from the deer—obviously. It came from below.

From Kai, who stood at the foot of the ladder, gazing up at her. He wore his outdoor work clothes, Carhartt pants and a dark green hoodie sweatshirt. With his wind-reddened skin and dark scruff, he looked so sexy she felt a jolt of heat.

"Jeez, you scared me." She put her hand to her heart, which was racing. "That wasn't funny at all. I could have fallen off this ladder."

"Nah. I'm right here, I would have caught you. What are you doing up there? Straightening Benji?"

"Benji?"

"My mom nicknamed him. She gave them all names based on their personalities."

Nicole squinted at the deer head. "That actually suits him."

"Right? So what exactly are you doing? Dusting? Need a hand?"

"I could probably use some help, thanks." She puffed out a breath of relief. This was definitely a two-person job. "I'm taking Benji down."

"*What?*"

Luckily, she'd worked out a perfect excuse for removing the deer heads. "I need to check for mold. One of the guests mentioned that the lounge made her wheeze. It's a public safety issue, so as a nurse aide, I feel obligated to check it out."

"That's ridiculous. Benji's been up there since I was six. He isn't starting to mold. Leave him be."

Trust Kai to make trouble. Nicole set her jaw. "Things change."

"Not Benji. He's not changing anymore, he's dead." Kai glared at her, hands on his hips.

Turning back to her task, she pressed the bit to the next screw and pulled the trigger. The high whine of the power tool drowned out Kai's next words.

The screw came out and bounced off the ladder. Kai picked it up.

With another burst of drill noise, she extracted screw number four. "You know, the whole dead animal decor is from another era. Don't you think it's time to try a more modern look? Stripes might be nice, in cocoa and sage."

His eyes narrowed. "You mean brown and green? We already have a lot of that. Have you looked outside?"

She moved to the next screw, ignoring that clueless comment.

He talked over the sound of the screw gun this time. "Everything's supposed to be on hold for a month. We agreed."

Obstinate. Stubborn. Pig-headed. Check check check. "Would you relax? I'm *just checking for mold.*"

"No, you're not. And there is no mold. Guaranteed."

"You don't know that." Flustered, she let her grip on the screw gun slip.

"Yes I do, because—"

The screw gun started to fall. She lunged after it, hitting the deer head with her elbow. The remaining two screws gave up the effort of holding it in place and Benji went crashing down, nearly sideswiping her on the way. She held tight to the ladder and the screw gun and squeezed her eyes shut, waiting for a crash, a boom, a shatter...what kind of sound would a stuffed head make, anyway? Could it survive a fall to the floor?

Had she killed a dead deer?

But the only sound was a grunt from Kai as he stepped forward and caught Benji in his arms. One of the antlers scraped against Kai's cheek, leaving a red mark.

"Are you okay?" she cried, clambering down the ladder, screw gun in hand.

"Are you asking me or Benji?" Kai asked with a snort.

"You, of course." She reached the floor and peered at the mark on his cheek. "It looks like the skin isn't broken, that's good." Then she examined Benji. "He looks fine too. Nice rescue."

Kai looked at his armload of deer head and smirked. "Right

place, right time. Except from his perspective. I'm twenty years too late if you ask him."

She laughed, starting with a giggle then giving in to a full-blown belly laugh. It took her over entirely, her body shaking with tremors of amusement and relief. "I thought I killed him," she gasped. "I mean, for the second time."

Kai was laughing too as he set the mounted head against the wall. He folded his arms over his chest and propped his hip against the reception desk, waiting out her laughing fit. "You're a stubborn woman, did anyone ever tell you that?"

"I prefer persistent." With the heel of her hand, she wiped tears of laughter off her cheeks.

"You were planning on taking all these guys down with nothing but a ladder and a screw gun? It's a good thing I came along. That sounds like a disaster waiting to happen."

"You're saying you'll help me?"

"I'm saying I'm going to talk you out of it." His green eyes gleamed at her.

"That's not likely." She examined the five remaining deer. Was it her imagination or did they looked unified in disapproval of her? She had to get them down. She had to get the shot Felicity wanted.

"I disagree. You want to know something about these deer? Want to know why I'm completely sure they're not moldy?" He picked Benji up by one antler.

"Why?"

"They're all plastic."

She stared at the head swinging from his looped finger. "No way."

"Yup. My mom didn't want real deer heads in the lounge. They made her cry. So she bought these instead. This is the wilderness out here. That's what people are used to."

"These are plastic deer? Like the kind on people's lawns during Christmas?"

"Yes, but much better replicas. Look closer. Touch them."

She'd avoided it before, but now she did. Yup—plastic. No doubt about it. "Plastic doesn't mold, does it?"

"Not as far as I know."

Crap. How was she going to get that photo?

She eyed Kai, who was staring at Benji with an odd look on his face, almost sad. Nostalgic.

Kai had an emotional connection to this place that went back to birth, she realized. Even down to the deer heads decorating the lounge. Every detail meant something to him. Which meant that one way or another, she was going to have to deal with Kai. She couldn't avoid him any more.

At first she'd though Felicity's idea of making Kai an ally was ridiculous, but maybe she was right. Maybe she could get Kai on her side. Wasn't that the Jedi way? Use an obstacle to make progress? Kai loved the lodge, but he didn't want to live here. If she could make him see the benefits of getting Max to sell...if he could see all the things the lodge *could be*...

"Listen, Kai. I have an idea. What if you give me a day?"

He frowned. "Give you a day? What do you mean?"

"Max may not have told you this, but the lodge is losing money. I know, because my paychecks are often late. That's why I started thinking of ways to shake things up."

He set down the plastic head and folded his arms across his chest. "Maybe Max just forgets to pay you."

"It's not just me. Renata's pay is late too. And I've seen bill reminders come in the mail. I asked Max about it and he admitted it's been tough."

A muscle clenched in Kai's jaw. "He didn't tell me."

"He's probably embarrassed. Or maybe he's just waiting for the right moment." She drew the conversation back to her plan. "Look, I really think that we can be on the same side here. The side of 'making the lodge amazing.' I propose that we call a truce and spend a day together. Or maybe just a morning, if things go off the rails." An entire day with Kai might really throw her off balance. "I'll explain my ideas. All you have to do is keep an open mind."

"I can do that. I have a very open mind."

"Good. Then we're on?"

One side of his mouth lifted in a devastating smile. "An entire day with Nurse Nicole? Can't pass up an offer like that."

A thrill went through her, from the top of her head to the tips of her fingers. Kai was like a shot of adrenaline packed into the hard-muscled body of a man. Was spending the day with him like throwing herself into a volcano? Sticking her finger into a light socket? Tossing a grenade into her own peace and quiet?

Didn't matter. If it helped her get that bonus, she'd take the risk.

~

THE NEXT MORNING, with the sun still flirting with the treetops, Kai met Nicole in the lounge for breakfast. He poured himself a thermos of coffee from the urn, and offered her some as well.

"No thanks, I have my own tea."

"And right away we hit a snag," he murmured as he screwed on the cap. "This is coffee territory. Steaming hot and black as tar, that's how the Rockwells roll."

"That's how the Rockwells *have* rolled," she corrected. "I'm here to open your mind. Would you like a sip of my tea? It has turmeric in it. Anti-inflammatory in case you have any muscle aches from all that hard work."

"Pass. I like to work up to healthy over the course of the morning. If I start out that way, it's a shock to my system."

She smiled at that, and took a sip from her tea.

He filled a bag with muffins from the breakfast buffet Renata set out every morning. "I've been wondering where you learned to use a screw gun."

"My father was a carpenter. He taught me a few things before...well, before he left."

Somehow, Nicole Davidson kept surprising him. "I pegged you for more of a...white collar girl."

"Not me. Blue collar family, at least while it lasted. But you've probably already discovered that." She offered him a teasing smile. She wore a fitted down vest over a cable-knit sweater, along with blue jeans and boots. Her eyes, that striking clear blue, held a hint of wariness. As if she still wasn't sure about him.

"Yes," he admitted readily. "I did a little investigating. You can't blame me for that."

"I didn't say I blamed you. I've been checking up on you too."

"That's not difficult. Just check the police blotter," he joked. "Or ask any random passerby. Nothing but trouble from an early age."

"Yes, I definitely picked up on that. Did you really skateboard down the mountain road?"

"Good times. Until I hit a bump and went flying into the underbrush." He touched the scar near his mouth, remembering the shock of that crash. "I was one of those kids who had to learn things the hard way."

"Well, that's why I think you'll like this great idea I had." Her face lit up, all pretty heart-shaped curves.

"About learning things the hard way? Definitely my area of expertise."

She smiled and took another sip from her thermos. "About bringing at-risk kids here to earn survival skills, like chopping wood, starting fires, basic field triage. Do you know that kids in some neighborhoods are teaching themselves how to treat gunshot wounds? They get called to the scene of shootings before the paramedics get there. Why not bring them here and train them properly?"

He blinked at her sudden passion. This was a side of Nurse Nicole he hadn't seen yet. "That would require funding."

She waved a hand. "Grants. Private donations. Rich people. We can make it happen. With the right investment, all kinds of things are possible."

Investment...the word rang an alarm bell. When people invested, they wanted a say in things. What exactly did she have in mind?

"Max said you've been talking about a healing retreat, whatever that is."

"Right! That's another of my absolute best ideas." She took him by the elbow. "Come on, let's go outside. We can get the whole picture there."

He discovered he liked her touch on his arm. More than he should.

With their thermoses in hand, they walked outside into the morning air, clear and crisp as cellophane.

"The retreats would be geared toward high-end customers who need a break from their stressful lives. Believe me, they'll pay anything to pamper themselves. The money would be *flowing* in."

His gut tightened at the mention of money. Was it really true that the lodge was in trouble? He hadn't seen Max yet this morning. But after his conversation with Nicole last night, he'd scanned through his own bank accounts and found some investments he could sell off if Max needed them. But would Max accept help from his banished son? Especially when he wouldn't even admit he was in trouble?

Nicole swept her arm at the wide lawn they were crossing. "We could hold *tai chi* classes on this big lawn here."

He laughed, imagining Max's reaction to something so different from the games of tag and snowball fights that usually took place on that lawn.

Nicole shot him an irritated glance. "Have you ever tried *tai chi*? It might really help with your stress level."

"I have my stress handled, thanks."

"Really? What's your favorite stress management technique?"

He gave her a smoldering look guaranteed to get under her skin. "I'm not sure we know each other well enough yet."

Even though her cheeks flushed, she lifted her chin and didn't back down. From what he knew of Nicole so far, that spunkiness was one of her most appealing qualities. She was no pushover; no wonder she handled Max so well. "Whatever it is, it's not working. You freaked out over a deer head. A plastic one."

"Hey, I take offense at that. You could at least call him by his name. Poor Benji."

She burst out laughing, a sound of such delight that a chill went up his spine. He shook it off.

"But for your information, I have no problem with *tai chi*. I like it. I think this is a perfect spot for it, at least in the summer. In the winter, we could make space in the great room."

He squinted at the lodge, finding it easy to picture a group of slow-moving *tai chi* practitioners going through their moves. When he turned her way, he caught her looking at him in surprise.

"I assumed you wouldn't be interested in that sort of thing."

"What sort of thing?"

"*Tai chi*, yoga, stuff that doesn't involve skis or a four-wheeler or a hunting rifle."

He gave her a mock-scolding shake of his head. "Haven't you heard my reputation for being a rebel?" He bent over her, bringing his face within inches of hers. "I decide for myself if I like something or not. I don't let other people tell me."

This close, he caught a whiff of her scent, nothing but fresh skin and clean lavender soap. Her pupils expanded, pools of black against clear blue. A pulse point beat in her throat. He felt as if he were looking through a macro camera lens in which he could see everything with perfect clarity.

His gaze dropped to her lips. Their shape was full and curved, tempting as a juicy summer peach. Those lips said something about her, that she wasn't always guarded and watchful. She had another side, a side filled with laughter and joy.

And why was he looking at her lips again?

She pressed them together, as if she was trying to keep him from seeing something. Maybe something he'd already seen, or maybe not.

He realized he was being rude, looking at her so closely. Forcing his gaze away, he uncapped his thermos for a long swallow of coffee. He didn't want to blow this opportunity to learn more about Nicole, or scare her off any more than he already had.

Capping his thermos, he took on a more businesslike tone. "Very interesting ideas so far. I like it. What else do you want to show me? Or is it my turn to show you a few things?"

"Your turn," she said, wetting her lips. Had she noticed the hum of electricity between them too? With any other woman, he might have cupped her face in his hand, brushed his lips across hers, slid his thumb across the tender skin of her cheek.

Bad idea. This unwelcome attraction was the last thing he needed. He was going to ignore it until it went away.

"I used to be the best tour guide at this place," he said. "It was my job to show the guests around. I know all the best views. I know where a secret hidden patch of wild strawberries is. We could bring a BB gun with us, shoot some plastic squirrels."

He winked at her to chase away the residual sexual tension that still hung between them.

She laughed. "You really know how to push my buttons, don't you?"

He smiled, a little strained, because the phrase made him think of other, more inappropriate buttons. "If you ask Max, that's my specialty. Don't worry, it's too early to make trouble. I'm all about peace and happiness this morning. Just follow me."

～

NICOLE HAD TO FACE FACTS—WHEN Kai turned on the charm, he was a lot of fun to be with. The rest of their day together passed without any more conflicts or awkward moments. He guided her all over the property, showing off his favorite trails and secret spots. A meadow dotted with scarlet wildflowers. An overlook with a stunning view of the ski lifts going up Eagle Mountain. The sweetest wild strawberries she'd ever tasted.

When he wasn't interrogating her, Kai was so easy to talk to, as if he was genuinely interested in hearing her ideas and thoughts.

And very, very easy on the eyes, even though she worked hard to block that out.

She told him about the special ed camp, the artists' retreat, the meditation sessions she imagined. He listened with interest, even threw in some ideas of his own. Corporate retreats. Trust-building exercises in the woods.

Then, remembering that she was supposed to talk about expensive ideas, she threw out her idea of expanding the lodge's tiny sauna into a full-service spa with private steam rooms and massage therapists, maybe a Turkish bath.

"You're talking major renovations," he said, finally balking.

"Yes, but think of how many wealthy people would come. Once they're here, they'll spend more money on things like branded Rocky Peak room fragrance and exclusive Rocky Peak bathrobes. It's a huge investment, but sometimes you have to spend money to make money."

"I'll keep that in mind. My very, extremely, entirely open mind...that never thought I'd see the day a spa came to Rocky Peak," he ended in a mutter.

She grinned. "Save the freakout for tomorrow. You promised."

"I did. Carry on. What's next, aromatherapy?"

"Now that you mention it..."

It was almost shocking how much she enjoyed his company. Now that he'd dropped his automatic suspicion of her, his attitude was completely different. He thoughtfully held branches away from her face as they walked. He listened carefully to what she said, and asked questions that proved he was paying attention.

Don't let a sexy man distract you, she kept telling herself. *Just because he's hot and smart and interesting doesn't mean he's on your side.*

They stopped for a quick picnic lunch near a waterfall on the property, one of her favorite spots. "It's probably out of the question, but I'd love to put a gazebo out here," she told him. "A meditation gazebo, a no-talking zone where you have to maintain silence."

"Is that some kind of hint?" he joked as he pulled sandwiches from the rucksack he'd brought. "You can meditate, I'll stick with my salami on rye. Besides, I have more questions for you. There's so much we haven't covered. Like what's better, mayo or mustard? Rye or sourdough? Chips or pickle?"

So much for silence—they talked all through lunch about everything from favorite books and movies to random pet peeves —they both hated goofy cell phone ringtones. She told him a few crazy stories about life with Birdie and he talked about his childhood running wild at the lodge with Griffin, the twins and little Gracie.

And then, when she was at her most relaxed, he snuck in a question that took her completely off guard.

"So this engagement you mentioned, the one that ended. I've been wondering. What'd the guy do wrong?"

She nearly choked on her last bite of roast beef sandwich. "Why do you assume it was his fault?"

"Well, wasn't it?"

"Yes, of course, but—" They both laughed, but that didn't distract him. He kept his gaze fixed on her, waiting for her answer. His expression was friendly, his smile warm. She *wanted* to share something with him, something real and personal. And that was...possibly dangerous.

She tucked her hands in the pockets of her down vest, digging her fingernails into her palms to remind herself not to reveal too much. "We disagreed about where to live," she finally said.

"That's it? Sounds like a real love match."

"Do those even exist anymore?"

"You have a point there." He gave her a wry smile. "Just look at us Rockwells. Not a single one of the next generation has gotten married and spawned."

"You're still young."

"I'm thirty-two. Seems like I would have felt the urge before now if it was going to happen."

"Maybe. Not necessarily. I wasn't thinking about marriage when I met Roger." She pressed her lips together as soon as the name slipped out. She hadn't intended to reveal that much, but she really wasn't very good at keeping secrets.

Maybe it didn't matter. This was just a friendly conversation, no need to be so paranoid.

He didn't seem to notice. "So what changed your mind about the M word?"

"I was getting my home health aide certification. It was taking me a while to finish because I had other commitments." Commitments named Birdie. "I met Roger when I fell asleep studying at a coffee shop near his office. Someone tried to steal my wallet while I slept and he stopped them, then woke me up. He was very sweet and worried about me. He asked for my number so he could check up on me. And that was it. I guess it felt nice to be the damsel in distress."

"I take it back. That is a very romantic story."

Of course, she'd left out a few details. Roger had told his driver to take her home, but she didn't have a home at that point. All her money went to pay for Birdie's housing and care. She'd missed too many rent payments and gotten evicted, so she was temporarily crashing with a friend until she found another place. Roger had offered her the guesthouse on his Queen Anne property. Then he'd shown up one night at her door, with a bag of Chinese food, and things had proceeded from there.

None of which she was going to tell Kai.

"Personally, I like your parents' version of romance better," she told him. "Married for decades, five kids, creating this amazing place to share with the world..." She swept her hand in a circle to indicate the lodge, the view, the wilderness. At the end of her motion, her hand brushed against his side. Even through his thick wool sweater, she felt the hard contours of his muscles.

She snatched her hand away.

"Sorry," she murmured. "Didn't mean to attack you with my high opinion of your parents."

"Hey, I appreciate it." Reaching out, he captured her hand and interlaced his fingers with hers for a brief moment, then released them. "But not everything is how it seems."

His cryptic comment barely registered as a swarm of butter-flies invaded her stomach. It was such a simple gesture, that short hand-hold, but it sent a spear of pure desire through her.

She cast around for a distraction. "Has Max ever dated anyone since then?"

"You're asking the wrong guy." Kai shot her an ironic look. "I haven't been here, as you pointed out to me."

Cheeks heating, she laughed. "Sorry about that. I swear I'm usually only confrontational when..." when she had to be, for Birdie's sake, "on special occasions," she finished.

"I'll consider it a badge of honor, then." He popped a wild strawberry in his mouth and lay back, hands cupped behind his head. His eyes closed as he savored the berry. She noticed the molding of his cheekbones, the scar near his mouth, the dark grain of scruff covering his stubborn chin. He was one intensely attractive man.

She asked the question that had been nagging at her ever

since he came back. "Why *did* you stay away for so long, Kai? I know Max can be a handful, but this place...it's so beautiful." She looked out at the wisps of mist still lurking in the deepest part of the valley, the thick stands of evergreen, the smooth slopes of the ridge. As always, it took her breath away.

Her question seemed to catch him off guard. He sat up, frowning at the view and propped himself on his elbows. "I had reasons."

Reasons he didn't want to talk about, obviously. Fine—it wasn't really her business.

Except that maybe it was. Felicity would say that it was. She'd say, 'learn whatever you can. Maybe it will come in handy.' *Be a spy.*

"Did you miss it here when you were gone?"

His jaw flexed. "Yeah," he said curtly, then fell silent.

He'd probably decided not to trust her, which was smart. If he had any clue about her secret mission here, he'd never trust her again.

But then he continued. "I left because Max and I had a bad fight. That happened all the time—basically I went through every day looking for a fight back then. At school, at home, wherever I could find it. But this one was different."

"What was it about?" she asked softly.

He was silent for a long time, his jaw working. "It had to do with my mom and the accident."

She held herself very still, torn between wanting to know more and hoping he'd keep his secrets to himself so she wouldn't have to report anything to Felicity.

"Anyway, that's all in the past. Max and I get along just fine now. Probably because we keep it simple. We avoid all topics that might get us fired up." He gave her that devastating one-sided smile, the one that always snuck behind her defenses.

And right into her heart, if she didn't watch out.

"Well, I'm glad. He's been great to me, very kind and welcoming. And I can tell he's happy you're back, even though he never says things like that straight out. You have to read between the grumbles."

He lifted one eyebrow at her. "Is this your Max-Whispering skill in action?"

Something about his tone of voice rubbed her wrong. "I never said I was the Max-Whisperer. That came from Gracie. I'm just a nurse aide doing her job."

He gave a short nod. She got the impression that he wanted to say more, but was holding himself back. "Doing it well, too."

And for the first time that day, an awkward silence fell between them.

Finally, with a powerful movement, he got to his feet. "Should we head back? It's getting close to dinnertime. You probably want to walk me through all the ways you want to change the menu. And just so you know, right from the start, the venison chili is going nowhere. I *will* put my foot down if you try to put tofu in it instead."

So they were back to joking around. *Good.* "Don't think in terms of *replacing*," she said lightly. "Think in terms of *adding*. Would it kill you guys to have fish on the menu, for instance?"

He hoisted his rucksack onto his back. "Around here all we catch is the occasional trout. But you're welcome to try."

"Hey, I only suggested fish because you were about to throw a tantrum over tofu. But we can stick with the tofu if you insist."

"Sneaky, lady. I'll see your tofu chili and raise you a wild turkey burger. Now that I can probably live with."

"Wild turkeys? Is there a BB gun involved?"

"You know absolutely nothing about guns, do you?"

She followed him up the footpath to the trail. "Kinda hoping to keep it that way."

They spent the rest of the hike back to the lodge bantering over menu items.

When she climbed into bed that night, she was wildly torn in two very different directions. One direction led right toward Kai, who was possibly the most attractive man she'd ever known— and not just physically. She sensed a lot of layers behind those storm-green eyes. She wanted to know more about him, every part of him, inside and out.

But that would require *him* knowing more about her. And she couldn't risk that.

There wasn't really a choice. If she had to choose between the lure of a sexy man and her responsibility to Birdie, Birdie would always come first.

9

AFTER DINNER THAT NIGHT, KAI FELT SO RESTLESS THAT HE HOPPED in his truck and drove into the town of Rocky Peak. With a population of only ten thousand or so, it offered little beyond the basics. Three grocery stores, a gas station, a post office, a bus stop, a combined police and fire department, a ski shop, a used bookstore, two churches, four restaurants, and three bars.

One of which belonged to his brother Jake.

Jake had bought the Last Chance Pub from an old-timer who'd nearly run it into the ground. But Jake insisted it had "good bones," and now that he'd spent so much time and money fixing it up, Kai had to agree.

It had the feel of an old London tavern, with a polished mahogany bar and candle sconces providing low, elegant light. Of the three bars in Rocky Peak, The Last Chance was the one you'd consider bringing a woman you were trying to impress.

But not Nicole, because apparently she didn't drink. Kai had forgotten to ask her why. So many questions still burned in his mind after their "one day." He wanted to know more about her broken engagement, more about those 'other commitments' that slowed her down while she was getting her certification. More about the way her hair smelled, more about what made her smile.

Face it, that one day with Nicole made him want another one. And then mostly likely another one.

He sat at the bar, nursing a ten-year old Laphroaig left from the original owner's stock, until Jake finally had a break between customers. His brother came over to him, wiping his hands on a bar towel, a warm smile in his gray-green eyes. His hair was long; its thick waves brushed his jawline. Kai noticed the appreciative female glances that followed his brother across the bar.

"The place looks great, Jake," Kai told him. "Sorry it took me so long to get down here."

"No worries. It wouldn't exist without you, so I'm just happy you're here."

Kai had provided some of the startup funds when Max had balked at the idea of financing a bar. Jake had paid him back within three years, but he still planned to claim the investors-drink-free card.

"So how's it going up there? You and Max blow the roof off the lodge yet?"

"Nothing but peace and quiet." Kai touched his whisky glass to Jake's tankard of foaming ale. "Here's hoping it lasts."

They both took a sip. "And Nicole? What's your take on her, now that you've spent some time around her?"

Kai shook his head, waiting for the smooth burn of the whiskey to subside. "Not sure yet. Sometimes she seems like a compassionate person who wants to do some good in the world. Her ideas for the lodge aren't *bad*, per se. Most of them," he amended, thinking of her crazy spa plan.

"That's what I thought, the two times I met her. My impression was "kind and hot." He grinned. "You didn't mention the "hot," so I guess she's not your type."

"I wouldn't say that."

Jake lifted his eyebrows.

"Because I don't have a type," Kai finished. "Types are too limiting. I like to keep an open mind."

Jake laughed and they clicked glasses again. "So what aren't you sure about? Any danger signs you've noticed?"

"Not exactly. I've noticed that when she talks about herself, she's very vague. She only gives the minimum amount of information, the least she can get away with. No specifics. If she slips up and reveals something, she panics. She hides it well, but I can tell."

Jake threw his head back and laughed, drawing more glances from the women in the bar. "You've been paying close attention, my brother. Told you she was hot."

Kai snorted as he took another sip. "That's what I'm here for, remember? I wouldn't be doing my job if I didn't notice these little details."

"Sure," Jake agreed readily. "Details matter. Like you can never really trust someone with brown eyes, so that right there—"

"Her eyes are blue. Sort of a light blue verging on turquoise color. But definitely not brown."

Jake was laughing so hard he had to rest his hands on his knees. "Glad you're on the case, bro. You're busting this thing wide open."

"Shut the fuck up."

Jake's phone rang. *Saved by the ringtone.* "Izzy," he said right away. "Guess who's sitting at my bar talking about blue eyes?"

Kai could hear her shriek all the way on his side of the bar. Jake listened to her, nodding and smiling, then handed the phone over to Kai. "She wants to say 'hi.' Among many other things."

"Hey, Iz." Kai greeted her as soon as the phone made its way to his ear. "Your twin is looking good. Just ask the unusually plentiful women at this bar."

"Oh, I know, it's ridiculous. Don't they know he's a big goober who drools when he sleeps?"

"I'll make sure to spread the word."

"I can't believe you're there and I'm not around to witness it! Did you make up with Dad?" He heard the nervousness behind her question.

"Why does everyone think I'm going to revert to my teenage rebel self as soon as I'm in the same room as Max? I'm a grown man now. He's not on my ass all the time about stupid shit. We're good now."

"That's so great, Kai. You know he was really sad after you left. Jake wouldn't let us tell you because he said it would be a guilt trip. But he was."

Kai fiddled with his bar napkin. The topic of his departure made him uncomfortable for many reasons. "It probably sucked having his best worker leave."

"*Best?* I used to chop more wood in an hour than you did in three. I could have been a pro. And just think, now I do surgery. Funny when you think about it."

"The world's first chainsaw surgeon," he teased. "Hopefully the only one."

"God, I still can't believe you're back in Rocky Peak and I'm in the freaking Sudan. I've never been so homesick! Normally I'm too busy to miss home, but just thinking of you there, with Jake and Gracie and Dad, I'm so jealous. Are you guys going to watch Griffin's race?"

Kai glanced at Jake, who pointed to the television discreetly mounted in the corner. "Yeah, Jake's going to show it at the bar. On this tiny-ass TV he has. Will you be back by then?"

"No, not yet. I have a few more weeks here. But I'm dying to get home and see everyone!"

Kai smiled, warmth expanding inside his chest. He hadn't really expected his return to inspire this much joy in his siblings. He'd been in constant touch with them all—well, mostly—and had seen them often over the years. He loved to show up out of the blue and take them out for some random fun thing like whitewater rafting or a flight seeing trip. He'd celebrated Izzy's med school graduation with a surprise trip to the Caribbean.

So it wasn't as if he'd been a stranger all these years. What difference did it make that he was back in Rocky Peak? Was it because of Max? Because their estrangement had been hard on his siblings?

That thought gave him a hard pang. He couldn't change the past, but he could be different going forward. Or he could try, anyway.

After he hung up with Izzy, he waited for Jake to finish a round of refills at the bar. Every time Jake served someone, he also spoke to them, listened, smiled. The best bartenders were like that—they offered a friendly ear, a sympathetic shoulder. Good advice.

Maybe he should pick his brother's brain about Nicole.

When he came Kai's way again, Kai had a question all ready for him. "I noticed that you're doling out advice along with the shots. I could use some."

"Let me guess. About Nicole?"

"Yes, about what my next step should be. I think she's holding something back."

Jake refilled his glass with another splash of Laphroaig. "Really, holding something back from the stranger who showed up out of the blue to scrutinize her motives?"

Kai laughed as he accepted his drink. "You have a point there. But I've been cool, I swear. Except for the first time, with the fireplace," he corrected himself. Then thought some more. "And the time with the antlers."

Jake threw up a hand. "I do not need to know about the time with the antlers. Sounds kinky. Have you done any other poking around? Online, say?"

"No." Kai made a face. "She has such a common name I didn't see the point. I did check the resume she gave Max, and her drivers license. Everything looked legit. But maybe I should take it deeper."

"Personally, I think you should just talk to her. But if it would put your mind at ease, yeah. Google her. Stalk her online. What could go wrong?"

Kai laughed and took a slug of his Scotch. There was nothing wrong with googling someone. Everyone did it. He'd once googled himself, just to see what came up. If Nicole had nothing to hide, she wouldn't mind if he googled her. And if she did have something to hide, he wanted to know about it. For Max's sake, of course. Not because he was more and more intrigued by her.

HE SPENT the rest of the evening flirting with a botanist studying high-altitude wildflowers. After he stumbled out of the Last Chance into the chill of midnight, he walked a few blocks to clear his head.

Flirting had been fun, but it hadn't chased Nicole from his thoughts. She was always there, percolating in the background with her clear blue eyes and her hopeful smile.

He pulled on his knit hat to keep the chill off as he walked. Quiet reigned in the little collection of homes that formed Rocky Peak. At this hour, everyone was snuggled into bed. Windows dark, vehicles tucked away. It was so quiet his own footsteps seemed obnoxiously loud. The only thing noisier was the stunning star scape suspended overhead. The sheer brilliance of the stars spoke as loudly as a marching band. *Here we are. Glory be. Sing back to us.*

Shaking off the silly thought, he spotted a bench in the little playground next to the elementary school. After he'd settled into it and his head had stopped spinning, he pulled out his phone. He didn't have to wait to google Nicole. He could do it right here on his iPhone.

After sorting through many wrong Nicole Davidsons, he finally found someone that matched the Nicole he knew. She'd gone to elementary school in Bellingham, where she'd won a spelling bee at the age of eleven. There was even a photo of her with her trophy and her missing two front teeth.

She'd graduated from college in Eugene, Oregon. With honors. So far so good.

Then something sad. Her mother had died of cancer. The obituary was very brief and mentioned two surviving children, Nicole and her sister Bridget. Nothing about a spouse.

Kai tried to remember if Nicole had ever said anything about a sister, but drew a blank. Not that she had any obligation to talk about her sister. Still, it seemed odd, considering all the family stuff they'd discussed.

From his fuzzy brain he dredged up the name of her fiancé. Roger. What would happen if he googled Nicole and Roger? He snickered as he typed it in. Probably not much.

Boy, did he get that wrong. He quickly pulled up dozens of gossip items, an engagement announcement, and a thorough writeup of their breakup.

Roger was *Roger Vance*. He ran one of the country's biggest hedge funds. Wealthy as fuck. He was *thirty years* older than Nicole. And there was tons of speculation about their relationship—none of it favorable to Nicole. She was painted as a clever, working-class gold-digger who'd wormed her way onto his fancy Queen Anne property and then lured him into her bed. She was referred to as "arm-candy," as a fortune-hunter, as a wannabe trophy wife.

Shit. Maybe his "worst case scenario" had been right all along. Maybe she was looking for another meal ticket. It had almost worked with Roger Vance. If they'd married, she would be worth millions now. Instead she was laboring as a home health aide for a cranky old man. A cranky old man who just happened to own a lodge worth millions. Sure, the lodge had fallen on hard times. But that didn't change its value.

Hadn't she asked if Max had ever dated anyone else? Maybe she'd been digging for clues!

Jesus. What was going on here?

10

A CALL FROM SUNNY GROVE WOKE NICOLE UP AT DAWN. BIRDIE had gotten into a food fight with Lulu at dinner, then smuggled some cookies back to bed with her and launched a sneak attack in the middle of the night.

Nicole heard the smothered amusement in the attendant's voice, but apparently Lulu hadn't thought it was at all funny.

"She's requesting an immediate transfer."

"Oh no."

"Yes. And you know what a hard time we've had finding roommates for Birdie. We're going to have to switch her to a private room for a while."

Nicole stuck her phone under her pillow and let out a not-so-silent scream. Why did Birdie always have to get into trouble? Private rooms were so much more expensive than shared rooms. *Crap.*

When she'd gotten a grip on herself, she brought the phone out again. "Is there any way to talk to Lulu about it? I'm sure Birdie didn't mean any harm. Lulu must know that."

"Maybe after a few days but right now her parents are insisting on an immediate move."

"What about another roommate? She gets lonely on her own."

"She definitely does better in a shared room," the attendant agreed. "We'll see who else moves in, maybe there will be a better match. Sorry, Nicole. I know this makes things tougher for you."

About twice as tough, to be exact. Birdie's disability payments only covered a certain amount, and she'd always had to supplement with her own income.

At least she still had some of the money from Roger's diamond engagement ring. He'd allowed her to keep it—probably out of guilt. She'd sold it and put all the money into an account meant for Birdie.

Sometimes she missed the way it made her hand sparkle. Like a fairy wand granting wishes.

"Okay," she said, resigned. "Maybe being on her own will convince Birdie she should be nicer to her roomies."

"She tries."

"I know she does." Now she felt guilty for blaming Birdie for her mischievous nature. She *did* try...until she forgot to try. "Please keep a close eye on her. If she starts getting depressed, let me know and I'll come down for a visit. I'm overdue anyway."

"Will do. Take care, Nicole."

Nicole hung up and lay back in bed. Mornings were always chilly in the dorm, and she loved snuggling under the duvet while the sky slowly lightened outside the window. Staring up at the ceiling, she traced patterns between the knot holes in the unfinished planks.

Oh Birdie. She could barely remember a time when Birdie hadn't been her three-o'clock-in-the-morning worry. Because of Birdie, she'd become interested in nursing. Because of Birdie, she'd assumed the role of guardian and responsible adult after their mother died.

Other things in life never seemed as dire. Job, school, relationships, even Roger—she'd never obsessed over those things the way she did over how best to care for Birdie.

And most of the time, she worried that she was getting it all wrong.

Did Birdie need special treatment or did she need to feel normal? Would she be better off at home or in a facility like Sunny Grove? Should she be surrounded with people or kept more sheltered?

Why was there no instruction manual for situations like this?

Birdie herself was no help. Every time Nicole asked her opinion, she agreed happily with anything. She didn't think beyond her present moment. It was part of the damage her brain had sustained.

Sometimes, during Birdie's most frustrating moments, Nicole had to remind herself. *At least she's still with me.*

Without Birdie, she'd be utterly alone.

The worst part was that everyone had an opinion, and they were all over the map. Different doctors offered different advice, as did therapists and counselors and social workers. Mom had insisted that she live at home, but after she'd died, Nicole couldn't afford to pay for live-in help, so Birdie had moved into a facility like Sunny Grove, but not as nice.

Then...Roger.

He was like a fairy tale prince swooping in and solving her biggest worry in life. But it was all bullshit. She and Birdie had moved into Roger's Queen Anne mansion for three months, until Roger decided Birdie had to go.

"You can't just kick her out!" Nicole had screamed at him— the first and only time she'd lost her cool with him.

"Of course I fucking can. It's my house. She keeps chasing the cat with her wheelchair."

"She's just having fun. She's not doing any harm."

"She comes into my office whenever she feels like it."

"Lock the door."

"I shouldn't have to. She should know better."

"She has *brain damage*, Roger."

"Which is why she needs to be somewhere with doctors around."

That was when he'd found Sunny Grove, which was extremely expensive but at least he paid for it. Until Nicole ended their engagement and started paying the fees herself.

Birdie was on the waiting list for a more affordable facility, but who knew how long that would take. A private room at Sunny Grove would drain her savings in no time.

Nicole did a quick calculation. The money from the engagement ring would run out in three months. *Three months.*

She *had* to make this sale go through. She had to get Max, and now Kai, to *want* to sell the lodge. When Felicity arrived with the offer from the Summit Group, they had to be primed to see the benefits of a big investment in the property they'd held for generations.

A pang in her jaw made her realize that her entire body was tense from the stressful direction of her thoughts.

She forced her muscles to relax, one by one.

Stress reduction.

I have my stress handled.

She smiled as Kai's voice filtered into her mind. She smiled a lot when she was with Kai. There was something so direct about him, so strong and magnetic, that she sometimes forgot to be on her guard around him.

She thought of Kai holding an armful of plastic deer head, looking up at her with that outraged expression, and laughed. He'd caught the deer, and she had no doubt he would have caught her, too, if she'd fallen off the ladder. He made her feel safe, which made no sense because she knew he still saw her as a possible threat.

But that was because of his protective nature—something she

appreciated. She didn't mind him looking out for his father and his family's legacy. She *admired* that.

Too bad it made them enemies.

Nestling deeper under the covers, she drifted into a half-dreaming, half-waking state in which Kai strode toward her across the wide lawn of the lodge. His t-shirt clung to his rippling muscles. It must have been raining because the wet shirt was completely see-through, revealing each flexing ridge and valley of muscle. His stormy eyes smoldered with heat as he closed in on her. He wanted her. He wanted to throw her across a bed and do incredibly naughty things to her. He wanted to make her scream. He wanted to get her wild and wet and trembling.

And she wanted all those things too. And more.

Then he was sweeping her off her feet, his hot gaze burning into her, causing her to melt into his arms. His mouth hovered over hers, sensual and tempting. Kai's kiss would be a whirlwind sweeping away all her boundaries, her fears, her worries. Whisking her to a place of pure sensation.

No.

She shook herself awake and sat up in bed.

No.

This was nothing but a dangerous fantasy. She'd done the whole "white knight riding to the rescue" thing. That was Roger's whole pitch—'I'll take care of you. You don't have to worry about a thing.' But it had been a huge mistake. No man was going to swoop in and solve her problems. That was her job.

Kai could be a good distraction though. Of that, she had no doubt. No man had appealed to her as much as Kai did in a very long time. Maybe ever.

Fix her problems? No. Give her a good orgasm? Absolutely.

Smiling at the idea, she slid out of bed and went to brush her teeth. Fantasy orgasms with Kai had to stay where they belonged —in her imagination. She had a mission to complete.

11

NICOLE WAS IN THE MIDST OF GETTING THE BLOOD PRESSURE CUFF set up when her fantasy came true—sort of. She and Max were in the family section of the dining room, where the Rockwells took their meals. Max sat in his favorite spot, overlooking the berry garden that Amanda had planted. She'd just noticed that the cuff needed a spritz of sanitizer, so she was hunting through her bag for the little spray bottle of alcohol.

One other group still lingered over their coffee; everyone else had already left for their morning adventures. Max's plate held the remains of buttermilk pancakes, which he should probably not be eating. Her bowl of oatmeal was almost empty.

Mundane details, which got swept away as Kai strode into the dining room.

Just like in her fantasy.

In a white t-shirt, just like her fantasy.

It wasn't wet, but then again she did have a very active imagination.

His hot gaze drilled into her, just the way she'd dreamed. But there was something more there, something beyond heat. Something unsettling. She didn't have time to figure it out, because he was at their table with just a few strides.

And then he was touching her arm and his mouth was hovering over hers — *just like in her dream.*

Granted, he hadn't scooped her into his arms the way he had in her dream, but that was understandable. She was no light-weight and this was a public dining room. She'd probably knock over a few water glasses if she got swept off her feet. Besides, that was her imagination going wild, whereas this—crazily enough— was reality.

Kai's mouth, inches away. Firm lips, surrounded by a subtle grain of stubble. The fresh smell of the outdoors clinging to his skin. That scar, that slightly broken nose, those fierce stormy eyes. His body heat, that electric chemistry, that magnetic pull.

"I need to talk to you." His low voice sent shivers up and down her spine. Her nipples responded too, peaking under her sweater.

"Sure, right after I take Max's—"

For some reason her mention of Max made his face tighten. "This can't wait."

"What's wrong?"

His eyes flicked toward Max, and she got the message. What-ever it was, he didn't want to talk about it in front of Max.

She bent over her patient, who was twisting his neck around to see what was happening behind him. "Sorry, big guy. Looks like something urgent came up. I'll be right back. Just hang tight and think peaceful thoughts." She squeezed his shoulder reas-suringly.

Max scowled.

So did Kai.

Suddenly their family resemblance really stood out.

"Fine, but don't be too long," grumbled Max. "All this waiting around is hell on my blood pressure. Bet my readings are going to skyrocket when you finally get around to taking them."

"Then we'll do some extra meditation sessions today."

"Threats don't work on me, chickie."

With a smile, she bent down and kissed Max on the cheek. For a grouch, he had a good sense of humor.

As she straightened up, she caught Kai's gaze and flinched as if he'd tossed a flame-thrower at her. He looked furious.

Was this about the plastic deer? The spa proposal? Tofu chili? She followed him out of the dining room feeling like a delinquent being called into the principal's office.

He led the way to the long, narrow room where the rental skis were stored. Its walls were lined with benches where skiers could gear up. A set of double doors let onto the back lawn, but generally no one used them in the summer. She'd only been in here once, on her initial tour of the lodge. Even now it smelled of ski wax and damp wool.

He closed the door with a firm click and faced her.

"Why didn't you mention that your ex-fiancé is Roger Vance?"

She stared at him blankly. This was about *Roger*? "Um... because why would I? It's over."

"Roger Vance is almost sixty."

"He's fifty-six," she corrected.

"And you're twenty-eight."

She took a moment to be touched that he remembered her age. "And you're thirty-two. Is this just a math lesson or do you have a point to make?"

"Roger Vance is extremely wealthy. He was on the Forbes list once."

"Yes, but apparently it was due to a clerical error. He never made it again, which bothered him to no end. You should have heard him rant about—anyway, yes, you're right. He's very wealthy."

"And old."

"He always preferred the term 'silver fox.'"

But Kai still wasn't smiling. "You lived on his property before you got engaged to him. You didn't mention that part either."

She folded her arms across her chest as familiar ripples of resentment coursed through her. "There's a lot I didn't mention. He's allergic to chocolate. He's very close to his chauffeur. He cheats at Hearts. Why don't you come on out and say whatever it is you're thinking?"

His jaw flexed, the only movement in his stony expression. "Okay, I will. I'm wondering why you broke up. And if it had anything to do with a prenup."

All color drained from her face, then came flooding back.

"Bullshit. You don't want to know why we broke up. You want to know if I specialize in preying on old men with big properties. You want to know if I'm getting my gold-digger claws into your father."

Finally, a crack in his granite expression. "I didn't say that. I'm just looking at the data and connecting dots and—"

"Want to know why we broke up?" she burst out, unable to listen to another second of his veiled accusations.

"Ye—"

"Because he wouldn't accept me as I was. He wouldn't accept my sister. He kicked her out of the house and didn't care how much that hurt her. When she hurts, I hurt *twice* as much. Ten times." Her words were stumbling over themselves in her passion. The harsh look on his face had vanished, and he was listening with complete and close attention.

"He only wanted me for arm-candy, that's all. He thought I'd be happy he bothered with me, a complete nobody with a sister in a wheelchair, always scrambling between paychecks, working two jobs, sometimes three—"

"I'm sorry." He reached out and caught her against him. Her breath caught in a hiccup of shock.

"I could have stayed, if I didn't care about my sister, and I'd already signed his stupid prenup anyway, if that's what you're so worried—"

A grimace flashed across his face. Then, in the next second, her face was in his hands and...oh my God...he was kissing her. As if to stop her words, soothe her pain...or his...

And she opened up to him like a flower desperate for rain. All her hot emotion poured out of her.

His kiss was every bit as tumultuous as she'd imagined. His firm lips moved against hers, his tongue swept across the sensitive inner flesh of her mouth, spreading wild tingles everywhere it touched. He took command of her mouth, exploring and claiming at the same time.

Her body went boneless against him. His hand gripped the small of her back, keeping her upright against the onslaught of sensation. She melted against him, nipples peaking against his chest, hot desire liquefying between her legs. Pressing close, she felt the hard bulge behind his jeans.

So he felt it too, this wild attraction.

But he'd just accused her of being a fortune hunter.

Screw him.

She pulled away from Kai and covered her mouth with her hand. He looked just as rattled as she felt. His hair was rumpled and he was trying to catch his breath.

"Sorry," he muttered again.

"You might need to narrow it down a little," she snapped. "Sorry for accusing me or sorry for kissing me?"

He put his hands on his head and turned away from her. "Fuck. I don't know anymore. Both. Neither." He spun around to face her. "I wasn't accusing you."

"It sure felt like it."

"Then I'm sorry." He dropped his arms back to his sides, causing her heart to leap into her throat again. The air hummed between them. Somewhere outside, a guest shouted something and a car started up. "As for kissing you, I guess I'm not as sorry as I should be."

～

KAI'S HEAD was still buzzing from that incredible kiss, so logic wasn't his friend right now. He needed some time to get a grip on what had just happened. But Nicole was still staring at him, the color coming and going in her cheeks.

He had to make this right.

"I didn't know about your sister."

Her expression shuttered. "Let's leave her out of this."

Right. That was Nicole's private life and she didn't owe him any explanations. He was the one who owed her.

"Did you really believe I was putting the moves on your dad? Oh!" Her eyes flashed fire at him. "That's why you got all huffy when I kissed him on the cheek. What exactly were you thinking?"

"I was thinking that you're beautiful." Honest answer, if not exactly to the point. He'd thought she was so beautiful that his dad didn't stand a chance. She was wearing a long skirt and boots, along with a turtleneck sweater in a charcoal gray color that made her eyes shine like liquid sky.

He shouldn't have kissed her. Why had he done it?

Because her passion had reached out and grabbed him by the heart and the only thing on his mind had been getting close to her. Tasting her. He'd forgotten everything else.

"Cut the crap, Kai. Were you trying to throw me off? Confuse me so I'd confess my nefarious plot?"

He scrubbed a hand through his hair in frustration. "No, Nicole. Nothing like that. It was one of those impulsive things. I didn't plan it. I didn't have some kind of hidden agenda."

Something flickered in her eyes.

A visceral memory of the taste of her lips came back to him. He'd kissed her, but she'd kissed him right back, wholeheartedly. It wasn't until her lips had parted, welcoming him in, that he'd taken that kiss deep.

Maybe she was regretting that now.

"Look, let's forget about the kiss. We never have to mention it again, we never have to do it again. We don't even have to think about it again."

She looked away, as if one of the Telemark skis had become the most fascinating thing in the room. Maybe she was thinking the same thing he was. *Fat chance. That wasn't the kind of kiss you forgot.*

"That goes without saying," she said, chin held high. "Of course we won't do it again."

"Of course."

"But I'm still hung up on the part about Roger. How did you know about him?"

"I googled you," he admitted. "Had a few beers last night and it seemed like a good idea."

She crossed her arms and tugged her lower lip between her teeth. "So what else did you learn?"

When he hesitated, she gave his chest a light shove.

"Come on, you owe me that at least. Let me defend myself. How do I know what other crazy things you think about me?"

He drew in a breath. "Well, it appears you went off the deep end after the engagement ended. Did a lot of partying in Mexico with your girlfriends."

"Never been to Mexico."

"There were rumors about a pool boy."

"Aren't there always?"

He softened his tone as he came to a more serious topic. "Your mother died of breast cancer."

"That part's true."

"I'm sorry." He didn't add that he knew how it felt to lose a mother. There was no need; she knew. He saw it in her eyes, which were starting to soften.

"Okay, what else? Come on, cough it up." Her tone was lighter now. *Phew.* Maybe he was going to get out of this alive after all.

"This next one is more of a guess, putting two and two together."

"Ha. So we're back to math again."

He smiled at that. "Okay, here it is. Pure theory and specula-tion. You're a former drinker, possibly a recovering alcoholic."

Her face went stark white. *Fuck.* He'd stepped in it all over again. "Because you don't drink," he added quickly. "Jake says you never come to his bar, and one of the articles said you'd been drinking heavily just before the breakup and Roger Vance was trying to get you into rehab and—"

In a complete shocker of a move, she hauled off and slapped him across the face. Not with full force, just enough so he felt it, and his cheek tingled. His jaw flexed in shock. He stood rock still, frozen. The skis rattled in their racks.

She clapped her hand over her mouth, then pulled it away and looked at it as if she could barely believe it was hers. "Holy crap. I just *hit* you. I used *physical force* on you."

He moved his jaw back and forth. The pain, such as it was, had already faded. "Guess I got that one wrong."

"You did. Way wrong. But that's no excuse." She lifted her stunned gaze to meet his. "I can't believe I did that."

The door swung open and Gracie came running in, followed by Max stumping after her with his cane.

"What is going on?" Gracie cried. "What are you two doing?"

"Boy, if you hurt her—" Max growled.

Hurt her? Kai curled his hands into fists. Max's face was an unhealthy red. So was Nicole's, come to think of it. His must be too, after that blow. Gracie looked like she was about to cry.

Shit.

"I'm sorry." He muttered the apology to everyone in general as he turned to go. "Sorry to all of you." How many freaking apolo-gies did that make in one day?

"Where are you going?" Gracie cried. He heard the fear in her voice. Maybe she was afraid he was about to leave again.

And maybe he should. He'd just brought more stress to the situation—just look at Max's red face.

"Gotta clear my head." He pushed open the double doors and burst into the outdoor air. How many times had he done exactly this—stormed out of the lodge, all messed up?

At least he knew exactly where to find an ice-cold creek to dunk his head in.

12

CLEAR CREEK RAN THROUGH THE EAST END OF THE PROPERTY. FED by melting snowpack, home to intrepid trout, it had always been Kai's favorite place to cool down. He stripped off every stitch of clothing and waded in. It felt like walking into a liquid ice cube. As if every cell of his body woke up and sounded the alarm—*we're going to die.*

He whooped out loud, his shouts echoing back to him through the forest. He swung his arms back and forth to amp up the BTU's in his body. Creek water churned over the rocks, tumbling head over heels, reckless and free.

Or maybe that was him—the reckless one. Why had he pulled out that wild theory about why she didn't drink? Why hadn't he asked Nicole about her engagement to Roger Vance in a civil manner? Why had he charged into the dining room, ready for war? Why had he kissed her, then turned around and insulted her?

He could still see the desire in her eyes, still feel the press of her lips against his. She'd trusted him enough to kiss him back. But now she'd probably never trust him again.

And that kiss—shit. That kiss had sent fire through his blood.

Even now, immersed in icy-cold water, his cock stirred at the memory.

That was officially a first. He'd never had anything approaching a hard-on in Clear Creek before. He hadn't known it was physically possible.

"Kai!"

Gracie came leaping down the trail like a gazelle in cutoffs. "Are you okay, Kai? Did you fall in?"

"That is the only sane explanation, but no." He snorted, immersing himself deeper into the water. "I'm naked, by the way. Fair warning."

Gracie didn't seem too fazed. She perched on a stump on the embankment above the creek. "I can't believe you swim in that water."

"Swimming is stretching it. I'm getting out in about forty-five seconds, so what's up?"

"I just wanted to make sure you're not thinking about leaving. You can't leave, Kai. Promise."

Her fierceness surprised him. Based on what happened in the ski room, Max would probably kick him out all over again. "Why?"

"I can't explain it." She rested her chin on her knees. "It's just a feeling I have. That you need to stay."

Gracie had always experienced flashes of intuition like that, even as a little kid. She'd had a screaming nightmare the night before the accident.

He trusted Gracie's "feelings," but they weren't the only factor. "I don't want to make things more stressful for Max. Seems like just being here, being Kai Rockwell, is enough to bring the stress. I'm not even fighting with him."

"I know. It's been great. It makes such a difference for Dad. You can't see it because you haven't been here. But I can. He's got an extra sparkle in his step, more zip. More zest." She smiled at her own goofy string of words. "More zip-a-dee-doo-dah."

"And that's thanks to me?" He pushed a clump of floating leaves away from him.

"Yup. So if you could just stop annoying Nicole, everything would be great."

"Stop annoying Nicole, huh? Not sure that's possible. Especially now that I basically accused her of being a fortune-hunter."

"You did? Yikes. That's bad." She plucked a blade of grass and stuck it between her teeth. "Very bad. You should be ashamed of yourself. If she was a fortune-hunter I'm sure she could do better than some falling-down old lodge in the middle of nowhere."

"Hey." He splashed water toward her. "You're insulting our legacy."

"Sorry, legacy." She made a little face at him. "There, see how easy that was? A simple apology goes a long way. I'm sure if you tell Nicole that you were in the wrong and that you deeply, *deeply* apologize, she'll forgive you."

Kai's hackles rose. Not only had he apologized, but Nicole was the one who had slapped him. But Gracie hadn't seen that part, and he wasn't about to tell her. That was between him and Nicole. "I'm not going to apologize for looking out for Dad. It's reasonable to investigate the background of someone who's with him all day. It would be negligent not to."

"That's true."

Nicole's husky voice made them both startle as she emerged from the trees. Gracie nearly fell off the stump, and Kai quickly checked to make sure the Clear Creek water completely covered him. And that it wasn't *too* clear.

"Nicole!" Gracie scrambled off the stump and blocked her line of sight to Kai. "Kai's in there naked and defenseless. How mad are you at him? I know he can be irritating, but he's my big brother and I love him. And he means well."

Nicole let out an astonished laugh. "You're protecting your tough rescue paramedic brother from me?"

"I don't need protecting," Kai called. "Although a towel would be nice."

"Should have thought of that before." Gracie shot him an impish grin. "Well, so long as neither of you is about to kill the other, I think I'll get on back to the house. I've got ice cream to dish, cones to fill."

She skipped off into the woods, leaving Kai and Nicole alone.

Nicole had added a zippered vest and a red beanie to her outfit. She shoved her hands in the pockets of her sweater and fixed her gaze on the ground.

"I'm very sorry I struck you like that," she said stiffly. "That's not the way I normally behave. All I can do now is apologize and try to do better in the future."

Nice apology, he had to admit. He eyed her thoughtfully, noting her embarrassed expression and flushed face. For someone like her, so cautious and guarded, it must have been truly shocking to lose her cool like that.

He noticed more details—shoulders a little hunched, knuckles white. Tension, wariness. He was really starting to know her body language well, he realized. Strange, with so many misunderstandings between them, that he would feel so in tune with her.

The chill was starting to seep into his bones, so in the interest of avoiding hypothermia, he dove right into his apology.

"Apology accepted, but not really needed. I jumped to conclusions and assumed the worst."

Looking unimpressed, she folded her arms across her chest. "Is that it?"

Didn't that about cover it? He clenched his jaw tight to keep his teeth from chattering. "That was supposed to be an apology."

"I just feel like there's something missing. Like the apology part."

His junk was going to be missing if he stayed in here too much longer. "Okay, I'll spell it out. I shouldn't have speculated about a prenup, your relationship with Roger Vance, or your relationship with alcohol. I'm sorry for all of the above."

She ran her tongue across her lips. "Thank you."

A loaded silence hung between them.

Nicole cleared her throat. "I also wanted to say that I don't blame you at all for checking into my background. Just like you said, that's a reasonable thing for someone to do. I would have done the same thing."

He narrowed his eyes at her, looking for the catch. It was such a fair and logical thing to say. There had to be a trick hidden in there somewhere.

There he went, getting suspicious of Nicole over nothing. *Give it up, Kai.* Maybe she was just a fair and logical person. "Then I guess we agree. I was right to google you. But I was an ass to believe things at face value."

"Finally we're on the same page."

He grinned. For a moment they looked at each other in silence, except for the noisy rush and tumble of the creek. And his teeth beginning to chatter.

"This is getting awkward," he told her. "If I don't get out soon, there might be permanent damage."

Her lips quirked. "Then there's one more thing I want to say."

"Go for it. I want to hear everything. Bring it on." *Quickly, please.*

"My father was a heavy drinker, probably an alcoholic even though he never admitted it. He left us when I was ten, lived on the streets, then died of a heart attack. *That's* why I don't drink."

"Jesus, Nicole." He sank underwater, icy water closing over his head, then surged up through the surface again, gasping. "Thinking I might drown myself for being such an idiot. I'm really sorry. If I'd known...shit. There's no excuse. I'm sorry. Want to push me under?"

She shook her head with a laugh. "No. Well, maybe a little. I just wanted to explain why I reacted like that."

"I get it. I really do." He shivered as a wisp of breeze chilled his wet hair. How inappropriate would it be for him to get out now?

She cocked her head at him. "It looks like I have the upper hand at the moment."

"Maybe." He shook his arms to generate some more body heat. "Probably."

"Then can I ask you something?"

"Make it fast."

For a wild moment he hoped she'd say something about the kiss.

But she didn't. "How attached are you to that old library room?" she said. "I have something in mind for it, maybe some healing crystals or aromatherapy treatments, and I never see anyone using it. I'm sure if Max knew you were okay with changing that room—"

"Oh sweet Jesus. *Now*? Seriously? You see a man freezing his dick off in a creek and you think, let's talk about crystals?"

She grinned. "Boom. Gotcha."

Damn. He'd been had. Completely.

"Oh, Nurse Nicole, you are in for it now. I'm coming out. And that's all the warning you're getting."

He rose to his feet, water streaming off his body, and waded toward the shore.

13

So much for maintaining her calm and dignified manner. At least she'd made it through her apology. And Kai's apology. But now he was rising up out of the water like some kind of god of the wilderness, muscles flexing, skin red from the chill. And he was the most magnificent sight she'd ever seen.

It took every ounce of willpower she owned—which was a lot not to openly ogle him. She quickly turned aside and averted her gaze. But even with a few quick surreptitious glances, she saw enough. Long, powerful thighs, taut stomach, not an ounce of fat anywhere. *Don't look at that dark patch between his thighs. Don't do it.*

"You know it takes a lot of confidence for a guy to walk naked out of ice-cold water," Kai was saying.

"All it takes is fear of freezing," she pointed out.

"That too." He crouched down next to his pile of clothes. The ridge of side muscles—what were they called again?—along his torso tightened. Her mouth went dry.

"Lats," she said faintly. She was a health aide, she shouldn't forget basic anatomy like that.

"Excuse me?"

Oops, she hadn't meant to say that out loud. "I said, *drat*. I should have thought to bring you a towel."

"Towels are for wimps."

Okay then. She flashed on a memory of Roger stepping out of his custom shower stall and wrapping three pre-warmed towels around himself—one for his hips, one around his shoulders, and one for his hair. He owned a special towel-warming rack that heated them to the perfect temperature.

Why was she comparing Roger with Kai? The two men were such complete opposites, as if they were barely the same species. She shielded her eyes while Kai pulled on his clothes.

Well, she *mostly* shielded her eyes. Not completely.

That brief glimpse of boxer briefs over his firm ass and the black t-shirt clinging to his damp muscles would probably keep her going for several busy nights of fantasizing.

When he was completely dressed, he came to her side. "I know you think I'm insane for going in that water, but it saved my ass many times growing up. Nothing clears your mind like a dip in icy creek water."

"So that was your blanket fort?"

"My blanket fort?"

They headed for the trail that led back to the house. "That's where I went when I had to get away from stress at home. I had a blanket fort that took up one entire corner of my room. I had a beanbag chair under there, a lava lamp. All my favorite books. An emergency stash of Reese's Pieces."

"It sounds a lot more comfortable than an icy creek."

She smiled. It was hard to believe that not too long ago, she'd been so furious with this man that she'd hauled off and struck him. Amazing that he was still willing to talk and walk with her.

"Your father doesn't give you much benefit of the doubt, does he?"

He looked at her sharply. "How do you mean?"

"His first reaction when he saw us was to ask if you'd hurt me. That's pretty rough."

He rubbed his hair, trying to get the water out of it. "I told you, I was a mess for a while. I got into a lot of fights. I can't blame him for thinking that."

"Well, I do. He had it completely backwards. And that was pretty unfair to you."

"I can take it," he said tightly. "I don't let Max get to me anymore."

"Well, except for exposing yourself to the risk of hypothermia. Pretty soon it's going to be winter and you can't go plunging into ice water when it's twenty below out."

"Pretty soon I'll be gone and it won't be a problem."

That was a relief. Or it should be, anyway. With Kai gone, she wouldn't be so worried about more secrets coming out. He knew about Roger, but so far almost nothing about Birdie or, God forbid, the Summit Group. Those things weren't really google-able, luckily. Birdie had never been on social media, was barely mentioned in their mom's obit. And Nicole had no connection to the Summit Group on paper.

But secrets aside...the truth was that she didn't want Kai to leave. He made everything more exciting—in a maddening kind of way.

He glanced her way with a smile. "Or maybe I'll switch to a blanket fort once winter comes."

She laughed, finding the thought of tall, broad-shouldered Kai curled up in a blanket fort completely adorable.

"So what kind of stuff drove you into your fort?" he asked. "Your father? Your sister?"

"Oh, mostly the usual childhood angst," she said lightly. She wasn't ready to say anything more about Birdie. She hadn't intended to mention her sister at all—it had just burst out of her.

"I'm serious. I want to know." He shot her a teasing glance. "Don't make me google you again. I learned my lesson."

"I didn't *make* you google me in the first place."

"Maybe you did, by being so mysterious and fascinating."

She paused on the trail and frowned at him. Mysterious and fascinating weren't the words she'd use to describe herself. "I'm a perfectly ordinary person. There's nothing exotic about me."

He stopped along with her. "Then why would I find you so fascinating?"

She swallowed, a little flustered. He was so powerful and male, standing before her, and yet there was that curious glint in his eye, that warm smile. Damp tendrils of hair curled against the back of his neck. She edged past him and kept walking.

"You know, I had a hard time picturing you with that hedge fund dude. That's what threw me off," he said as he caught up with her.

"Are you saying you can't imagine me as a trophy wife?" A meadow butterfly flitted past them, on its way to the nearest wildflower.

"Trophies are about ski races, not people." He cocked his head at her. "When I hear 'trophy' I think marlins on a wall, or a rack of plastic deer antlers. Not a wife."

She laughed at that. "By the way, if I'd married Roger I would have been his fourth wife. And I *did* sign a prenup. It was a boiler-plate agreement, believe it or not. He literally deleted the name of his former wife and put mine in."

"He sounds like an ass. I'm glad you didn't marry him. You deserve better."

She tripped over a tree root, and he caught her arm in his firm grip. Everything about Kai was so direct, so strong. But did she deserve better? Was a spy any better than a fortune-hunter?

Kai bent to pick up a crushed soda can someone had tossed to the side of the trail. "Maybe that's why I couldn't picture it. You don't seem the type."

"If that's a compliment, I'll take it. It makes a nice change."

He threw his head back in a laugh. "I've been *thinking* plenty of complimentary things about you. In between the moments where I wasn't."

Did she want to know those things? Yes, she did. She wanted to know every little detail. But that would be trouble. *Don't go there. Don't ask. Change the subject.*

"You're not the only one who can google, you know," she told him. "I've been doing some research too."

"Oh yeah?" She heard tension in his voice.

"Yes, and I have a few questions. Does Max know you rescued an Outward Bound group from a crazed gunman?"

"No." He quickened his pace as they drew closer to the lodge.

"Does he know that you got a million-dollar reward for chasing down a runaway fugitive with your truck?"

"No. Of course not."

"*Of course not?* Why not? You're kind of a hero and it's like you don't want him to know."

"You're right. I don't want him to know." He stopped on the trail and turned to face her. "And don't tell him. Please."

"But why?" She was completely mystified. Why wouldn't he want everyone to know all these amazing things he'd done?

"Because with me and Max, it's complicated. He thinks the worst of me. That's his right."

Confused, she reached out and touched his arm, which felt tense as steel. "Maybe it's his right, but that doesn't mean it *is* right."

"Look. Stay out of it. Do your Max-Whisperer thing, put crystals in the library, whatever. Just don't get in the middle of me and Mad Max. That's a guaranteed disaster zone."

Tension sang between them, like the vibrating bowstring of a violin.

Her curiosity was going crazy now. There was some kind of wild story here, something beyond what Renata had told her. But his tense expression, his set jaw, his hard eyes, told her to keep her questions to herself.

She drew in a long breath. What did it matter? Kai was a distraction anyway. She had two jobs here, and neither of them involved Kai. The sooner he left, the better off she'd be. Getting to know him—his history, his heart—wasn't part of her mission.

Her gaze dropped to his mouth, those firm lips surrounded by stubble. Kissing definitely wasn't part of her mission. And yet she'd done it.

And that kiss was the best thing that had happened here so far.

She swallowed and tore her gaze away from him, fixing it on a tall spruce tree next to the trail instead. Now that all her wildest fantasies about kissing him had been confirmed, was she just supposed to block that from her mind? Pretend it had never happened? Move along, nothing to see...

"Should we talk about that kiss?" he asked, as if he'd read her mind—or noticed her staring at his lips. "Or pretend it never happened?"

"The kiss was a mistake."

"Not all mistakes are bad. In fact, I've heard it said that there are no mistakes and no accidents."

It definitely hadn't been an accident. She hadn't tripped over her shoes and fallen into his lips. Although that would have been easier to explain.

She drew in a long breath. "Okay, let's talk about it. Clearly, there's an attraction. But I'm here in a professional capacity so that's all there is to say."

"I'm not your patient," he pointed out. "There's nothing standing in the way of us kissing again, if we choose to."

"I don't choose to."

That was a big fat lie. She'd love to kiss him again. It was probably written all over her not-very-good-at-lying face. "It's much better if we keep things on a friendly basis. That's what's best for my patient."

"So that's your medical opinion?"

"Absolutely. I can't be distracted from my responsibilities. And I wouldn't want Max to feel neglected."

"True. Because Max definitely isn't the kind of man who would scream bloody murder if he felt neglected. He's the stoic, suffer-in-silence type."

His sarcasm made her laugh. "You know what I mean."

"Put it this way. I know what you want." That phrase, in his rough velvet voice, sent thrills through her.

"What, then?" *She* knew what she wanted—she wanted him to toss her over his shoulder and carry her up to his bed. She wanted him to slide his hand under her sweater, up the curve of her waist, to her breasts. She wanted him to tug her against him, press his long body against hers, damp clothes and all.

"You want to ignore the heat between us. You want to pretend like we aren't drawn to each other. You think it makes things too complicated. Too hard to manage."

A wisp of wind tugged at her beanie. She tucked it around her ears to keep it on. Everything Kai said was true, and yet it wasn't even close to the whole story. It left out the fantasies she kept having about him. "You're right. It is too complicated. It's also incredibly inconvenient that I find you attractive."

His smug grin made his eyes gleam. "Sorry to make life difficult. That's kind of my thing, in general."

She rolled her eyes. "On the other hand, you're obviously doing everything in your power to kill the attraction."

"And yet, it lives. Must be some pretty powerful chemistry."

She couldn't deny that, and didn't try. "Luckily, we're both grown adults who know that you don't always have to act on every little attraction you feel. We can follow our better judgement. We can make good choices, do the smart thing."

He nodded thoughtfully, with a hot, quick, sweeping glance up and down her body. It left tingles, that look. Delicious, tempting tingles. "Good choices. I like the way you put that." He winked at her. "It's good to be a grown adult, isn't it? We can make all the good choices we want."

With one of his charismatic smiles, he set off toward the lodge, waving at a group of hikers just setting out for the woods.

She hurried after him, feeling out of balance and confused. And at some deep-down level, unbearably excited.

~

THAT NIGHT, she filled Felicity in on *some* of what had happened, though she left out the kiss.

"He's been googling me."

"Shootskies. Did he find anything connecting you to me?"

Nicole rolled her eyes. "No, you're perfectly safe. It was all personal stuff about me. We're still fine."

She swallowed hard, since "fine" didn't really fit. Felicity had never mentioned that it would feel so sleazy to be a spy. Every word of these calls made her feel like a lowlife.

"At dinner tonight, Max asked me to put together a presentation," she told Felicity. "He wants me to show the family my vision for the lodge."

"Uh oh."

"But that's a good opportunity, right? That's what we wanted, to get Kai on our side."

"Yes but..." Felicity drummed her fingers on her desk. Still hard at work, this late at night. Nicole marveled at her workaholic ways. "Is Max trying to convince Kai to stay? Is that what he's up to?"

Nicole thought about that for a moment. Max would never come out and say that he wanted Kai to stick around. He was too damn proud. But would he try more underhanded methods? Absolutely. "Yes, there's a good chance of that."

"Damn. I knew this prodigal son returning from exile thing

would be trouble. Do you think Kai will move back permanently?"

"He hasn't said a word about that. I doubt it because he has such a tense relationship with Max. It's like a tinderbox just waiting to explode."

More drumming. "Okay, here's what you do. You do that presentation. But you present a vision of the lodge that's so crazy and so far out there that Kai will *hate* it."

Nicole took the phone away from her ear and blinked at it for a moment. "You are the devil," she told her friend.

"Thank you. After your presentation—think all your nuttiest New Age stuff—any reasonable proposal will sound good to them by comparison. That's when the Summit Group will swoop in and make an offer and they'll be so relieved they'll jump at it."

"Are you drunk? Have you been getting enough sleep lately?"

"Of course not to both questions. I never get enough sleep and I'm a disaster when I drink. Why do you ask?"

"Because you sound *insane*. Why not just present your offer and go from there? They'll either take it or leave it."

"Because Mad Max Rockwell is a tough nut to crack. I mentioned the shotgun, right?"

"He's mellowed out a lot, thanks to me."

"Well that's nice but I'm not counting on Mad Max turning into Mellow Max. This will work, Nico. Make a PowerPoint. I'll send you whatever materials you need. I want all your craziest, wackiest ideas in one place. It'll be gold."

"You've lost it, Felicity. You really have."

"Bonus for Birdie, remember?"

"Emotional manipulation, remember?" Nicole ended the call and threw her phone across the room, into a stack of freshly laundered blankets. How, how did she get herself into these situations? *How*? And how could she get out?

14

KAI THREW HIMSELF BACK INTO HIS TRAIL WORK. NICOLE'S questions about his relationship with Max had rattled him. It reminded him that he and Max still had a huge gulf between them. They'd been getting along only by avoiding awkward topics.

He kept asking Max about the lodge's finances, but the frustrating man refused to give him a straight answer. Neither Gracie nor Jake knew much either. Why did Nicole know more than any of them?

It seemed strange.

One more mystery surrounding Nicole.

In the meantime, autumn was coming.

The days were getting shorter and crisper, the nights more brilliant with stars. Forecasters kept warning about early storms, either rain or snow or even hail. Kai wanted to finish tidying up the trails before the first snowfall. He gave the generator system a tune-up and made sure all the handheld radios worked. Prepping for winter felt good, and more than once the thought crossed his mind...what if...?

He always dismissed the thought before it finished forming. He couldn't stay. Not unless he and Max cleared the air about a few things.

A group of birdwatchers booked the lodge for the fall warbler migration. He strolled into the lodge one morning as Nicole was helping out at the reception desk.

She had a way of lending a hand when it was needed, even if it wasn't her actual job. He'd seen her helping in the kitchen, doing loads of laundry, weeding in the garden.

While he poured himself coffee, out of sight, he listened to her chat cheerfully with them. Her friendly manner put them at ease as she handed them trail maps and keys to their rooms.

Casually eavesdropping, he heard her respond to a question with a light laugh. "No, I know nothing about birds. But my sister loves them so much she renamed herself Birdie. We used to have a hummingbird feeder and she'd watch it all day. One day, she just decided that was her name. Birdie. We thought it was a phase, but nope. She's Birdie to this day."

So Nicole's sister was named Birdie. The sister in the wheelchair, the one Nicole had never mentioned after that time in the ski room. Should he google Birdie? What was the point? Nicole had no obligation to share details of her personal life with him. She was here to take Dad's blood pressure, that was all.

The fact that she raised Kai's blood pressure just by walking past him, with those long legs and curvy hips, that wasn't her fault. He had to stop treating her like a threat.

The deadline for saying 'yes' to the Montana job passed. He made no effort to look for another one.

Did that mean he was staying? He wasn't sure what it meant, only that he wasn't going to Montana.

One day, when he needed a break, he drove into town and met with the fire department guys. They shot the shit about the old days—the kitchen fire that nearly burned down Majestic Lodge, the wildfires that had come so close when he was a kid.

They pestered him about signing on as a volunteer fireman like his brother Jake.

"Can't. I'm not sticking around. I'll be back in the real world soon."

"Ain't nothing more real than the mountains, you know that," the chief said.

"Yeah, I do, but these aren't the only mountains."

"Wash your mouth out." They all laughed, since loyalty to their piece of the Cascades ran deep.

After that, he stopped for a burger at the Black Diamond Grill. His high school crush, Betsy Polaski, ran it now. They flirted for a while, but his heart just wasn't in it.

Finally he stopped at the Last Chance to see Jake. He was training a new waitress, a bombshell redhead who would have rung all his bells a month ago. But her lack of clear blue eyes and soft lips was a real problem. That is, her lips might have been soft, but he didn't even notice.

"I heard Nicole's giving some kind of presentation about the lodge tonight," Jake told him. "You're going to check it out, right?"

"Wouldn't miss it. You coming?"

"Nah, dude. I'm leaving it all in your hands. That's why you're the oldest. I get to kick back and sling drinks while you defend the Rockwell legacy."

Kai exchanged a forehand grip with his brother, then grinned at the new waitress. She wore square black-rimmed glasses and a diamond stud in her nose. "Good luck with your new boss. You're going to need it."

"Don't scare away my employees," Jake warned. "Or I'll tell her to charge you, for once."

"Is he on the freeloader list?" the new waitress asked innocently, pretending to mark him down in her notes.

Both the brothers laughed, and Kai headed back up the twisty road to the lodge, each curve so familiar it felt like a part of him. Light spatters of rain hit his windshield. He tuned the radio to the local weather channel, where the forecasters had been warning about a front moving through. The familiar sounds of the weather report—winds out of the northeast, gusting up to thirty miles per hour, possibility of local flash flooding—made him smile.

The truth settled into his bones. He liked being back at Rocky Peak. He liked being near his siblings. In many ways he belonged here.

Except that he didn't, not really. Not the way things were with Max—polite and distant. With so much still unspoken. With Max and him at odds, he'd never really belong here.

BETWEEN CARING for Max and helping Renata pack brown bag lunches for the birders, it took Nicole some time to put together her ridiculous PowerPoint. Keeping an eye out for Kai also kept her busy. Every roar of a four-wheeler had her snapping to attention. Every glimpse of a broad back, long legs and work boots had her heart skipping a beat.

But finally she got it done, and Kai, Gracie and Max gathered in the TV room, where she hooked her laptop up to the big flat screen. Kai's vibrant presence made her heart skip a few beats. He was the target of this presentation, but now that it was really about to happen it felt so underhanded.

Selling is the best option for them all, she reminded herself. *They can't afford everything the lodge needs.*

She passed around a platter piled high with chocolate chip cookies Renata had made for the occasion. Kai helped himself to an entire handful, then sat back with a wink, crossing one ankle over the opposite knee.

"If you're trying to soften us up, it's working."

"That's good." She smiled at him nervously. "Cookies improve every situation, if you ask me."

"I second that!" Gracie, already in her pajamas, sat cross-legged on the couch. "Maybe we should turn the whole lodge into a bakery."

Max snorted. "We ain't turning my legacy into cookies."

"You could do worse." Gracie tapped his arm with impish affection.

Kai popped a cookie in his mouth and motioned for Nicole to get underway. Max ignored the cookies and chewed on the end of an unlit cigar instead.

She cleared her throat and clicked play on her PowerPoint presentation. A vintage photo of a pared-down version of the lodge appeared on the screen. A group of skiers in old-fashioned gear posed in front of it. One of them was Max's grandfather, the original founder.

"Max asked me to put together this presentation because as soon as I arrived here, I started spouting ideas about other ways to use the lodge. Finally he asked me to put them all in one place. Think of this as a kind of vision board of what the lodge could be."

She glanced at her audience of Rockwells, who were all gazing at their ancestor. It was hard to tell, with his sheepskin-lined leather hat, but Nicole thought he had a strong resemblance to Kai.

"As you all know, Rocky Peak Lodge has been in the Rockwell family for four generations. It has a wonderful and historic legacy going back seventy-five years. In the early days, only the most intrepid outdoorsmen made the trek to this lodge, drawn by the pristine wilderness and remote ski trails. Over the years, as the lodge was built up and expanded, it became more accessible to guests of all ages and skill levels. The demographic base is wider and more diverse today."

She switched to another slide, with a graphic breaking down the demographics of the guests.

"Nonetheless, you can see that the guest composition skews

toward the male, thanks to the preponderance of hunters and outdoorsmen who book the lodge. This is rugged territory, so that makes sense. However, in my view this creates a golden opportunity to appeal to a broader spectrum of people."

"What if the broader spectrum of people isn't especially interested in a wilderness experience?" Kai asked.

"We *make* them interested. And who says it has to be a wilderness experience? Do you have any idea how much women will pay to be pampered in a gorgeous setting?"

Kai was frowning at her latest slide, which showed a breakdown of the average cost of treatments at the upper echelon of West Coast day spas. "Is that a typo? One thousand dollars for a massage?"

"It's more than a massage. It's a four-handed massage with an added volcanic hot stone age-defying treatment."

"So you defy age by getting thrown into a volcano? I like it." Kai smile grimly. "Who gets to do the throwing? I can volunteer."

She rolled her eyes. "Mock all you want, but this gives you an idea of the financial potential. We wouldn't have to charge that much, but we *could*."

"I thought you were talking about fresh air camps for kids, that sort of thing. What happened to that part of the plan?"

Yeah, well...that part didn't fit in with Felicity's scheme.

"First things first. We need a new model in order to bring in more profit. That will open up all kinds of possibilities." She switched to the next slide, which showed a topless woman face down on a massage table with a practitioner dripping oil on her back. "Now we get to the good part. Raindrop therapy is *the hottest* trend in holistic health. Imagine a place where each precious raindrop brings peace and healing."

Kia peered at the slide. "I'm sorry, you want to sell *rain*?"

"It's not rain. It's essential oils applied in a certain sequence."

"I'll take *that* kind of raindrop therapy." Kai pointed to the window. Rain from the storm was pelting it hard.

"You're being obtuse. Raindrop therapy isn't—"

"And what building is that?" Kai interrupted, leaning even closer. "That's the fire station."

Nicole tried not to flinch. Of all the crazy changes she'd thrown into this PowerPoint, that was the one most guaranteed to annoy Kai. She'd taken a photo of the fire station outpost and made a few digital cosmetic changes to it.

Gracie's eyes widened. "Oh wow. It looks completely different. You want to paint it gold?"

"It's not gold, it's saffron. A very healing color. And it's not technically a real fire station. It's just a nice-size building with lots of open space. It hasn't been staffed in years, right, Max?"

Max grunted and chomped on his cigar.

"It doesn't have to be staffed," said Kai. "That's where we store the rescue gear and other equipment. Not to mention the fire truck. The fire department uses it when they need it."

"But how often does that happen?"

She already knew the answer to that question. Not very often.

"Also, the equipment is outdated. For it to be really useful, it would have to be modernized. When I spoke to the fire chief, he seemed to think they could get on just fine without the station up here."

Kai waved at the screen. "Whatever you want to call it, that fire station is the heart and soul of this lodge. That was the original inspiration. The whole reason for building up here. Old Man Rockwell saw himself as a kind of guardian of the ridge. Back me up, Max."

Max scratched at his beard. "That's what the family legend says. But that's history. We're talking about the future now."

Kai shook his head, slumping deeper into his seat. "Hey, it's your sandbox, Max. What else, Nicole? Let me guess, you want to change the name too. Rocky Peak is just so...masculine, am I right?"

"It is, a bit," Nicole agreed. She hadn't intended to bring it up so soon, but since he'd asked, she skipped ahead to a later slide. "I came up with a list of alternative names. They would all work well, staying with the mountain theme, and of course you guys would have the final say."

She scanned the list projected on the screen and smothered a grin. Meadow Sweet Retreat and Day Spa. Lilith of the Valley Day Spa. Rivers and Rainbows.

"We don't have a river here," Kai ground out. "Or any fucking lilies of the valley."

"It says *Lilith* of the Valley," Gracie pointed out. She was leaning forward, peering at the screen with a perplexed frown. "Who's Lilith?"

"Lilith is a very popular figure right now in certain circles," Nicole said. "She represents uncontained female energy, magnificent and angry. But these are just a few suggestions for new names."

"Here's another," Kai growled. "How about 'Overpriced and Ineffective Beauty Treatments for Spoiled Celebrities,' is that about right?"

"Kai, that's mean," said Gracie. "Personally, my favorite is Meadow Sweet, because we actually have a meadow."

Kai rubbed his temples, as if a bad headache was growing. "Flip ahead to the slides about the kids' camps and good causes and so forth."

"I don't have any slides, but just off the top of my head, fresh-air camps for juvenile offenders."

"*What?*" Kai's head shot up. "You want a bunch of junior criminals up here?"

"Don't be so judgmental. Everyone deserves a second chance. I've also thought about survival skill instruction, as I mentioned before. The lawn would be a great place for a paintball tournament. Then there's art therapy for the disabled, as long as we can add more ramps. But that can all come later. Step one is a complete transformation of the lodge from the ground up."

"So if we're *really* going to be literal here, the name would be Afterthought Camps for Poor People as a Fig Leaf to Justify all the Spoiling of the Rich Celebrities." Kai unfolded himself from the seat and stood up. "I think I get the gist here. How much more do you have in those slides?"

"Kai," Max said sharply. "She's just trying to shake things up a little. Don't get your panties in a bunch."

Kai's gaze clashed with hers, as an image of his "panties"— form-fitting boxer briefs—swam into her mind. "Like I said, it's your sandbox, Dad. If you want Real Housewives of the Cascades in here, it's your call." He headed for the door grabbing another handful of cookies on his way out. "I kind of like the bakery idea, myself."

All the energy in the room seemed to rush after him. Nicole gazed at her two remaining audience members. "Too much? Too fast?"

"Oh yeah, you definitely lost Kai." Gracie snagged another cookie.

"What happened to all those other ideas you had before?" Max grumbled. "They weren't all so fruitcake."

"They're haven't gone anywhere," Nicole assured him. "They're all right here in my head."

Gracie cocked her head thoughtfully. "But I like some of these new ideas, like art therapy for the disabled."

Nicole swallowed hard. Trust Gracie to home in on the one element that Nicole herself would most love to bring to Rocky Peak, if she had any say in it. Birdie would adore it. But it would never happen. The Summit Group couldn't care less about art therapy. There was no money in it. Not like timeshare condos or high-end luxury suites.

She shut down her laptop. "How about I tweak a few things before we go any further?"

"Nah, don't bother. That son of mine has his mind made up," growled Max through his cigar.

Aaaaand...her job was done.

Too bad she felt like shit about it.

15

LATER THAT NIGHT, NICOLE WOKE FROM A RESTLESS SLEEP BECAUSE a light was flashing outside her window. At first she thought it was lightning, because the rain was still pouring down in relentless sheets. But it came from below, not above. Someone was loading gear into a four-wheeler, running in and out of the old fire station outpost.

She pulled on jeans, added a sweater over her pajama top and a hooded rain slicker, then ran downstairs. No one else was awake, the lounge dark except for the flicker of the last ashes of last night's fire in the hearth. She ran outside, her face instantly feeling the sting of raindrops.

Kai was in the midst of heaving a duffel bag onto the back of the four-wheeler. He wore a yellow firefighters' rain jacket with white reflective stripes. For a wild moment, she wondered if she'd already managed to drive him away from Rocky Peak.

"What's going on?" she called to him over the drumming of the rain.

He looked toward her, his headlamp nearly blinding her before he adjusted it upwards. "Birdwatcher got lost. Didn't come back with the others. They've been searching on their own, but finally called it in. The fire department radioed me."

"I'll go with you," she said instantly.

"No need, the fire department's standing by. If I haven't located him by daybreak, they'll send a search chopper out."

"But what if he's injured?"

"I'm a paramedic."

Of course he was. Saving lives was second nature to him, according to his google history. But she was a certified nurse aide, damnit. And she wanted to chase the bad taste of that presentation out of her mouth.

"It's always good to have backup," she pointed out. "Especially if you're searching. You can focus on the driving and I'll be the lookout." Before he could argue any more, she slid onto the passenger seat. When he scowled at her, she gave his attitude right back to him. "If you want to waste time trying to evict me, good luck. Otherwise, let's go."

He shrugged finally and fastened a bungee cord around the supplies he'd loaded. "Anyone ever tell you you're stubborn as fuck?"

"About as often as you've been told you're a jerk."

That got a laugh out of him. "Fine, have it your way." He swung onto the rig. "Hang tight. This is going to be a helluva ride."

That applied to time spent with Kai in general, in her opinion.

She hung onto the safety bar while they zoomed onto the westernmost trail.

"He was last seen near Skyfall Ravine," Kai yelled over the tumult of engine noise and rain. "Spotted a Rocky Mountain bluebird, apparently. Way out of its range, according to the group."

He flashed a grin at her. He looked energized and fired up. She realized that he was in his element now. Riding to someone's rescue, braving rain and cold and ravines and whatever else might come. It sent a sharp thrill through her.

She focused on scanning the forests for signs of anything out of the ordinary, but saw nothing all the way to the ravine.

"Where are the other birders?"

"They're searching on the near side of Skyfall, where they last saw him." He gestured into the dark depths of the forested slopes. "I have a theory that he came this way because there's a creek bed that runs through here. He could have easily gotten turned around and gone the wrong direction. We can only go so far on the four-wheeler, so I hope your boots are in good shape."

"Don't worry about me."

He parked the vehicle as close to the top of the ravine as possible. The rain had turned it into something more like a mudslide.

"You stay here," Kai said as he set the emergency brake. His manner changed into something intense and focused. He handed her a handheld radio. "Keep this in your pocket. Be ready for anything. If I need your help I'll call."

She nodded and cinched her rain slicker tighter.

He slung a gear bag over his shoulders and scrambled down a narrow trail that zig-zagged down the slope. It was covered with scrubby bushes, and he lost his footing a few times, nearly sliding down the slope, which was a virtual mud bath. She held her breath until he made it to the bottom, then veered upstream. Soon she lost sight of his dark figure.

The handheld in her pocket crackled. "You okay up there?"

She drew it out and clicked the button. "All good. How's that mud treating you?"

"I'm thinking we could bring the ladies down here and charge a couple thousand for a dip in this stuff. I feel ten years younger already."

She laughed. "I knew you'd come onboard sooner or later."

"It's because you're so irresistible." Holy crap, was he flirting with her over the handheld radio? In a rescue situation? "Signing off now," he said, abruptly more serious. "Stay alert. You hear or see anything out of the ordinary, call me immediately."

"Stay safe," she told him.

"Safe is overrated." He clicked off and suddenly she was all alone in the dark wilderness. The rain poured down, dripping through the dense forest, rattling onto the four-wheeler. And she realized—right here, right now, she felt more alive than she had during most of her life. And a lot of that had to do with the maddening man out there charging into the wilderness.

About half an hour later, another vehicle roared up behind her; it held a small crew from the fire department. One of the firefighters jumped out and ran through the rain to talk to her.

"Where's Kai?"

She pointed in the direction he'd disappeared in. "He said he'd call if he needed help."

"The storm's getting worse. They're warning about microbursts. He needs to come back," the firefighter shouted over the din of the rain. He took the handheld radio from her. "Come in, Rockwell. Kai Rockwell, come in."

No answer. He handed the radio back to her.

"You should get back to the lodge, ma'am. It's about to get worse out here."

"But what about Kai?"

"Kai can take care of himself." He turned to go, but she clutched at his sleeve.

"You aren't going after him?"

"No, we have more folks out there to warn. Possible evacuations in the flood zones. I'll give you a ride back if you want to leave the four-wheeler for him. That's the best I can do."

"But what about the missing bird-watcher? Aren't you supposed to be helping him?"

"Yeah, we are. That's why we sent Kai." With a stern look, he tugged his jacket out of her grasp. "That birder couldn't be in better hands. Kai's got this. Now come on, you need to come with us. That thin little slicker isn't going to do a thing for you.

He was right about that part; she was already soaked through to the skin. But there was no way she was leaving with Kai still out there. She shook her head. "I'm a nurse, one or both of them might need me. I'm not going anywhere."

He started to argue when a shout came from the direction of the ravine. "A little help here!"

Kai.

The firefighters ran toward him as he crested the ravine. Someone shone a light on him. The white glare illuminated the bizarre sight of Kai crawling on hands and knees up the muddy slope. Clinging to his back, piggyback style, was an elderly black man in a fishing cap.

Nicole scrambled off the four-wheeler and joined the group. The firefighters, one on each side, grabbed Kai by the upper arms and dragged him up the last few feet. One of them unfastened the harness that attached the victim to Kai's back. He extracted the poor confused man as Kai, still on his knees, gasped out the details of the situation.

"Fell out of a tree and broke his left leg, probably the tibia. Lost his cell phone. Skin is clammy, pulse is thready. Disoriented, possibly hypothermic."

One of the firefighters wrapped a reflective space blanket around the shivering man.

"You carried him?"

"Yeah, about a quarter mile, not too far. The hardest part was keeping him from letting go. He kept spotting imaginary birds. I had to strap him on."

"Saw a three-headed yellow-eyed warbler, right there in the next tree," the man said through chattering teeth.

"Three-headed, huh?" One of the firefighters took charge of the victim and whisked him into their rig. The other—the same one who'd told her to leave—offered a hand to Kai and helped him stand. Kai staggered as his feet touched the ground. Nicole came to his side and wrapped her arm around him to give him more support.

"This one refused to leave without you," said the fireman with a smile. "Not even when I warned her about microbursts."

"Yeah?" Kai glanced down at her. She noticed deep lines of fatigue etching his face, and the pale tone of his soaked skin. How much strength had it required to carry another person a quarter mile, then *straight up* a muddy cliff? "I'm not surprised," he said softly, then turned back to the fireman. "What's this about microbursts?"

"Storm's worsening. We've already taken too long here. Can you two make it back on your own?"

Kai gave him a thumb's up. "You'll take the vic to the ER?"

"On it." They clasped each other's forearms, then the fireman jogged back to join the others. Their rig executed a tight three-point turn, then they disappeared back down the trail.

As soon as they were gone, Nicole helped Kai to the four-wheeler. "I'll drive," she said firmly. "You rest."

He didn't argue, which she greatly appreciated. It was probably a sign of his exhaustion. She helped him load the harness and ropes, everything sopping wet and even heavier than before. They didn't speak. The rain was getting louder by the second and a fierce wind howled through spruce trees, making their tops whip wildly back and forth.

"There's a hunter's cabin out here," he shouted over the din. "That's the closest shelter. Take that path to the right." He gestured at a very overgrown trail she hadn't even noticed.

"You need warm clothes and a bed," she yelled back.

"Just until the danger passes."

She nodded and hopped in the driver's seat. Once they were underway, she realized why Kai was allowing her to drive. As they wended their way through the thick brush, he used his exhausted body to hold back the worst of the branches from her face. He'd given her the easier task—typical Kai.

As she drove, the rain slashed their bodies and faces, and the wind buffeted the little vehicle. The engine kept making whining noises that made her worry it was about to stall. None of the city driving she'd done in her life had prepared her for this. She had to wrestle with the wheel just to keep the rig on the trail.

The drive seemed endless, more rain, more gusts of howling wind. She'd never been so glad to see a tiny dark structure in the middle of nowhere in her life. Kai directed her to drive right up to it and park as close to the entrance as possible. Then the two of them dashed inside just as a mammoth thunderclap sounded overhead.

16

Kai had nearly forgotten about this hunter's lodge, but clearly someone had been taking care of it. Firewood was stacked next to the wood stove and cans of food filled the shelves over the stove. There was even a bed pushed to one corner, with a pile of clean bedding stacked neatly on top.

The one-room cabin wasn't insulated, but it was a well-built structure that would keep them cozy while the storm raged.

He dropped his wet gear just inside the door. He was so exhausted all he wanted to do was fall into that bed. But first things first.

"I'll get a fire going and some lanterns lit, if you want to heat up some soup or something," he told Nicole.

"Why don't you just rest, I'll take care of all that."

"You sure?" That sounded like an incredible plan to him. His muscles were sore and aching from that climb up the ravine. Thank God, Jim had been on the small side, probably even lighter than Gracie.

"Absolutely. You look ready to drop."

He nodded wearily. "In a minute." He crossed to the kitchen and found a lighter, then lit a hurricane lamp and hung it from a hook embedded in a rafter in the center of the room. It cast a wide circle of light in the tidy space.

"In case I didn't mention it before, I'm really glad you came with me."

Her face brightened with a wide smile. "I'm glad you're glad, even though I didn't do much."

"Oh yes you did. All of this would be harder by myself." He handed her the lighter. "You can use this for the fire. I'll make the bed."

"You're supposed to be resting." She crouched down next to the wood stove. "But I suppose you'd have to be literally incapacitated for that to happen."

"You know me so well." Which was a strange—but possibly true—thought. Maybe sparring with someone was a good way to get to know them. He bent over to make up the bed. When he shook the sheets out, he got a whiff of lavender. "Gracie."

"Excuse me?"

"Gracie's the one who's been keeping this place alive. She loves using lavender soaps and so forth." He grinned. "I wonder if she's been meeting someone out here? Out of sight of Max?"

Nicole laughed from her position next the wood stove. "If so, my lips are sealed. She deserves all the happiness she can find."

"Agreed."

She'd taken her wet raincoat off, but he noticed that her thick sweater was soaked through, and that her hands were red and chapped, and shaking slightly. She stacked kindling on top of a round log, which had exactly zero chance of starting a fire.

City girl.

He shook the blanket over the sheets and watched her touch the lighter to a piece of newspaper in the stove. It sent a puff of smoke into the room, then expired.

He winced. What was the tactful way to tell her that she was about to smoke them out of here? "Hey, how about I start the fire and you make the soup?"

eyebrows drew together. "Are you doubting my fire skills?"

I'm sure you can start a fire. I'm just not sure the cabin will survive it."

"Ha ha." She peered inside the stove, her hair sliding over her shoulder, as rich and thick as chocolate. Great, now he had to worry about her setting her hair on fire. "Okay, I admit it. I skipped Girl Scouts. A lighter, some paper and some wood isn't enough?"

He laughed. Honestly, he was feeling better already. Just being around Nicole made him less tired. "You have to open the damper, otherwise there's no oxygen flow and the smoke will pour into the cabin." He squatted next to her to show her the lever on the chimney. "Want a quick tutorial?"

"Remedial Girl Scouts?"

He chuckled, then walked her through the basics of building a fire in a small wood stove. She watched him attentively each step of the way. He let her do the honors with the lighter, just so he could witness her delighted expression when the fire took hold and the smoke went up the smokestack rather than into her face.

"Nice work." They exchanged a high-five. It was really only then that he realized how close their bodies were to each other. Her face was flushed from the effort of starting the fire, and her hair curled in damp tendrils around her face. Her lips were parted in a relaxed smile.

Uh oh. Relaxed-and-sweaty Nicole was always dangerously appealing to him.

Something had shifted between them since they'd ridden into the woods after the lost birder. Life-and-death situations always changed things. They made you take life more seriously, and focus on what was important. Like the fact that he and Nicole were here alone, and more attracted to each other than ever.

She was watching him too, something deep and hot stirring in her gaze.

His cock responded. He wanted her, tired as he was. Ten minutes ago, he'd been ready for bed. Now he still wanted to get into that bed—but for completely different reasons.

He brushed a stray lock of hair away from her face. "You shouldn't look at me like that. I'm too tired to exercise good judgment."

"Good judgment is overrated." Her smile held sass and promise, and sent another rush of lust through him.

He cupped his hand around the back of her head. "You know, that's what I always thought, but people kept telling me I was wrong."

Gazing into each other's eyes, they knelt there by the stove, basking in the waves of heat coming off the cast iron. Or maybe they were generating the heat themselves. Either way, wisps of steam were rising from his wool sweater. Slowly, watching her reaction every step of the way, he brought his lips close to hers. He hovered next to her, breathing in the rain-washed scent of her wet hair, and the fresh fragrance of her skin.

"I want to kiss you," he told her in a low voice. "But I don't want to screw it up like last time."

"I wouldn't call that a screw-up," she whispered.

"I need to know you want this."

"The fact that I kissed you back doesn't give you a hint?" She tilted her head back, her hair sifting across his fingers.

"I've pissed you off a bunch of times since then."

One corner of her mouth danced with humor. "Do you have to sound so proud of that?"

He threw his head back and laughed. It felt so good to be there with her in this cozy little universe of two, with the wind wailing outside and a fire crackling cheerfully inside. "I swear it's not intentional. At least not completely." He winked at her.

"I knew it!" She launched herself at him, toppling him onto

his back, then straddled him. He couldn't stop laughing at her comical expression of outrage. Even though two minutes ago he'd been sore as hell, he felt no pain in this position, flat on his back. Just pure heat and arousal.

She pinned his arms to the floor. "Admit it—you like all my crazy ideas."

"Never."

"You think I'm a genius."

"I think you're incredible." Very true. He saw her register his sincerity, then move on.

"You'd like to try that raindrop therapy as soon as possible."

"Isn't that what we just did? Some genuine Rocky Peak raindrop therapy. It's working for me." He winked at her again, loving the wild sparkle in her eyes and the flush on her cheeks. This was exactly what he'd been after all this time. Wild, unrestrained Nicole Davidson. Sexier than ever.

A hard bulge was growing in his trousers. His cock pounded and throbbed, eager to be free of the stiff fabric of his work pants. Why did they both still have all these wet clothes on? She'd already seen him naked, even though she'd pretended not to look. He'd definitely seen her sneaking a couple of peeks. Not that he minded.

Her glance slid down his body, pausing on the lump in his pants. "Oh," she said softly.

"Yeah, oh. Don't tell me you're surprised. I've been hot for you since—"

"Since when?"

"The sports bra," he admitted with a grin. "Round about then."

A slow smile spread across her face, all the way to those gorgeous clear blue eyes. "You could have just said so, you know."

"I did. In my own way."

She leaned forward, gently lowering her face to his. The rain fresh softness of her lips brushed delicately against his. He held

very still, as if a butterfly was landing on him, one he didn't want
to scare away. The light touch of that sweet kiss made something
settle deep inside him.

He'd go a long way for this woman. A long way in an
unknown direction.

She drew back, touching her tongue lightly to her lips, as if
savoring the taste of him.

He lifted the hem of her sweater and slid his hands underneath, onto the smooth warm skin of her lower back. She shivered deliciously as he ran his hands up her back, across each
little knob of her spine. Her eyes went half-closed and she arched
her back to make it easier for him. She shifted on his thighs, a
sensual rotating move that made him groan.

He pressed his fingertips into the muscles alongside her
spine. With his two hands spread open, he could span the width
of her back, which meant his thumbs were able to just brush
against the sides of her breasts.

Her quick snatch of breath told him she felt that—and loved
it. He dug deeper, working out the tension in her muscles.
Tension that was probably always there, he realized. Nicole lived
with a lot of stress. From working for Max? Something else? The
sister she'd mentioned once, then never again?

Her skin was so tender, so sensitive. Every time he came
closer to her breasts, a full-body tremor passed through her. And
every time that happened, his cock hardened even more, until it
was pushing painfully against his fly.

"Oh my God, Kai, that feels incredible," she moaned. "You
could definitely get work at the new spa."

He chuckled. Right now, all of his opposition to the spa idea
seemed so distant. "Might be a nice change from scrambling up
and down hillsides."

The reminder made her snap to attention. "Wait a second
here. You're the one who's tired and sore. I should be giving you a
massage, not the other way around." She rolled off him, landing

on the floor with a thump. "And this floor is so hard! Why didn't you say something?"

"I didn't feel it," he said honestly. "I was feeling something else."

She rose to her feet, then offered her hand. "How about we continue in bed, and you let me take a turn with the muscle massage."

When they were both on their feet, it took a moment for the room to stop spinning. Holy shit, he was dehydrated, he realized, astonished that he'd allowed that to happen. She noticed it too, trained nurse that she was. She hurried to find a water bottle, which she brought over to him.

"Thank you," he said when he'd drained about half of it. "Basic wilderness protocol, small regular sips of water, and I totally forgot about it. That's how damn distracting you are."

She pointed to the bed. "Lie down."

"Bossy."

"I'm not kidding. You're at the end of your endurance. Even a stud like you has limits."

"I never said I didn't. Never said I was a stud, either." He knew his limits very well, especially in a wilderness context. "In the rescue field, I'm known as the over-prepared type, not the reckless type." He swayed slightly. Damn, it had all caught up to him now. Or maybe all his blood had rushed to his erection, leaving nothing for other vital functions.

"Bed. Now. Well, after you take your clothes off," she added.

"You should too," he murmured as he unfastened his trousers. "Shared body heat, best way to combat hypothermia."

"You're not hypothermic."

"Also best way to snuggle."

She laughed, a delighted sound that made his heart turn over. "I'd love to snuggle with you, Kai Rockwell. I'd love to do a lot of other things too, but first we have to get you stabilized. Come on, strip. I will too."

She tugged her sweater over her head. Her hair crackled in a riot of static as her head emerged. But he was more focused on what she wore underneath—a damp silk shortie camisole printed with a pattern of dancing kittens. "Is that your pajama top?"

"I was in a hurry," she admitted. "I just threw on some clothes and ran out to see what was going on."

He ran a hand up the smooth skin of her arm and slid the thin strap off her shoulder. "I'm not complaining, but next time you're in a wilderness rescue situation, you might consider proper gear." He slid his thumb along the curve of her collarbone and watched her shiver.

"You're supposed to be in that bed," she said weakly. "Is it always this hard to get you into bed?"

"That sounds like a dangerous question to answer."

She took him by the shoulders and turned him around, pushing him toward the bed.

"I'm a terrible patient. Might as well know that going in, Nurse Nicole."

"I've been warned. Now go. I'll be right behind you."

That bed did look tempting, and the heat from the wood stove was warming his skin, relaxing him. As much as he wanted to keep bantering with Nicole, the need for rest won out. He stripped off the rest of his clothes, peeling off the clammy layer closest to his skin. As soon as he stretched out on the bed, his eyes began to close.

"This is embarrassing. First time I have a chance to see you naked and I crash," he mumbled as sleep dragged him under. "Not fair."

The last thing he saw was her teasing smile as she slid the other strap of the camisole off her shoulder. "To be continued..."

17

Awake or asleep, Kai was the most compelling man Nicole had ever known. Even his snore was kind of fascinating, a soft wheeze, like the wind whistling through cracks in the siding. But mostly it was the magnificence of his body at rest, how he still radiated vitality even when he was unconscious. The firelight flickered across his chiseled muscles, turning his skin a warm gold.

He'd pulled the blanket over most of his body, but his chest and shoulders were uncovered. She noticed a raised scar on his chest, and a small tattoo of a jagged mountain on his upper arm. Rocky Peak?

That thought made her heart twist. Kai loved this place, even though he'd left and stayed away so long. It was clear to her how much Rocky Peak was a part of him.

And the Summit Group was trying to take it away, and she was assisting them.

But the lodge was a financial disaster in the making. Was it so bad, helping someone else take over the place? Kai didn't want it. None of the kids did, not even Gracie. In Nicole's opinion, Gracie needed a kick in the pants to go explore the world.

Anyway, she was just a small piece of the puzzle. Max wouldn't sell unless he wanted to. She was just...offering a vision.

She took a moment to dry her panties by the fire, then slipped them back on and climbed into bed with Kai. She settled against his side as if she belonged there. Without waking, he adjusted his position to tug her closer.

Well, that was her purpose here, after all—she was supposed to be warming him up. She flung one leg across his, feeling the iron bulge of his thighs and the soft prickle of his body hair. Everything about Kai was so ... manly. Except that there was another side to him, too. A sensitive, surprisingly thoughtful side.

Not to mention an irritating side. She couldn't let herself forget that part. Just because he was unbelievably sexy and attractive to her didn't mean she should get involved with him.

Just because she was snuggling naked with him didn't mean that either. This was just a one-time snuggle for medical purposes. He was still "the enemy," someone standing in the way of her "bonus for Birdie." So technically, she was sleeping with the enemy.

And wow, did it feel good.

She drifted off, dreaming of running through the halls of Rocky Peak Lodge, the way the Rockwell kids must have grown up, except she was chasing Birdie. Birdie was laughing and running on her own two legs, as if she'd never needed a wheelchair. As if she'd never lost oxygen to her brain.

When she woke up with a start, Kai was watching her, his head propped on one hand. The firelight gave his eyes a deep tender glow. "What were you dreaming about?" he asked her softly. "You have the happiest smile I've ever seen."

"I dreamt that—" She stopped abruptly. She still hadn't told Kai anything much about Birdie. But why did she have to be a secret? The thought of her sister swelled in her heart—almost like a bird trying to break free.

"I was dreaming about my sister."

"The sister you mentioned before?" Kai cocked his head, waiting for more. As if he really wanted to hear, as if he'd stay right there, patiently listening, until she said whatever she needed to.

"Yes. Her name is Birdie and she's disabled, she uses a wheelchair. But in my dream she was running and laughing. Like she used to before—" To her utter surprise, her eyes filled with tears. Maybe it was thanks to Kai and his empathetic presence. "She has brain damage."

"What happened?" Kai asked the question like someone experienced in disasters, someone who knew what a traumatic event felt like.

For some reason that freed her to spill it all out. "She nearly drowned. She was only eight. Mom was at work, I was at school. She always went to her best friend's house after school, and they had a pool. She was practicing holding her breath with a friend and she saw a necklace on the bottom. She went after it and got her foot stuck."

Nicole had pictured it so many times in her mind. Birdie spotting something sparkly, her deep inhale, her push to the bottom, grabbing the necklace, then her big toe snagging the grate over the filter. Her confusion, her panic, the necklace drifting back to the bottom. Five minutes and fifteen seconds before her friend called out for help.

"But that was many years ago. I don't know why I would have a dream like that now."

"Where does Birdie live?"

"She lives at an assisted-living home in Seattle. I miss her a lot," she admitted. "I'm used to seeing her several times a week. Talking on the phone just isn't the same. She has a very short attention span. It's much easier if I'm right in front of her."

Kai caught one of her tears on his thumb and lifted it away before it spilled down her cheek. "Are you her guardian?"

"Yes, ever since Mom passed away. But even before, I was very close to her. Mom worked a lot, so I was the Birdie-sitter." She smiled at that old nickname, which was similar to Max-Whisperer, now that she thought of it. "I can't tell if she misses me or not, if I should call her more, or if she's just fine."

"It sounds like you beat yourself up about her."

She cast him a surprised look. "Yes, I really do. How did you know that?"

"I can tell. I did the same thing after I left home. I worried about my brothers and sisters. I second-guessed myself. Maybe it's an oldest-child thing."

She became aware of Kai's big body, so close to hers, their legs touching, their shared body heat radiating between them like the sweetest fire imaginable. "Finally we have something in common."

"Except that you miss the Birdie who is and the Birdie who *was*. That's twice the missing."

Her mouth fell open. Where had that insight come from?

"Just doing a little dream interpretation." He smiled at her, looking so handsome her heart nearly stopped.

"Well, that's pretty dead-on. Except that I don't normally miss the old Birdie. I love her how she is. She's still my rascally little sister who I will love forever. She gets into just as much trouble with that wheelchair as she did without."

His eyes darkened as he studied her. A long moment passed while she held her breath, wondering what was going through his mind. What judgments was he forming, what conclusions was he making? "Thank you for telling me," he finally murmured. "I appreciate that." And then, "Damnit. This was easier before."

She didn't really know what that meant, and the intensity of his scrutiny made her want to squirm. He was supposed to be the patient, not her. Her first duty was to his health.

She forced herself into medical assessment mode. His color was better, the shadows under his eyes were gone. Her job in his bed was done.

And yet she had no desire to leave.

Outside, the wind was still keening through the treetops, but the lash of rain had slowed to a patter. The fire was still merrily heating up the tiny cabin. All the sounds and sensations wove together into a kind of spell. A soothing, tempting, seductive spell that made her muscles refuse to even contemplate getting out of bed.

She cleared her throat. "Are you feeling better?"

"Fantastic." His gaze heated, making her shiver. "There's this incredibly beautiful woman in my bed and she's wearing hardly anything." He spread his hand across her lower belly, his little finger tangling in her panties. "I want to touch her. Lick her all over." His voice lowered to a growl. "Make her moan."

Her heart raced to triple its normal speed. The heavy warmth of his hand sent a wave of desire through her, so strong it snatched all her words. "Mmm, hmmm?" she managed.

"So if she doesn't want that, she should let me know." He widened the spread of his hand, slid it up her rib cage. Her nipples, anticipating his touch, pebbled hard against the blanket covering her and Kai.

"She's not crazy," Nicole murmured, arching her back under his slow caress. "Trust me, she's fine with that."

"Fine with it, huh?" He tugged the blanket down to expose her breasts. Under his heated gaze, her nipples hardened even more. He let out a sigh and lowered his head to touch his tongue to the left one, closest to him. She felt the electric sensation all the way from her nipple to her sex, as if an invisible cord connected them.

"I'm hoping for more than just 'fine with it.' I'm aiming for something more like, 'Yes, by all that's holy, let's do this thing.'"

His warm breath on her nipple made her crazy, especially when he licked it again afterwards, swirling his tongue around and around, teasing and taunting.

"Yes," she moaned. "What you just said. But Kai—"

"Yeah," he mumbled, his mouth full of her right breast, which felt so good she wanted to open her mouth and sing.

But she had to establish some rules first. "This can't be a *real* thing."

His warm mouth left her nipple, and of course she craved it again, right away. "What are you talking about?"

"We have to agree about what this is, before we do anything. It can't be an actual relationship. I just want to make sure we're completely clear about that."

He studied her closely, one hand still splayed across her stomach. Her body ached for him, her sex throbbed with need. She wanted him, she wanted this. But she couldn't add one more deception to her list. Especially not this one. She couldn't permit a real relationship. She couldn't take the risk of hurting him.

"What's the big deal?" she said lightly. "You're Mr. Don't Tie Me Down. Mr. Wanderlust. Mr. Travel Bug. Mr. Show Me a Mountain and I'll Climb It, or Rescue Some Dumbass Who Tried to Climb It."

He didn't fall for her jokes. "Don't put this on me. I'm not the one laying down rules."

Ugh—why did Kai have to be the only man who would resist an agreement to not get involved?

"We're both going behind enemy lines," she pointed out. "This cabin is like a safe zone, but when we get back to the lodge, we'll be right back where we were. I'll be pushing crystals and you'll be googling my third grade boyfriend."

He caressed the curve of her waist, making her skin shiver. "Have to admit, it's hard to see you as the enemy right now."

But she *was*. And he didn't know the full extent of her enemyness. That was why she couldn't allow this to mean anything.

She stared at him helplessly, torn between giving in to the sensations coursing through her body, and wanting to be real with him.

"Ah, fuck it," he finally said with a grin. "I don't know what's on your mind, but have it your way. I'm a guy, not a monk." He rolled on top of her, stretching her beneath him, pinning her arms to the bed. "But I get to call the shots on everything else."

"Like what?" she asked breathlessly as a rush of heat shot through her body.

"Like what I'm going to do to you." His voice deepened to a lust-struck growl. "Like how many times I'm going to make you come. Like how many *ways* I'm going to make you come."

He nudged his knee between her legs, spreading them apart. He dragged his thigh against her mound, which made the silk of her panties rub against her clit. Her body arched and she pressed up against him. His grip tightened on her arms, holding them locked in place. But instead of making her feel restrained, it made her feel free. Free to let her mind take a back seat, and her body revel in the moment.

"Let me do the work," he murmured. "You stay just like that, you gorgeous woman."

He lowered his head so he could kiss her. This wasn't just any kiss. It was a ravaging, claiming, soul-rocking kiss. It left her trembling, completely at his mercy. Every sweep of his tongue sent fire streaming through her body. This man knew how to kiss, knew how to take command, how to adapt to her responses, how to stoke the flames higher and higher.

When she was gasping and breathless, he moved farther down her body. Still holding her arms pinned to the bed, he nuzzled her neck, the point of her jaw, the sensitive skin below her ear. He pressed kisses into her neck, nibbled his way down the tendon to her collarbone. His hair brushed against her chin as he delicately licked the base of her throat, where her pulse must be going absolutely mad.

She inhaled the smoky scent of his hair, which held the memory of rainstorms and forests and wild journeys into the unknown. This was another journey like that, except they were going there together and it felt so good she wanted to cry.

Now his mouth was on her nipple again. Already sensitized, it practically sizzled under his deep suckling. He switched from one nipple to the other, gathering each breast into his mouth with ferocious appreciation. He swirled his tongue around the delicate skin of her areola, sucked until she felt it deep inside her sex.

"Kai," she pleaded. "Touch me. I'm dying."

"I'll get there. I got you, sweet thing. Don't you worry." The lust in his voice mingled with laughter. He released her arms so he could make his way lower, licking his way down her abdomen. Her skin jumped everywhere he touched, as if he'd turned her into one big nerve ending.

His big hands wrapped around her hips. She still wore her panties, though she wished she could magically remove them from her body. Make them vanish in a wisp of smoke.

On the other hand, if she did that, Kai wouldn't be able to play with them the way he was now doing. Tugging them with his teeth this way and that, dragging them against her clit. Using them to create the most sweet and maddening friction.

"Jesus, Mary and Joseph," she sighed as she opened her legs for him. *Take me*, that gesture meant. *Take me and never let me go.*

"There's one detail we forgot." His words sent warm air through the fabric, onto her swollen, aching mound. "No condom."

"Oh!" She'd forgotten about that part of the equation. Need pulsed between her legs. It felt as if the entire world was centered right there. Nothing else mattered. "Oh no."

"Oh yes. Luckily, there are two million ways to make you come that don't require a condom." He slid both his hands under her panties, his thumbs landing on the plump folds that shielded her clit. Again with his teeth, he drew down the upper edge of her undies, exposing her to his hot gaze.

She nearly came just from that, from the nearly physical sensation of his eyes on her, and the actual physical sensation of his thumbs pressing into her sex. But that was nothing compared to the electric effect of his mouth claiming her clit.

A blinding bolt of pleasure streaked through her. She nearly came off the bed as her body arched under the rough strokes of his tongue. Or maybe it was more than his tongue. She hardly knew what he was doing, just that it felt unbelievable. His firm lips took total, absolute command of her body. His iron-strong hands pinned her hips to the bed, while he worked magic with his mouth.

His dark hair felt like sable between her legs. She peeked down at him, and went dizzy at the sexy sight of his powerful body crouched down there. Big hands holding her legs apart, wide shoulders hunched, muscles bunching

Good God.

She lay back and surrendered everything to him, all control, all restraint.

The wild pleasure unleashed a part of her she'd nearly forgotten. A greedy side, a selfish side, the part of Nicole that wanted something for *herself.* That wanted to feel good, no matter the cost to anyone else. *Because there was no cost.* Kai was here for her, like a rock in a storm, or maybe more like the wind in her sails. He was urging her on with every tool he had—hands, mouth, words.

"Go after it, babe, get it, get what you want, you're so fucking sexy, I want to hear you scream. I want to watch you come apart on my tongue. I want you to explode, baby. Fucking explode. You got me so hard my cock's like a fucking pile-driver."

The words he muttered in between tongue-fucking drove her even crazier. He was so shameless. So open. So demanding. And yet so *generous.*

Her pleasure was his—there was no separation. And that was what sent her right over the edge. She rocketed into a screaming orgasm that wiped her mind clean. She clutched at the sheets, digging her fingers into the mattress as if she might spiral off the edge of the earth. Wave after wave of ecstasy swept through her.

Kai was relentless, pushing her into new spasms, another, then another.

With each one, she screamed again, sometimes his name, sometimes a random curse word, sometimes something incoherent like, "So good, oh my God, please don't stop."

At least that was how it sounded in her head, but it came out more as incomprehensible mumbling.

Finally the waves of pleasure slowed and she flopped back on the bed, covered in sweat, completely wrung out. So satisfied and happy that she could leap tall buildings. Maybe run down cliffs and carry lost hikers on her back.

"Jesus, Kai, maybe you should have warned me," she said, half-laughing as he lifted his head away from her sex.

His eyes were so dark with lust they barely looked green anymore. He came up onto his knees and she saw the massive erection jutting between his thighs. Thick and swollen, spectacularly aroused, it made her mouth go dry. It had been *so long* since she'd been with a man. She wanted to revel in it. She wanted everything with him. All of it, over and over.

He gave her a strained smile. "Never going on a rescue mission without a condom again. At least not with you along."

A powerful sense of wellbeing welled inside her. This was just the beginning. The beginning of something wonderful—not a relationship. They both knew that. They were clear about it. But something amazing nonetheless.

She scrambled onto her knees and shuffled across the bed until she faced him. "Sit up," she said softly. He came off his heels so he was kneeling on the bed, his arousal right at her eye level. "Perfect."

As he watched, eyes burning, she brought her lips to the tip of his shaft.

18

IT HAD THE FEEL OF AN X-RATED FANTASY, BUT SO MUCH BETTER because this was the very real Nicole with her lips wrapped around his cock. He held himself as still as he could, even though he craved the feel of the back of her throat. This was just the start; he didn't want to scare her off with his more rough-edged side.

But that was before she began sucking him with deep, almost greedy draws. Before she surrounded him with the wet velvet of her mouth. Before she skimmed her fingers up and down the backs of his thighs, across his ass cheeks, between his legs. The contrast between the lightness of her touch and the intensity of her sucking made him lose his mind.

He gripped the back of her head, tilting it so he could thrust deeper. Her cheeks hollowed and her eyes half-closed.

"Fuck, that feels good," he ground out. "Tell me if you want me to stop. Promise me. Cause I'm about to lose it."

She winked at him. Winked!

He clenched his jaw to keep from exploding right then and there. Face it, he didn't know where this was going to go, or whether they'd ever do this again. She might go right back to her arm's-length manner as soon as they returned to the lodge. He didn't want this moment to pass too quickly. He wanted to draw it out as long as he could.

But his cock didn't care what he wanted. That beast was swelling bigger with every sweet pull of her mouth. A ball of energy built in his spine, tightening his balls, drumming through his veins.

He thrust forward, catching her by surprise. She quickly adjusted and caught onto his rhythm. Her hair tumbled across her naked back, nearly reaching the tender twin curves of her ass. Wild images bombarded through his head. He wanted to fuck that hair, feel its rich waves against his cock. He wanted to toss her onto her back, plunge inside, bury himself in her, lose himself.

Find himself.

And then he gave in and let the pleasure swamp him. Let the orgasm seize him and turn him upside down and inside out.

THEY LAY side by side afterwards, Nicole tucked against him, his chest heaving as if he'd just run up and down...well, another cliff. Funny when he thought about how this whole night had started — with a call from help from the Rocky Peak FD.

When the call had come in, he'd been asleep, after going to bed furious with Nicole and her crazy raindrop therapy plans.

Which he still opposed. *That* wasn't changing. But something else was nagging at him. A detail from that presentation in the media room.

"Art therapy for the disabled," he said out loud.

"Hm?" She stirred against him, a warm, silky bundle of sexy female goodness.

"You mentioned art therapy for the disabled. Were you thinking about your sister?"

She nestled even closer against his side. "Yes. Well, the

thought was inspired by Birdie. She loves art. They have a class at Sunny Grove that she never misses."

"That's where she lives?"

"Yes, for now. She's on a waiting list for another home but those spots are in big demand. Roger found Sunny Grove after he—"

"After he kicked her out? Isn't that what you said before?"

"She liked to chase his cat around. We couldn't get her to stop," she said ruefully.

He chuckled, then stopped—was that rude, to laugh at her sister's mischievousness? His Rockwell irreverence might get him in trouble again here.

"You can laugh, it's okay. Birdie is actually hilarious, but getting her to follow rules, forget it. She lives in the moment, completely."

"Not a bad quality. Is she happy at Sunny Grove?"

"Sure. I mean, if she lived somewhere else, she'd probably like that too, unless it was horrible. If she hates something, it's pretty clear. She won't say so, but she gets very quiet, like a turtle going into its shell. You have to know how to read her signals because she doesn't communicate like other people."

He stroked her hair, sifting the soft strands through his fingers. "I hope I get to meet her."

But that was the wrong thing to say, apparently. She sat up, shaking her hair away from him and twisting it into a knot. The old Nicole, cautious and on guard, stared back at him. He couldn't imagine *this* Nicole taking his cock into her mouth, or coming so hard. Why did she keep such a lid on her wild side? "She won't get on an airplane. Terrified of them. Besides, that's a relationship type of thing, meeting my sister. We're not in a relationship, remember?"

He stared at her. What kind of crazy reaction was that? "Why does it have to be a relationship thing? Why couldn't it just be a human thing? She's a human. I'm a human. You're an amazing human I just had sex with. Or close enough. What are you freaking out about?"

She snapped an elastic tie around her hair. "I'm not freaking out. I'm just making it extra clear that we have to keep this," she sketched a box with her finger, "within the lines. No coloring outside the box."

"Are we back to art therapy again?"

Humor burst through her wariness as she let out a laugh. It was a damn good thing she found him amusing. Otherwise they'd never get anywhere.

"Maybe you should tell me exactly what's in the box. Or what isn't in the box."

"Birdie is definitely not in the box. She's a sensitive subject and I'm shocked I even told you about her. I don't know why I did."

"Probably because deep inside you know I'm trustworthy."

With a cautious glance at him, she drew her lower lip between her teeth. "Do I? I told you, I've been burned in the past."

He hated being compared to Roger Vance, who probably only cared about his money and his image. "I'll prove you can trust me. I'll stay in that little box of yours, as long as you're in there with me."

Her smile spread all the way to her eyes, which shone in the glow from the lantern. "We'll make it the best box ever."

"Can we be naked in the box?"

"Yes. It's a clothing optional box."

He grinned. "Then I don't see a problem."

But in the back of his mind, he did see a problem. Trust went both ways. And he still sensed she wasn't telling him everything. If she was, why would they even need a "box"?

He'd never been good at coloring inside the lines. But he'd try.

He rolled out of the bed and walked to the window. Cupping

his hands to block out the light, he peered into the still-dark outside world.

"It's about an hour until sunrise and the rain has died down. We should probably head back."

Nicole was already pulling on her wet pants, which she'd draped next to the fire. "Wow, these feel pretty dry. Thank you, secret wilderness cabin." She stripped the sheets off the bed. "I think I'll take these back to the lodge and wash them. I'll have to sneak them back here before anyone notices."

He watched her bundle everything up, so efficient, as if the lovemaking they'd shared had already been forgotten, except for the logistics.

Good thing he knew that wasn't entirely true, because she kept giving him surreptitious little glances and her cheeks were still flushed.

He should probably put some clothes on, but her businesslike attitude irritated him. Even if it was a one-time non-relationship thing, it was a *damn good* one-time thing. Their time together didn't deserve to be instantly forgotten.

He strode over to her and lifted the bundle of sheets from her arms, then stuffed them into his duffel bag. "You know this changes things, don't you?"

Her eyes widened, and a pulse fluttered in her throat. "What do you mean? Why does it have to change anything?"

"Because now that I know you have a wild side, I'm going to want to see it again. Rock climbing, maybe. Skydiving." He winked at her. "Fair warning, the challenge is on."

She relaxed. What had she *thought* he was going to say? Something more menacing? More obnoxious?

"And what about the lodge?" she asked carefully. "Does it change anything with respect to the lodge?"

"Hell no," he said promptly. "Enemies to the end when it comes to raindrop therapy."

She laughed. "You know, someday you're going to try it and eat your words."

He pulled on his clothes, still slightly damp but nothing his body heat couldn't fix. "Maybe. But imagine if the rescue outpost was already a treatment room. What if I hadn't been there? Poor Jim the birder might still be lost in Skyfall."

"That's a good point." She was quiet for a moment, then snapped her fingers. "We'll keep the fire outpost because having sexy firemen around will be an added bonus for the spa crowd."

"*Added bonus?*"

"See?" She smiled at him mischievously. "I'm open to change. As long as it's sexy change."

"I hope that means you think I'm sexy."

"Do you seriously have any doubt about that?"

Completely dressed now, he walked over to her and cupped her chin in his hand. He searched her face, looking for some sign of how she felt about him, about what they'd done, about what came next.

Her heart-shaped face told him nothing. She ran her tongue across her lips. Nervous? Excited? Regretful?

"I guess we'll find out. In the box."

"In the box," she agreed.

It felt like a date.

"Let's go, the sun'll be up soon." All business now, he closed the damper on the wood stove, returned the hurricane lanterns to their storage spots, put everything else back in order.

Outside, the rain had transformed into more of a mist. It kissed their faces with cool welcome as they made their way to the four-wheeler. Without saying anything else, they loaded up and headed back into the woods.

As they passed the first ridge with a view of the sky, Kai saw rosy fingers of light starting to appear on the horizon. Sunrise always began like this in the mountains. Darkness lifting to gray, then fingers of coral painting the horizon.

Love for Rocky Peak and these mountains grabbed his heart so fiercely it felt almost like a heart attack. How had he stayed away from this place for so long? How could he ever bear to leave?

And then it came to him, like the rays of the rising sun lighting up the valley. The idea had tried to emerge before, but he hadn't allowed it to. Now he couldn't stop the images flooding his thoughts.

What if he stayed?

What if *he* ran the lodge the way it ought to be run? The way it used to be run? Ski parties, dances, family reunions, hunting parties, fishing parties? Outdoor adventures...ski races...hiking expeditions? The lodge was losing money because Max was getting older and had less energy to spend on it. If he took over...

He could still do the rescue work he loved—right here at home. He could still spend time in the mountains. Still feel like he was making a difference. But he'd be based *here*. The place he'd grown up. With his family.

With Max.

He inhaled a long breath as they cruised through thick forests touched with the tender light of the new day.

Right....Max. The reason he was getting along okay with Max was that they weren't talking about anything painful. They were coexisting. Avoiding battles. Keeping things cool.

But if he stayed on, that wouldn't work. At some point, they'd be at each other's throats again. He should do what he should have done years ago, but hadn't known how to.

He should hash out all that painful history with his father.

Maybe with medical assistance standing by. Nurse Nicole, for instance.

If he decided to stay, what about Nicole and all her plans? Maybe he could adopt some of her ideas. They could expand the sauna a little bit. They could add camps for kids, even art therapy. Her ideas weren't *terrible*.

Okay, maybe some of them were.

He dropped Nicole off at the front door. "I ... uh...might call on you for some Max-whispering later."

"What kind of Max-whispering?" Her eyebrows quirked with curiosity.

"I need to talk to him, and it might get his blood pressure up."

"Talk to him about what? Not about..." She waved a hand back and forth between them. Her face was flushed from their ride and her hair a wild tangle. He fought back the urge to touch it. Anyone could be watching right now. Hell, Gracie was probably up early with her watercolors, laughing her ass off at their four-wheeler ride of shame.

"About the box?" he asked. "Nope, the box is completely private. What goes in the box stays in the box."

"Starting to regret that metaphor," she murmured.

He smiled at that. "This is about me and Max and it goes way back. I need you to make sure Max doesn't blow a gasket."

"Humans don't have gaskets, you know that, right?"

He leaned closer, lowering his voice to an intimate level guaranteed to bring back hot memories of their night together. "Baby, any time you want to share more anatomy lessons, I'm there."

She tilted her head forward so her forehead touched his. "Keep your door unlocked and maybe I'll feel educational one of these nights."

Bam. Was she serious or just teasing him? His cock didn't have any doubts. He went rock hard at the idea of her showing up at his door. "You got it," he managed.

She took a step toward the lodge, then turned back, lowering her voice. "Also, where is your room? I wouldn't want to end up in a random birder's suite."

So she *was* serious. Hot damn.

He grinned at her. "I'm in one of the guesthouses. I'll put some plastic antlers on the door, you can't miss it."

19

WHEN NICOLE GOT BACK TO HER ROOM, SHE COULDN'T SIT STILL. Pacing around her cozy space, she sorted through every delicious detail of the night, committing everything to memory. What an incredible, once-in-a-lifetime experience.

She couldn't do that again. She couldn't! It was deceptive. But was it deceptive, now that they'd established "the box"? They both knew where things stood. She wasn't deceiving him.

Oh, who was she kidding? Of course she was deceiving him. Until she told him all about the Summit Group and their plans for the lodge, she was keeping something a secret from him.

An idea stole into her mind, so tempting it almost made her cry.

What if she told Kai the truth? What if she laid it all out there —the coming offer, her part in it, its huge benefits for the Rockwells? The millions of dollars they'd make?

Just as quickly, she shut down the thought. Kai was an honest, straightforward guy who rescued people from life-threatening situations. He wouldn't understand her reasons for coming to the lodge. He would just feel betrayed.

Also—he might send her away once he knew the truth.

Which meant that she'd also lose this job and the best opportunity she'd ever had to take care of Birdie. She'd lose everything and gain nothing.

Telling the truth was out of the question.

Which meant she should not get any more involved with Kai. No more being alone with Kai, no more getting naked with Kai, no more feeling his touch on her skin, his kiss on her—

She jumped when her phone buzzed. She'd left it behind during their rescue mission, which made last night the longest time she'd been separated from her phone in forever. Usually she had it practically implanted in her hand in case Birdie needed her.

But it wasn't Birdie, it was Felicity.

Status report, please.

Nicole's heart sank. She was supposed to relay everything to Felicity, but did that extend to the night she'd just spent with Kai? Hell no.

The presentation went really well, she texted back finally. *Kai hated it.*

Great. Along with a big thumb's up.

Nicole thought about her conversation with Kai, about the rescued birder. Maybe she could do something right now to keep that piece of the lodge intact.

From your eyes and ears on the inside, a recommendation. The fire station needs to stay. It should be part of the sale contract.

Right away her phone rang with a call rather than a text.

"What are you talking about?" said Felicity. "That piece is a relic. It needs to be torn down."

"Then replace it with a better building. But last night I saw someone get rescued and I think it's important that some form of the fire station stays."

"Someone got rescued? By who?"

"Kai."

A brief moment of silence, along with some finger-drumming. "Oh Nico. You aren't getting involved with Kai, are you?"

"No! What are you talking about?" She looked around the room in a panic, as if Felicity had a camera hidden somewhere. She wouldn't put it past her.

"It's the way you said his name. He means something to you. Nicole, don't get distracted. Get it together. No fucking the rebel Rockwell."

Nicole set her teeth. "Are you done, Shark Tank?"

"I don't know, am I? Do I have to come out there? Because that's the *last* thing I want to do. I'm not a fan of mountains, I'm a skyscraper girl."

Oh sweet Jesus, that would be the worst possible plot twist. "Don't be ridiculous. There's no need for that. When are you planning to make the offer?"

"As soon as possible. My boss is worried that word is getting out and someone might beat us to it. All those acres of pristine, unprotected land. That just doesn't exist anymore."

Unprotected land. All those tall spruce, the ravines, the flitting birds. To Felicity, it was just "unprotected land."

"Don't worry. I got this. Kai said he was staying for a month, and there's only a week left. Trust me, okay?"

She ended the call and headed for the shower, but all her happiness had leached out of her. If only she could tell Felicity and the Summit Group to shove their stupid job and do their own dirty work.

It hadn't sounded so bad at first. *A little light espionage. Eyes and ears on the inside. Ocean's 8.*

But now that she knew Max and his family, and Renata and all the other people who worked here, it felt like the sleaziest job in the world.

This was for Birdie, she reminded herself, for the umpteenth time. And besides, selling the lodge was the best thing for the Rockwells. None of them wanted to run it. Especially Kai. So she had no reason to feel all this guilt.

20

THE BIRD-WATCHING GROUP THREW A BIG "THANK YOU" PARTY FOR Kai and the crew from Rocky Peak FD. Nicole chatted with a scientist from New Zealand and tried not to stare at Kai, who was surrounded by grateful birders.

Max seemed thrilled with the whole event. He chomped on a cigar and told stories about the old days when rescuers used wooden toboggans and routinely lost fingers to frostbite. "That's how it's always been here. Everyone's got each other's backs," he kept trumpeting. "That wilderness out there will kill you if you give it half a chance. Rocky Peak, the people here, sticking together, that's the real deal. Good going, Kai."

He was in such a good mood that she stopped babysitting him and allowed herself to enjoy the party.

Until a couple hours later, when she realized that somehow Max had acquired a bottle of Scotch, and was helping himself freely as he held court from his favorite leather chair.

She'd never seen Max drink before—he was supposed to avoid hard alcohol. She hurried to his side as he lifted up the bottle for another pour. "Max, please. You're not supposed to drink more than one glass a day, and it's supposed to be wine, not the hard stuff."

"Haven't had a drink in a week."

"That doesn't matter." She lifted the bottle out of his hand before he could fill his glass again.

"Damn it, girl. You work for me, you forget that?"

"This is me, working for you. Doing my job. And having such a fun time doing it, too."

"Sassy," Max grumbled. But she'd gotten a smile out of him, which was the first step.

From across the room, Kai glanced over at them, and shot her a secret smile that sent a thrill down to the soles of her feet.

Then he sketched a box in the air.

"What's that?" Max asked sharply. "What'd he just do?"

"Um, nothing. Just a...nothing."

"Kai! Come over here." Max called to him. Kai said something to the group around him, then walked their direction. He looked sexy as sin in his hunter green sweater and evening scruff.

"Nice party, huh?" he said to them both. "I told them it wasn't necessary, but they wanted it."

"What was that ..." Max imitated the 'box.' "That sign you made? Looked fishy."

"It's nothing, Max. Personal. Private."

"Personal and private? With Nicole? You keep your hands off my nurse now."

Holy shit, her patient was wasted.

Kai's smile dropped and a muscle flexed in his jaw. He glanced at the bottle of Scotch Nicole had set back on the table. "How much have you had to drink, Max?"

"Not relevant," he growled. "Nicole is a sweet, kind girl. You... you never met a...a rule you didn't question. S'what Amanda said. Always said."

Nicole exchanged a look of alarm with Kai. This was her fault.

She'd been distracted, ogling Kai, and let Max go overboard with the liquor.

"Max. Pipe down," Kai murmured. "This is a party."

Max went red and leaned forward in his big chair. "Pipe down," he mimicked. "This is a party. Want a party? Invite the fishermen."

"What?" Kai froze, his head rearing back. "What did you just say?"

Something had just happened, something big, but Nicole had no idea what. The two men stared each other down while she searched her mind for anything related to fishermen, and came up blank.

"I said, where are the fishermen?" Max slurred the words ever so slightly.

"What are you talking about?" Kai asked carefully.

"You know what I'm talking about."

Nicole looked wildly from one to the other, totally out of her depth. Where was Gracie? Maybe she could interpret this scene. But Gracie must have ditched the party already, as she was nowhere to be seen. It was up to her to keep the peace here. "Guys," she said. "Let's all just take a breath—"

But Kai lifted one hand to interrupt her. He kept his gaze pinned on Max.

"Are we doing this?" he asked Max intensely. "Now? Right here?"

"No," Nicole tried again. "Whatever this is, no."

But Max raised his voice. "Curfew time!" he bellowed, the sound like a pressure wave through the room. "Don't you bird-watchers like to get up at dawn? Get the hell out of here. Go. Nice party, time to go."

Whoa. Nicole had heard stories of "Mad Max"'s temper, but she'd never seen it in action before. White waves of hair rippled around his head as he sent a scowl blazing through the room, chasing their guests away.

Within ten minutes, the restaurant was empty except for the three of them.

Kai stood before his father, arms folded across his chest, staring him down. It felt like an electric storm was gathering between the two of them.

"Should I leave?" Nicole asked tentatively, with a longing glance after the last of the birders.

"No," said Kai. "Max might need you. This could get ugly."

A splash of red appeared on Max's cheeks above his bushy beard. He kept his gaze fixed on Kai, virtually ignoring Nicole.

"She was leaving me," he choked out. "Wasn't she?"

Nicole's eyes went wide. "She" could only be one person. Amanda—Max's wife.

Kai nodded slowly. "Yes. She was."

"I wondered. All this time. It *was* that fisherman. And you *knew*."

"I knew. I'm sorry." Kai's tone was tight and even, as if he was using all his willpower to keep a grip on his emotions.

"You could have stopped her." Max's words wrenched out of him in a kind of primal cry. "Why didn't you stop her?"

Kai's face turned to stone. Nicole put a hand on his arm and felt the muscles tense like wrapped steel cables. She felt his titanic struggle for control.

"This is a bad time for a fight," she began.

"Fight!" Max burst out. "He doesn't fight. He runs!"

"I didn't *run*," Kai said through clenched teeth. "You kicked me out."

"Because I couldn't look at you. You could have stopped her." Nicole heard the pain running through Max's voice, under the anger and the alcohol. Did Kai hear it too?

Kai bent down so his hands were on the arms of Max's chair. Max shrank back, but Kai kept his voice perfectly even. "You don't know what really happened, Max. You never *wanted* to know. You wanted to think you were right, that I was a punk ass kid who failed you."

Max grabbed the bottle of Scotch, while Kai took a step back. At first Nicole thought he was going to throw it, but he just poured himself another glass. She gnawed on her lip. She should stop him. This was bad, so bad. But how was she supposed to step between these two forceful men, both vibrating from sheer intensity? It would be like trying to stop a storm.

Max tipped the glass to his lips and took a swallow, as if he was bracing for something terrible. "Tell me then. Tell me, son. Tell me what happened."

Kai's jaw worked and his eyes went hooded as he stared down at his father. "Mom asked me to drive with her into town, and as soon as we were past the driveway she told me she was leaving. She mentioned a fisherman staying in Rocky Peak. I got upset and yelled at her. I told her she shouldn't go, that we needed her, all of us kids. How could she just leave us, she was our mother! She started crying. I wanted her to pull over so we could talk about it more. I kept saying, 'pull over, pull over. Just for a minute.' But she wouldn't."

Max made a choking sound. Alarmed, Nicole knelt next to him to feel his pulse. It was racing, but still strong. "What else?" he managed.

"She said she was tired of Rocky Peak, tired of the mountains. She wanted to go to California, then send for us kids. I kept telling her that was nuts. We wanted to stay where we were. We wanted to stay here."

Max passed a hand over his eyes. "And then?"

Kai glanced at Nicole, a look of warning, and maybe a little embarrassment. She had no business being part of such an intimate moment between a father and son, but she was fascinated anyway. They were both so powerful, so magnetic, each in their own way. It was like watching two goliaths face each other down.

Kai shoved his hand through his hair. "Then there was someone in the road."

Max's head whipped up. "What?"

"He was on the side of the road, but he'd taken a few steps in, like he was trying to get our attention. He was waving. I don't know who it was, but I thought maybe it was the fisherman she was meeting. Mom swung the wheel really hard to avoid him. Much harder than she had to, and all of a sudden we were headed for a tree."

Kai clasped his hands behind his neck and turned away, hiding his face behind the screen of his bent elbows.

"I didn't tell the police any of that," came his choked voice. "I didn't tell anyone she was leaving. No one, not Griff and the others, not you. But you knew anyway, all this time."

Nicole longed to go to him, to offer whatever comfort he would accept, but her primary concern was Max. His shoulders were hunched, his fists clenched, his big body shaking.

The moment spun out into silence. Max stared at the floor, as if he was a million miles away—or maybe seventeen years ago, on a dark mountain road.

"I thought—I was afraid—" He broke off.

"What, Dad? What were you afraid of?"

"I thought...you might blame me. You looked at me different after it happened. Scared the living hell out of me."

Kai lowered himself into a crouch next to his father, so Max would meet his eyes. "Maybe I did. But I blamed myself too, because I couldn't make her listen."

"Make Amanda listen?" Max snorted as if the thought was absurd.

They were both quiet for a moment. Nicole caught Max eyeing the bottle again, and moved it out of his reach.

"That's why you kicked me out," said Kai. "That's why we kept fighting."

"I didn't kick you out. You left."

Kai rose to his feet and let out a snort. "Are we back to that again? Yeah, I left. Because you wanted me out. Because we couldn't say a word to each other without blowing up. Own up to it, Dad. It's okay. I get it. I got it then, too."

Max's beard moved back and forth as his mouth worked. Nicole fought the urge to rush in with a visualization, something with a soothing waterfall or a tranquil lake.

"I'm sorry I kicked you out," he muttered.

Kai's gaze flew to meet Nicole's. He looked astonished, as if he wasn't sure he'd heard right. "Did you just—"

"Yes. And don't make me repeat it," Max snapped. "Wore me out the first time. Shit."

Nicole bit her lip to hold back the laugh that wanted to spill out. The release from the tension of the past few minutes was tremendous.

"What are you snickering at, girl?" Max grumbled.

"Oh, I was just thinking about that study about the healing power of an apology."

"Bunch of bull crap. I don't feel any better at all."

"Blame the Scotch for that, not the apology." Nicole retrieved his cane from its resting spot in the corner. "How about I help you to your room? I think that's enough drama for one night."

Max nodded and yawned widely. "Why'd you let me have all that liquor? Oughta know better. That's your job, to keep me out of trouble."

Over his head, Nicole exchanged a glance with Kai. He still looked shell-shocked. With her entire heart, she wanted to go to him—comfort him, support him, embrace him. But her duty to Max came first.

She mouthed, "see you later," at Kai. Once again, Max caught it as he was getting to his feet.

"What was that?" Max asked her.

"What was what?"

"What did you say to Kai?"

"Nothing much."

"I saw your mouth move. More secrets? Why all the secrets all of a sudden?"

She took his arm while he got his cane under him. "Nothing important. I was just...well, it was something about antlers, if you want to know the truth."

"*Antlers?* What is wrong with you, girl?"

She took a peek at Kai and saw his smile flash. *Message received.*

21

NICOLE TUMBLED INTO HIS ARMS AS SOON AS HE OPENED THE DOOR to her later that night.

"Are you okay?" She actually felt him all over, as if that painful conversation with his father had left physical bruises on his body. It had been tough, no doubt about it. But it had also lifted a huge weight off his shoulders. All those years, protecting his siblings and his father from the truth had taken a toll.

"I'm not sure. I could probably use a comprehensive evaluation from a professional."

"That's what I'm here for. I'm the consummate professional."

"Consummate? I like the sound of that."

He lifted her up and wrapped her legs around him. The warmth of her body, the secret luscious heat of her, pressed against his cock. Exactly how he'd been fantasizing all day.

At least he had been, until that crazy scene with Max had chased all other thoughts away. Since then, he'd been in his little guesthouse, pacing the floor and wondering what came next. Should he tell the rest of his siblings that Mom had been trying to leave them? Did they have a right to know?

Nicole tilted her head back to look at him. She was wearing a clinging silvery turtleneck that he'd wanted to run his hands under all night long. "Seriously. How are you? I barely took a breath the entire time you and Max were talking."

Since she was determined to be serious, he walked her over to the seating area in the guesthouse. With its high peaked roof and rafters, and its panoramic view of the back ridge, it suited him perfectly. Gracie had offered it to him, after he balked at moving into his old bedroom.

He lowered onto the couch, Nicole still in his arms, so she was now straddling his lap. "That? That was nothing. Not a single stick of broken furniture. No unforgivable insults. In Rockwell terms, that was practically a peace talk."

She sat on his lap and splayed her hand across his chest. "That's a pretty big secret you were keeping."

"Yeah, it was. It took a lot of fucking willpower. Then it turned out he knew the whole time—or suspected. Pretty wild. Honestly, I probably deserve some kind of medal for not throwing it at Dad earlier."

"You do," she said sincerely. "You actually do."

"No, I don't. But that's one reason I left. I was afraid I wouldn't be able to keep my mouth shut if he kept riding me. All this time, I was trying to protect him…" He shook his head to chase away all the bad emotions that had haunted him ever since. Guilt. Doubt. Anger.

"You know, you're not at all what I used to think," she said slowly. "You're not an arrogant hothead."

He laughed. "Listen to that. A compliment, almost."

She gave him that mischievous smile he loved as she traced her hands along his ribs. "I can think of a few other compliments, just off the top of my head. But I wouldn't want you to get all puffed up."

He looped his arms around her waist and dropped a kiss on the top of her head. "Thank you for being there. It helped, oh mighty Max-Whisperer. From your perspective, did he handle it okay?"

She cocked her head, screwing up her face in a whimsical way that made him want to kiss her senseless. "I really think he did. It's always hard to tell with him, but his blood pressure stayed stable and his color was good. Pulse normal."

He laughed and ran his hands up her thighs, then back down, appreciating the sleek firmness of her legs. "Nurse Nicole, you turn me on."

She winked at him. "You should see me in my scrubs."

"Sign me up." His cock twitched at the vision forming in his mind. "Do I have to develop a heart condition to get a shot at that?"

She swatted him lightly on the chest. "You shouldn't joke about heart conditions. That's morbid."

"Have you met my family yet? Us Rockwells love nothing more than to laugh our asses off at something completely inappropriate. It's a survival mechanism."

"You know, that definitely explains a few things. Like the undead deer."

"My mother had a dark sense of humor. On my fourteenth birthday she made me a zombie cake, it was supposed to look like brains, with bloody icing and two ears on either side. Luckily she wasn't a very good baker, so it looked just like every other cake she made, kind of messy and lopsided."

He drew in a breath, bracing for the emotion that usually struck him when he thought of his mother. But it didn't come— maybe because the sexy woman on his lap was so distracting.

"She sounds like my kind of woman," Nicole said lightly. "I can't bake for shit either. I even ruined *brownies* once. I used a cup of baking soda instead of a tablespoon, and they practically blew up in the oven. Birdie literally cried when she saw them. Actual tears running down her face."

He laughed along with her. "We'll have to keep you out of the kitchen. And in my bedroom," he added in a hot growl that made her giggle again. He shifted his hands to her hipbones and scooted her closer. "You know, you did great out there last night. A little training and you could be rappelling down cliffs rescuing crazy black diamond skiers."

She laughed it off. "I'll pass. I don't mind patching them up, but someone else has to rescue them."

"See? We're the perfect team." He grinned at her and nuzzled her forehead with his. "I don't know why you're fighting it. Give it up, Nicole. Admit you want me."

"I never said I didn't want you." That breathless tone...the way she shifted on his lap...the light lavender fragrance that made him think of last night's sheets...

With their foreheads touching, he couldn't see enough of her face to read her expression. But he sensed the conflict running through her, and could guess at what she was thinking. She didn't want to get involved—he got it. They were at odds with each other when it came to the lodge. But did that mean they shouldn't enjoy the fantastic chemistry they shared?

"Nothing's changed," she finally murmured. "Since last night, I mean."

But *something* had changed. She was here, wasn't she? "Not true," he said. "Something very big has changed. And I do mean big."

She tilted her head back to meet his eyes. "What are you talking about?"

Deploying his most devastating smile, he winked at her. "We have condoms now."

~

KAI CARRIED her to the big bed that dominated the guesthouse. Wild excitement coursed through her, sweeping away all her reservations. Kai was a big boy. He was an adult, a grown man who'd shouldered many burdens in his life. He'd kept secrets to shield his family. He'd rescued strangers at the risk of his own life. She didn't have to worry about hurting him.

And maybe that was part of what drew her to him so much. She'd had enough Birdie worry to last a lifetime. Being with Kai —the whirlwind of Kai—made all of that other stuff disappear.

He tossed her on the bed and unzipped her pants. "Need to say a little hello first. Don't want to be rude."

She laughed as he yanked down her underwear and buried his face between her legs. His hair tickled her thighs as he nuzzled her. Not to arouse, just to flirt and tease. Then again, she was already aroused from the feel of his iron thighs under hers. Sitting on Kai's lap, listening to him talk about his mother, was an incredibly powerful aphrodisiac. His love for his mother shone through, along with his protective nature. Sure, he was a "rebel," but the impulse behind his rebelliousness was protectiveness.

Face it, her respect for Kai was growing the more time she spent with him. And the more she respected him, the more she wanted him.

Give it up. Admit you want him. Take this joy. Grab this pleasure while you can.

He stripped her sweater off, then the rest of her clothes, until she was entirely naked.

"I'm going to feast my eyes for a minute, don't mind me."

Under the scalding weight of his stare, she couldn't have moved if she tried. He made quick work of his own clothes, that magnificent physique revealed bit by bit, muscles already tense, erection jutting between his thighs.

She reached for him. "My turn to say hello."

"Nice to see you. It's been too long," he said, almost formally. "We really must do this more often."

Laughing, she touched the velvety skin of his penis. "At this rate, we're talking once a day."

"Exactly. How about every hour on the hour?" He crouched

over her and licked his way up her inner thigh—Lord almighty, how did he know that was one of her most sensitive spots? She moaned and parted her legs farther.

Oh please. She wanted more of last night, more of his rough tongue on her clit, his warm mouth doing those magical things.

She felt his body heat, the slide of his skin against hers, the soft brush of his hair, and all of a sudden she was on fire. She grabbed his hand and brought it to her mound. "Touch me, Kai. Touch me everywhere."

He looked up at her, eyes flaring with wild heat. Then he *was* everywhere. Mouth on her nipples, hands stroking between her legs, along her sides, over the knobs of her hipbones, along the curves of her breasts. She lost track of everything except the sparks igniting everywhere he touched.

Then he turned her over—oh God—and spread her out on the bed. Nibbled the backs of her thighs, tongue sweeping across the crease between her ass and her thighs. She felt so exposed in that position, and yet so deliriously free.

One hand stole around to her front and found the little nub screaming for attention. He pinched her clit between his fingers, drawing a wild shriek of pleasure from her. His hot shaft pressed against her lower back. He surrounded her with hard, hot maleness, with muscles and hands and cock. He whispered a flood of hot words into her ear—*I can't wait to bury my cock inside you, come for me beautiful, let me hear that scream, I can't get it out of my mind, come on you hot sexy thing, you wild woman, I'm going to fuck you so long and hard...*

And then she was coming, suddenly and completely out of control, bucking against his hand, against the sheets, exploding again and again, crazy sounds spilling from her mouth.

She was still gasping and trembling when Kai flipped her over onto her back. She'd never seen that expression on his face —so hot, so focused, so intent. He reached to the nightstand and pulled open a drawer with so much force that it toppled over.

But he managed to snag a condom first—he held it up in triumph.

She laughed weakly, still rocked by that incredible orgasm. "Nice rescue."

"Count on me when it matters." With a strained grin, he tore open the package and tossed it aside. He rolled the condom over his raging erection. She could still remember how it tasted, how it felt against her tongue, but now wasn't the moment for that.

Now she wanted more. She wanted Kai inside her, over her, all around her. She tugged him down so the full length of his front was joined with hers. The light scatter of hair on his chest created a delicious friction against her nipples. She felt it all the way to her sex, which still pulsed from her climax.

He parted her thighs with his knee, a little rough, as if he was hanging onto his control by the barest thread. And that drove her own lust even higher. This powerful, sculpted, passionate wild beast of a man wanted her just as badly as she wanted him. Talk about an aphrodisiac.

He placed his hands, so strong, so calloused and capable, on her thighs and pushed them back, opening her even farther. Her sex practically wept with anticipation. "God, you're sexy," he muttered as he ate her up with his eyes. "Are you ready for this? I sure as hell am."

"So ready," she breathed. "Any more ready and I might explode."

"I like it when you explode." He took his cock in his fist and found her entrance. The sexy sight of his corded muscles bunching as he moved into position made her wild. She arched her back, offering herself, offering everything. He made a rough sound in his throat, as if he were giving up on words and going for grunts instead.

The blunt tip of his penis pressed into her—so wide, so thick. Her throat closed as the rest of her opened up. Inch by glorious inch, he entered her, watching her every step of the way. She felt his gaze on her face, but kept her eyes closed so she could focus on the sensation of being filled to the core. By the time he was fully seated inside her, she brimmed with heat, overflowed with it, a fountain of pleasure coming to life inside her.

Had sex ever felt like this before?

Nope, never. She might as well be a virgin, because nothing she'd ever experienced had come close to this. No reason bothering to even remember those other, forgettable times. They'd never mean anything to her again.

Kai slowly withdrew, almost all the way out, while her inner tissues clung to him. With a powerful flex of his hips, he thrust all the way in again. Parting her flesh, piercing her with pleasure, sending her mind into a freefall. The grip of his hands on her thighs, the way he dragged against her clit, the restrained power behind every move he made—it all sent her out of her mind.

"Oh my God," she babbled, all dignity gone. "Go more. Harder. It feels so good."

He pushed her thighs farther back and drove deep. "Oh yeah, sweetheart. That's it. Jesus," he muttered, just as incoherent as she was. "Fuck, you feel good. It feels so fucking good to be inside you."

He set up a rhythm that took her breath away, that she couldn't wrap her head around. Didn't matter, because her body took over. She met his every move with one of her own, wanting him deeper, feeling the hot sensation expand within her, the explosion just out of reach, waiting for her, taunting her. "Please," she begged. "Oh please, Kai…"

"I got you, sweetheart. I'll always take care of you. I got you, honey." His low mutter, almost out of her hearing, made some hidden tension release inside her. She didn't need to worry because Kai was the kind of man who would make sure she came. That was his nature—to take care of the people he was with. Especially in bed. This amazing man was on a mission, and it was all about pleasing her.

And that did it—she fell over the edge, streaks of pleasure shooting through her, blinding her to everything except the incredible ecstasy. Her climax must have swept him along with her. She heard his shout of release, as if from very far away.

She held on to his sweat-slick back, where the muscles felt like steel, rigid with tension. They rode out the waves together, like skydiving off the edge of a cliff. She floated, spiraling, blissful, powered only by pleasure.

Then everything relaxed, his muscles uncoiled, and he rolled over next to her. She curled onto her side, so deliciously spent that she wasn't sure she'd ever move again.

"Damn," he breathed.

She could barely breathe, let alone answer. He kept talking, something about how amazing she was, but not even those sweet words could hold sleep at bay. She drifted off, snuggled close against his side. The last thing she felt was his arm pulling her closer, and his lips dropping a kiss on her hair.

The last thing she heard was his soft whisper somewhere above her head. "You go ahead and sleep. I got you."

22

AFTER THAT NIGHT, NICOLE SPENT AS MUCH TIME WITH KAI IN their "box" as she could. Either she waited until everyone else was asleep, then ran across the property to his guesthouse, or she left her dorm room door open for him. It didn't make a difference to her, although she allowed herself to scream and shout more at his place. Which he *loved*. His favorite thing to do was use his magic tongue on her clit until she came —which in turn made him so hard *he* came almost as soon he slid inside her.

Other times he liked to draw it out. They'd snuggle on the couch, watching movies, as he lazily stroked her. Not just the obvious places—but also secret spots like the inside of her forearm, the back of her neck, the small of her back. Time seemed to slow like honey while he caressed her like that. She'd be like a trembling rag doll by the time he drew her skirt up her thighs and slid his hand under her panties.

"Open for me," he whispered in her ear. Right there on his lap she spread her legs apart. And came as soon he slid his big thumb along her sizzling clit. After that he tumbled her onto the couch, had her kneel, gripping the back, while he flipped her skirt up and drove into her from behind. She came then, too.

Wherever he led, she followed because it always took her to a place of bliss and joy.

They didn't always make it to one of their suites. One day he cornered her in the old library, where she was reorganizing the books the lodge had accumulated over the years. With a wicked grin, he pinned her against the wall between the mystery section and the field guides.

"Did I ever tell you about my naked librarian fantasy?"

"Shhhh." She scolded him with the most severe frown she could manage. "No talking in the library, you naughty boy."

"See, that's exactly how it goes. Unbutton your top, lady. Show me those tits."

She loved it when he talked dirty like that. As he lifted her up and wrapped her legs around his hips, she undid her blouse, fingers already trembling.

"Hold on tight," he muttered as her breasts came into view. She tightened her legs around his hips and rested her head against the wall. With a groan, he cupped her breasts in his hands, thumbing the nipples into aching peaks, stroking the sensitive undersides. With his hands still filled with her flesh, he claimed her mouth, kissing her so deep and hard her head spun.

Then he abandoned her breasts and gripped her upper thighs, his fingers digging into her flesh. His fingertips brushed the edge of her panties, then found their way inside. He stroked her until she was right on the edge, shaking and frantic.

A book fell to the ground in a little cloud of dust. Someone rattled the doorknob, which Kai had locked.

None of it mattered. There was only her and Kai, and this amazing, compulsive chemistry. A finger inside her now. Then another. Those long, strong fingers that knew exactly where to press, and how hard and how deep. When he brushed his thumb against her clit, she exploded, burying her head into his neck so as not to scream out loud. He came too, groaning along with her, rubbing against the place where his hand met her pussy.

"Are you crazy?" she hissed when the last spasms had died away and reality set in. She relaxed her legs from around him and planted her feet back on the floor. "This is a semi-public place. Guests wander in here all the time."

"Which is why I locked it." Kai smiled smugly. "Besides, you know that saying, rules are made to be broken."

"I know that saying, doesn't mean I live by it."

"Are you sure? Maybe my motto is rubbing off on you." He winked at her, then winced as he looked down at himself. "Gotta go change. You're really a distraction, you know that? A million things to do, and here I am, making trouble with you again."

"Don't pin this on me." Buttoning her blouse, she made a face at him. "I was innocently minding my own business."

"You were impersonating a naughty librarian, which happens to be a longtime fantasy of mine. If you saw Miss Thurston, the Rocky Peak librarian back in the day, you'd understand."

Stupidly, she felt jealous of that long ago librarian. She wanted Kai all to herself. She wanted all his fantasies focused on her.

Which was wrong and bad in so many ways.

Because outside of their sizzling sexual connection, nothing else had changed.

The end of the designated month came and went, but Kai stayed.

She started avoiding Felicity's calls. Things had shifted since that confrontation after the bird-watching party. Max wasn't interested in new ideas anymore. He deferred to his oldest son on just about everything. He asked his advice about which plumber to hire to fix the bathroom. He allowed Kai to hire a mechanic to come to the lodge for a day and give all the rigs a tuneup.

And then one morning at breakfast Max announced that he wanted Kai to become an official signatory on the lodge's bank accounts.

Everyone at the table knew what that meant. It meant Max was doing the unthinkable and asking for Kai's help.

But of course Kai reacted to it in his own way. "You're trying to torture me, aren't you, Dad? Send me screaming back to Colorado?"

"Nah, that's just a bonus," Max said in his rumbly voice. "An extra-nice bonus."

Kai's laughed, while Gracie tossed a blueberry at her father. "Stop that, Dad. Kai is not allowed to leave. Not yet."

"Good to know," Kai said mildly. "Let me know when that changes."

Nicole bit down on her lip. She didn't want him to leave. No, it wasn't that, since she too would have to leave soon. It was that she didn't want anything to change. She wanted to stay with him, in their cozy little box, as long as she possibly could.

But how long would that be? Where was this headed?

Was there any way to reach some kind of harmonious resolution that didn't involve the Rockwells finding out the truth and then despising her? Could she disappear before Felicity made her offer? Could she deny any connection to the Summit Group?

Of course she could, but that would mean leaving the lodge. And the truth was, she was becoming more and more deeply attached to it. Not just because of Kai, though that was a huge part of it. She was discovering her own favorite spots—a rise where the wind smelled of flowers she couldn't see. A bramble patch with the biggest, juiciest blackberries imaginable. An over-grown path that led to a bench situated with a view toward the winding road that led into town.

The bench made her think of Amanda Rockwell, and all of Kai's revelations about the accident. Had Amanda sat on this bench, watching for arrivals? Or dreaming of the day she could go back to the beach?

Even though Nicole had grown up on the coast, she didn't miss it. She didn't miss sand in her shorts or the smell of diesel boats. She loved the crisp clear air and the swaying spruce forests. She loved the homey, authentic feel of the lodge. She loved Max and Gracie, and the whole Rockwell attitude. Work hard and laugh your ass off, as Kai put it.

And Kai...yes, she loved Kai too.

She loved him in a detached way, because she had no faith that they'd ever really "be" together. She loved him because he was so fierce, so strong, so kind, so outrageous. Because he made an impact just by walking into a room. Because he made her laugh, because he freed her to be herself—a forgotten self that had been buried under worries and responsibilities. And because he cared, because he would always care. Even when it hurt to care.

"Everything okay, Nicole?" Kai was looking at her with concern, and she realized she'd blocked out everything after Gracie's comment about his leaving. She'd been staring at her oatmeal bowl, lost in thoughts of Kai.

"Yeah, sorry. I was just putting together a shopping list in my head. We're out of Mason jars." She'd been helping Renata with the garden harvest, putting up green beans and making sauerkraut from big-headed cabbages.

"You're driving into town?" Kai asked.

"Yes. If anyone needs anything, let me know." She cast a general smile around the table at all the Rockwells.

"You need something," grumbled Max. "You need a chauffeur. You freeway drivers don't belong out here."

"Oh stop. Just because I'm a city girl doesn't mean I can't adapt."

And they shifted into one of those Rockwell joke-fests that she loved so much.

⁓

AFTERWARDS, she drove her Jetta into town. Despite the family's teasing, she loved the drive down the mountain road. It was so beautiful, winding through birch and spruce. She routed her phone through her speakers and called Felicity to pass on the news about Kai being made a signatory on Rocky Peak's accounts.

"We need to make a move," Felicity said right away. "We're way past that month mark. We have to make our offer before Kai gets his hooks too far into this."

"His *hooks*? Felicity, it's his lodge. He has a lot more stake in it than you do."

"Not true. I've invested a lot in this project. I told you my partnership in the firm is on the line. If I don't come through, I'm pretty sure they'll fire me."

Nicole heard the fear in her voice. "I know how important this is for you, Felicity. I get it."

"Not just for me," she said, her voice rising. "For you and Birdie."

Was the bonus really worth it? Maybe there was another way to provide for Birdie that *didn't* involve taking away Kai's legacy.

"I don't know, Felicity. It feels more sleazy every day."

"Oh pooh, would you grow up? People do sleazy things all the time. Sleaze sleaze sleaze. It's like sleep and easy put together. How can that be bad?"

"Are you okay, Felicity?"

"You can stop asking me that, it's fucking annoying."

Nicole shook her head as she took one of the sharp curves in the road. Where was her friend, the Felicity from before she'd turned into such a damn shark?

She changed the subject. "Have you seen Birdie this week?"

"Yesterday. I promised I'd visit her twice a week, and I have." Felicity's irritated tone softened. "She's fine, but she doesn't like her private room."

"I don't like it either. It's frickin' expensive. Any chance you can get her to make up with her roommate?"

"Do I seem like a relationship counselor?"

Nicole laughed. Felicity was many things—a loyal friend, a cutthroat competitor, a sharp businesswoman—but personal relationships were definitely not her forte. "Okay, never mind. I'll check in soon, Felicity. Promise you won't do anything without warning me."

"Sweetie, you're getting much too attached up there in the mountains. What's going on with you and Kai? Are you keeping something from me?"

"You don't have to worry about me and Kai."

That much was true. No need to worry, because there was no possible way it could end well.

23

After she'd made her purchases, on impulse she stopped in at the Last Chance. She wanted to talk to Jake, to confirm that he wanted nothing to do with running the lodge. To assuage her guilt, to be honest.

But Jake wasn't there. Instead a curvy redhead who introduced herself as Serena brought her a bar menu.

"I was actually hoping to talk to Jake."

Serena rolled her eyes. "You and every other woman in this town. He's training with the fire department right now."

"Oh, not like that!" she said with such indignation that Serena laughed.

"My bad. Well, would you like a drink of water at least?"

"Sure." She slid onto the stool and gratefully received the water Serena poured for her. They chatted for a while, discovering that they were both new in town, both transplanted city girls. Both working for Rockwells.

"It's a good thing they're good-looking," Serena joked. "Makes up for the my-way-or-the-highway attitude."

"Jake? He seems so easygoing."

"You'd think so, right?" Serena refused to say more than that, and they segued to a conversation about Netflix shows and small town culture shock. They exchanged numbers and decided that two new girls in town ought to stick together.

And now it would be even harder to leave—she had a friend. A friend who wasn't a shark.

~

WHEN SHE GOT BACK to the lodge, Kai, Max and Gracie were hovering over Kai's phone, which was planted in the middle of the table.

"Come here," Gracie hissed as Nicole walked in. "It's Isabelle."

"Am I on speaker?" came a female voice from the phone. "That's supremely irritating, but I'll try to act normal anyway. Normal being relative, *of course*, so don't bother saying it, Kai."

Kai pulled an innocent, 'who, me?' face, then winked at Nicole.

"I hope you have good news, Isabelle," Max shouted. He never understood that it wasn't necessary, that the phone could pick up his voice just fine.

"You don't have to yell, Dad. Anyway, it is good news, at least *I* think it is. I'm coming back for Christmas. Kai promised me a ski race. You know it's the one thing I can't resist."

Nicole swung toward Kai. "A ski race?"

More importantly—did that mean he was staying into winter? She celebrated internally with a silent whoop.

Wait, no—it was bad news. It put a huge wrench in the Summit Group's timeline. Felicity would freak out. *Crap.*

She schooled her expression so as not to reveal all her conflicting emotions.

"Isabelle is a phenomenal cross-country ski babe," Kai said. "We used to put on a race every winter against the Majestic Lodge crew. I talked to the people over there and they agreed it's time to bring the tradition back."

On the phone, Isabelle gave a hoot of excitement. "I've been stuck here in the desert with no skis, so I'll have to come back a little early and get my groove back."

"The race is set for the end of January, so if you came back for Christmas, you'll have plenty of time. I'll get your skis tuned up for you."

Kai *was* staying. Until January. *What did this mean?*

"You let me know when you're getting in and I'll pick you up at the airport, Izz," he told the phone.

"I can't wait! Now we have to talk Griffin into coming back too. Are you guys going to watch his race?"

"Yup. Jake's holding a watch party down at the bar."

"We have a perfectly good TV right here at the lodge," Max grumbled. "No need to drive down the mountain just for that."

Nicole's heart sank. She'd been looking forward to the watch party— to a night out with Kai. But if Max wasn't going, she shouldn't either. She couldn't allow him to get overexcited unless she was standing by.

"Well, my plan is to drive thirty miles across the desert to the one café with a black-and-white TV from the fifties and beg them to turn it to ESPN, which they probably haven't even heard of. Wish me luck. See you all in a few months. Gotta go now, someone just came in with an infected knife wound oozing pus and—"

Kai ended the call before it got too graphic. "That's how Isabelle gets people to hang up," he explained. "It's her way of saying goodbye."

"Is every member of the Rockwell family so..."

"Weird?" Kai winked at her. "Yes. Thanks for noticing. So, Dad, what you think? Ski racing returning to the lodge. A big family Christmas. Pretty exciting, huh?"

Even growly old Max had to agree that it was pretty damn exciting.

But after her first thrilled reaction, Nicole plummeted back to reality. By Christmas, she'd be back in Seattle. She always spent Christmas with Birdie. She brought her a pile of gifts and a much-inferior version of Mom's German chocolate cake. Sunny Grove always had a Christmas tree and one of the orderlies dressed up in a Santa suit. They did their absolute best to make the holidays fun for the residents, and Nicole was so grateful for that.

But going home at the end of the day, back to her quiet apartment, would suck. She had her own personal Christmas tradition that involved a hot bath, lots of bubbles, a TiVo full of an entire season of *Scandal* and a bottle of sherry.

"Don't look so down in the mouth, girl." Max nudged her with his cane. "We'll give you a few hours off for Christmas."

"Don't get carried away, Dad," said Kai dryly. "Maybe an hour, no more than that." The two of them grinned at each other.

A sharp pang twisted her heart. She wouldn't be here to take any hours off. By Christmas, she'd be permanently off.

Everything was slipping away. Not just her purpose here, her secret mission. Not just the bonus that would be so helpful for Birdie. But also—the lodge itself. Her life here. Felicity was right. Even though she'd always known it would be temporary, she'd become deeply attached to Rocky Peak, to the quiet forests and forbidding peaks.

But she couldn't stay. After the Summit Group made their offer, she had to get back to Birdie. If the Rockwells remembered her, it would be as that girl who'd infiltrated the lodge as a kind of double agent home health aide.

Kai might remember more—he might remember hot nights tumbling around in his bed. But it would be a bitter memory once he knew the whole story.

Try as she might, she couldn't figure out a way to get through this without revealing the truth about her role here—except to take the coward's way out and simply disappear. Hop in her car in the middle of the night, while a blanket of darkness cast a spell of peace over the lodge, and drive down that winding road one last time.

It was tempting. But she wouldn't do it. She wanted every last second of Kai, of the lodge, of the Rockwells.

IN THE GUESTHOUSE, Kai stared at the numbers flying across the computer screen and took another swig of bourbon. Ever since Max had given him access to the lodge's bank accounts, he'd put off the moment where he actually looked at the bottom line. He was no accountant, but he managed his own finances well enough. It was easy. Earn money, don't spend too much. Invest here and there. It seemed to add up just fine. He was able to be as generous as he wanted with his money, and that was what mattered most to him.

But these numbers...ouch. As far as he could tell, the lodge had been running at a loss for a few years. Could that be true? Why hadn't anyone told him?

He dug up the phone number of the lodge's longtime accountant, Greg Sanders.

"Hey there, Kai Rockwell. Great to hear from you."

"Not too late to call?"

"No. I'm mostly retired now, and I stay up as late as I want."

"You still handling the lodge's accounts?"

"Yes, I am. I've been hoping you'd call. I told Max he needed to loop one of you kids in. Stubborn bastard didn't want to listen to me."

Kai's heart sank. "How bad is it? Just hit me. No sugarcoating."

"It's bad, kid. The lodge has been losing money for the past six years. Max has covered the bills by dipping into his personal savings. I told him to contact you, but you know how proud he is. He kept insisting he had a handle on things. He made me promise not to reach out to any of his children or I would have by now."

"He finally gave me access to the accounts and they sure look grim."

"Grim but not hopeless. It's a sad situation because the lodge itself—buildings and land included—is worth multiple millions of dollars. It's the very last viable piece of property in this area. Everything else has contingencies. The day Max—or any of you—decide to sell is the day you'll become very very rich."

Kai took another throat-scalding swallow of bourbon.

Sell the lodge.

A month ago, he would have shrugged and said "why not?" Now that he was back … the thought made his stomach twist in revulsion.

But his feelings weren't the important thing. He had to think logically.

Was it time to cash in on the Rockwell family's investment?

He had enough money already. He didn't need more millions. Griffin had plenty of funds as well—all his endorsements and prize winnings added up. Jake's bar was finally operating in the black, all debts repaid. Isabelle, with her medical degree and wanderlust, never talked about a need for more cash. And Gracie —what did Gracie want? That was still a bit mysterious to him. Maybe selling the lodge and becoming a millionaire would be at the top of her list.

What about Max? He'd be taken care of for the rest of his life if he sold the lodge. On the other hand, the lodge was his passion and the only place he'd ever lived. He even hated going on vacations. That had been one of Mom's complaints, that she never got to see the ocean because Max refused to travel anywhere. These days, he even hated going into town.

He cleared his throat. "Thanks, Sanders. If we decided to sell..."

"No one would blame you. The Rockwells have been part of this community since the beginning. But that doesn't mean you need to stay. You all have your own lives to live. Even Max understands that."

"Do you think it's possible to turn it around? Get the lodge profitable again?"

"Oh well, I guess anything's possible. It'd take some serious investment, not to mention time and energy. "

On that note of doubt, Kai ended the call. Not even another swig of bourbon could wash the bad taste out of his mouth. If he'd come back six years ago, ten years ago, would the lodge be in this position today?

Had his own anger and hurt destroyed the Rockwell legacy forever?

Or was there another way?

He closed his eyes, images from the lodge's glory days flitting through his mind. Epic snowball fights on the snow-covered lawn. Snowshoeing though the silent winter forests. Families pushing tables together in the dining room for one big chili-fest.

That was it. *Families.*

Nicole was right. They had to find ways to bring in more business. But he didn't see why it had to be wealthy women who wanted pampering. To him, the real beauty of the lodge was the opportunities it offered for families and for kids. Nicole kept talking about camps for kids, and that was something he could get behind one hundred percent.

Why did he and Nicole have to be opponents? Why couldn't they work together? Why not implement some of her ideas—the good ones—no raindrop therapy—but keep the lodge in Rockwell hands?

Added bonus—working with Nicole. Another bonus—*being* with Nicole. Not just in bed, but in every way. In his workaholic, adventurous, footloose life, he'd never spent this kind of time with a woman. He loved their verbal sparring almost as much as their bedroom adventures. He enjoyed her inventive brain, the way she kept coming up with new ideas. He really appreciated her kindness to Max, and the way she cared for him. Her teasing manner was exactly what Max needed.

He liked the way she interacted with the guests. She listened and paid attention, and found ways to make them feel special. She welcomed guests with a vase of wildflowers in their rooms. She'd talked Gracie into offering every kid a gift coupon for a free double scoop cone. In the evenings, while parents were enjoying a drink in the lounge, she organized games of freeze tag for the kids on the lawn.

She was doing so many little things like that, and it wasn't even her job. She was Max's nurse. Whatever she did beyond that was due to her generous nature...and to her desire to convince Max to implement her ideas.

Last night, after dinner, Max had pulled him aside and told him that as long as Kai was at Rocky Peak Lodge, he wasn't going to make any major changes without his agreement.

"Don't tell Nicole yet," he'd insisted. "I want to break it to her myself. She's got a vision, but as long as you're around, you've got final say."

"I don't know how long I'll be—"

"Doesn't matter. If you leave, you leave. If you're here, I want you weighing in."

The trust on his father's face was something new and freaking sweet to him. Man, had things changed since he'd come back.

But what about Nicole? What about her quirky, ultra-feminine ideas for Rocky Peak?

He shut down his laptop and sent her a quick text. *You still up? Got an idea to run by you.*

When she sent back a "thumbs up," his heart lifted. He knew she was going to love his idea. It made perfect sense. It would make everyone happy. He couldn't wait to see her face when he proposed it.

He also couldn't wait to see her face when he made her shatter into her umpteenth orgasm after they'd worked out all the details.

24

It took him some time to present his plan. First they fell into bed like a couple of ravenous beasts. Then they took a long hot shower together. Soap bubbles never felt so good as when they were sliding across Nicole's naked body.

Finally, with their lust temporarily satisfied, he got down to business. He sat next to Nicole on her couch, where she was drying her hair with a fluffy towel.

"You're right about the lodge's finances. Things are pretty bad. But not so dire that we can't fix it."

"Oh?" She briskly rubbed her long hair, hiding her face from him.

"I've decided to stay on for a while, until we can get the lodge back on its feet." Her face was still hidden by the towel, but he assumed she was eager to hear his proposal.

"Oh. Well, that's great. Good for you. That's a lot to take on. Are you sure?"

He hesitated, since she didn't seem nearly as excited as he'd expected. "For now. Yes. I think I can make a difference here. But it's not just about me. This can be good for you too. I want you to stay on as lodge manager."

"As what?" she mumbled from behind her towel.

"Manager. Max likes your ideas, and I think only some of them are crazy. I think we can work well together."

She really was taking her time drying her hair.

"Your ideas, my history with the lodge, what could be better? I've seen you talking to guests, dealing with the staff. We'd pay you more, obviously. Probably not a lot more, at first. But it will build. I know we can make this a success."

"What about Max?" Finally she took the towel away from her face. Her damp hair curled in wild tendrils around her pink face. Her wary, not-excited face.

"Max can find another nurse. Or you could divide your time, the way you already are."

"And us?" She waved her hand at her bed with its nest of tangled sheets, half on, half off the bed. "You're talking about working pretty closely together. We'd have to stop this...affair, or whatever it is."

He was silent for a moment. *Affair or whatever it is.* What was it? They'd never defined it, other than as her crazy "box." He got to his feet, needing to put a little distance between them. "I don't know about that part. We can work it out. We're mature adults, why not?"

She tucked her toes under her. He loved her toes, so ticklish that she shrieked whenever he touched them. He was tempted to tickle them now to chase away her serious expression. "No, it would never work," she said. "I appreciate the thought, but I'm sorry, Kai. The answer is no."

He stared at her, sure he must be missing something. "You're saying you don't want to partner together to manage the lodge because you don't want to stop sleeping together. But you also don't want to be in an actual relationship. So you're willing to sacrifice a real role at the lodge for a non-real relationship?"

She tugged her bottom lip between her teeth, but said nothing.

"This isn't making any sense, Nicole. What am I missing?"

"I just don't want—it's just 'no,' Kai. No, I can't run the lodge with you. It won't work," she cried. "Can't you just believe me and let it go?"

He scrubbed a hand across the back of his neck, still damp from their steamy shower. He remembered the look on her face as he made her come under the warm water streaming from the showerhead. That look wasn't just about sex. There was so much more there, but for some reason she didn't want to acknowledge it.

"Is it Birdie? You don't want to be so far away from her? I've been thinking about that too. She can live here, with us."

"Stop!" She jumped to her feet, looking so shaken he wondered if they were speaking the same language. "The problem isn't Birdie, it's you!"

"Me?"

"How long until you leave again?" She threw those words at him like rocks at a stray dog.

"Excuse me? I'm not seventeen anymore," he said evenly, holding back his anger.

"No, but you have other things in your life besides this place. You'll start missing all those ski bunnies. You'll want to get back out there on a rescue squad or a ski patrol. Or Max will tighten the leash, he won't let you do what you want, and you'll take off again."

In nothing but drawstring pants and bare chest, he stood frozen to the floor for what seemed like an eternity. Was that really what she thought of him? Despite the time they'd spent together, despite everything she knew about why he'd left...did she still see him as untrustworthy? As someone who wouldn't stick around?

"I guess there's nothing else to say, then." Stiffly, he reached for his t-shirt and pulled it over his head. "I withdraw the offer. It was a crazy idea anyway. What made me think we could work together? We'd be like cats and dogs, right?" He pulled on his sweater and pulled his phone from his pocket, making a show of checking the time. "I, uh, have some emails I need to return. I'll see you tomorrow."

"Kai—"

He waved her off. "Don't worry about it. You're being honest, and that's all I ask."

Her stricken look stayed with him for a long time.

NICOLE SPENT that night crying herself to sleep, which was such a babyish thing to do, but something that always made her feel better in the end. Not this time. If only she could *actually* be honest and tell Kai the truth. If only she could explain that *nothing in the world* would make her happier than to stay at the lodge as the manager.

Especially if Birdie could come too.

It was like every fantasy she'd ever had rolled into one.

But none of that was possible. The Summit Group wanted this lodge and they were going to get it. She'd seen them in action. She knew how relentless they were.

Ruthless, too. If Max refused their offer, they'd expose Nicole in a flash. No one would want her around after that.

So the dreamy scenario of her and Kai living and working at the lodge could *never happen*. She needed money, more money than the Rockwells could pay her. The lodge needed money too. Selling it was the only logical solution. She simply didn't see another way.

But if she told Kai the full story, he'd hate her for deceiving him. He'd kick her out and she'd get no bonus from the Summit Group. No help for Birdie. And—she'd never see Kai or the lodge again. Lose-lose-lose-lose.

What a mess.

By the time she came down to breakfast the next day, she'd cried all the tears she could manage. All the guests had eaten and left already, judging by the plates of half-eaten pancakes littering the tables. Only Max was left. He stood at the big picture window, leaning on his cane and gazing out at Amanda's berry garden.

"Morning," he grunted, in his usual brusque way. "Sleeping on the job, are you?"

"Sorry, I had trouble slee—"

But then he surprised her by interrupting. "Dreamed about Amanda last night."

"Oh?" She paused in the midst of loading her plate with pancakes.

"Happens now and then. I think she gets a kick out of haunting me." His laugh made his bushy beard dance on his chest.

"What happened in the dream?"

"She was playing cards. She loved cards. Played solitaire when she couldn't sleep. Anyway, she was playing cards with you, up on the roof. I was on the ground yelling like a banshee, telling you gals to climb on down before you fell. But she just laughed and opened an umbrella like Mary Poppins. And off she went. Floating away."

"And me? Did I fall off the roof?"

"You turned into a...cat, I think. That part's fuzzy. I think it was a cat. Might have been a rat."

She flinched, but he didn't notice.

"Amanda loved cats. She fed all the strays that wandered around here. Never understood how stray cats found their way all the way up here."

He grew quiet, gazing off at the berry bushes. He was having one of his more disoriented days. Nicole's heart ached for him.

As grouchy as he was, she'd come to care deeply for Mad Max Rockwell. How could she contribute to this old man losing the only home he knew—losing the legacy that he'd inherited, that he'd built into something so wonderful?

She couldn't. That was the decision she'd come to during her sleepless night. Time to tell the truth, no matter what it cost her.

She opened her mouth, ready to spill everything, to throw herself on his mercy. To beg him to forgive her, and to never, ever sell the lodge unless he really wanted to. No matter how many tens of millions were in the offer from the Summit Group.

But just then, Kai walked in. She snapped her mouth shut. Telling Max was one thing, but she wasn't quite ready to face Kai's scorn yet.

"Son," said Max, lighting up with delight. "Remember how Amanda used to play solitaire? She had those worn-out cards she'd gotten at a casino."

"Wagon Wheel Casino, Reno Nevada. I could never forget those." Kai nodded to Nicole casually, as if they hadn't made love in the shower last night. As if they hadn't...fought. Or broken up? How did you break up something that wasn't real to begin with?

Her heart ached again. If only she could have said yes to his offer. Or if only she could have said 'no' in a way that didn't hurt his feelings or make him suspicious.

Ugh, this situation was impossible. Kai filled his plate with an overflowing stack of six pancakes, then poured a river of syrup over it. He went to stand next to Max, and the two of them looked out the picture window at the deep forests beyond.

"Looks like another storm coming," Kai said as he stabbed a fork into his pancake.

"Looks like," Max agreed.

"Oooh, a storm!" Gracie skipped into the room, wearing rubber boots and a flirty short skirt. "Any chance of snow? Twenty bucks says the first snow flies before October."

"Done." Kai held out his hand for a smooth low-five, after which she bent down to kiss Max on the cheek. The three of them stood watching the first dark clouds skimming into view.

Nicole shoved aside her plate, unable to eat another mouthful.

She loved this family, and she couldn't deceive them for another minute. She'd figure out another way to take care of Birdie. Time to come clean.

She opened her mouth again, but once again Kai forestalled her. "It's race day for Griff. Everyone got their lucky underwear on?"

Kai put an arm around Max and helped him to his chair. Gracie danced alongside them. "I always wear black and white checkers, like the flag."

"I wear pink because he dared me to once, and had his best result ever." Kai laughed. "The things we do for family, right?"

"I never wear underwear on race days," Max rumbled. "Works every time."

All the Rockwells burst out laughing. Nicole fisted her hands so tightly one of her fingernails bent backwards.

She couldn't ruin their joy. She'd tell them after race day.

25

Kai slid onto one of the stools at the Last Chance Pub. From the other end of the bar, Jake caught his eye and gave him a grin and a thumbs-up. The viewing party for Griffin's big race was mobbed. Everyone who lived in Rocky Peak wanted to see one of their local celebrities on national TV. Those who were visiting didn't want to miss out on the party.

There were so many people here that the crowd spilled out onto the street. The only reason Kai got a seat was thanks to the reflected glory of being Griffin's brother. The excited chatter of the horde of customers melded into a deafening din. People were talking about the race, about the amazing fact that a Rocky Peak local was favored in a nationally televised competition, and—of course—when the first snow dump would happen.

Over in one of the banquettes, Gracie gave him a wave. She was apparently on a date, since her other hand was being held by a good-looking kid across the table. The dude couldn't stop staring at her, which made Kai's teeth clench. Of course Gracie looked amazing—she'd woven herself a crown of rose hips, which she wore over the softly flowing waves of her hair. Total hippie-chick vibe, and her date was eating it up.

Kai eyed him with distrust. He didn't recognize the guy, but then again there were plenty of people who'd moved here since he'd left. But this guy just didn't look local; you could always tell. How could a stranger possibly recognize how special Gracie was? She ought to stick to locals, people she knew, people who could be held accountable if they messed up.

Get over yourself. Kai gave himself a mental slap across the face. Gracie was a grown woman. She could choose her own dates. She'd been handling her own business for a long time and didn't need Kai barging in and acting all big brother-ish

And it wasn't like he had any real wisdom when it came to relationships. Look at him and Nicole. All this time he'd thought they had something pretty phenomenal happening. And then she turned around and threw him a curveball he still hadn't figured out.

Jake finally worked his way through the thicket of customers and reached Kai. They gripped hands, and managed a brotherly hug over the bar separating them.

"Glad you made it down the mountain," Jake said. "Dad wasn't up for it?"

"I think he's turning into a hermit. Not sure what it would take to get him away from the lodge. I left him holed up in the media room with no-salt peanuts and apple cider."

"Apple cider?"

"That's as close as Nicole will let him come to an alcoholic drink."

"The nurse is holding the line, huh? I thought you would have chased her away by now. You were all growly about her the last time you were in here."

"I was doing my due diligence, that's all."

"Yeah? And how'd that go?"

"I'm nothing if not diligent." Kai grinned at his own inside joke. But Jake got it right away, and lifted his eyebrows.

"I see how it is."

Responding to an order from the new waitress, who'd just appeared at Kai's elbow, Jake filled a beveled glass tankard with foaming Guinness and passed it across the bar to her. Someone else called an order to him, which he acknowledged with a nod.

He seemed to be doing ten different things at once—washing glasses, drawing drafts, filling orders from the waitresses, all with a calm that seemed almost Zen.

"You really love this gig, don't you?" Kai asked the next time he had a chance.

"I really do. It's the best of both worlds. You get to talk to people and hear the wildest fucking stories, and you can step away whenever you feel like it. Built-in excuse." A dimple flashed in his cheek, that devastating dimple that had caused girls to fall at his feet from about the age of fifteen. "Take that woman near the TV, for instance. She's been drinking pretty hard since she got here. She's been saying some wild shit. I'm trying to keep a little distance here."

Kai took a discreet look at the woman in question. Asian, thin as a licorice whip, in a black blazer that belonged at a conference table instead of a pub, she radiated nervous energy. She was drinking a fruity drink through a straw, her gaze fixed on the television. Occasionally she said something out loud to anyone listening.

"What kind of wild stuff?"

"Lot of name-dropping. Says she knows the ESPN guy calling the race. Then she said she has a Jaguar F-Type convertible, this year's model. She's a little intense."

"What's she doing *here*?"

"Don't know. She acts like it's a big mysterious secret. Says she can't talk about it, but it's basically to check up on a friend."

Kai eyed the stranger. "Sounds cryptic."

"Yup. Then again, I don't really care much what she's doing here as long as her credit card doesn't get declined." Jake winked at him. "In which case I can always confiscate her Jag."

"I wonder how many drinks it would take for her to spill this big secret?"

"Well, she's already had three, and I'll probably cut her off soon. Also—I can't have you harassing my customers. Let her be."

A shout went up as the scene on the TV switched to the line of helmeted riders waiting at the start of the race.

Kai felt the familiar grip of excitement and nerves that he experienced whenever he watched Griff race. Motocross was a dangerous sport. Griffin had broken bones, sprained a wrist, gashed his leg once when he'd veered off course. He always shrugged it off and did whatever surgery or rehab needed to be done. But for his siblings, watching him race could be excruciating.

Kai had a routine he stuck to during Griff's races. He always made sure to have a drink nearby. He would watch with one hand covering half his face, so if he needed to block his vision for a second, he could. Other than that, he never changed position from the start of the race to the end. He had a strange superstitious belief that something bad might happen if he did.

The flag dropped, a horn blew, and the racers were off. The jostling between the bikers was unnerving, as if they'd just as soon crash as let someone else take the lead. And then there was the angle of tilt as they rounded curves in the packed-dirt course. The way they put their hands down to keep from crashing out... Kai had to use the fingers-over-his-face trick whenever Griffin did that.

Even though all the riders wore similar gear, he recognized Griffin from his jacket, which displayed the logo of his main sponsor in bright red over white. Besides, Griffin had a way of moving that set him apart. He was so fluid, so in tune with his bike and the terrain he was navigating through. He always seemed to find a line of approach that shaved seconds off his time. He saw things his competitors didn't.

At the third turn, Griffin nearly wiped out. He overcompensated in the curve, and only his quick reflexes kept him from crashing.

Everyone in the bar gasped. Kai cringed, barely able to watch.

"He's got this," Jake muttered next to him. "Wait, what's he doing? He's slowing down."

Slowing down *coming out* of the curve, which was the opposite of what he should be doing. "Looks distracted," said Kai. "Shit."

"Yeah, something's up. He doesn't look like himself," Jake agreed. "He's thinking too much."

As the race went on, Kai noticed more problems. Griffin wasn't attacking the way he usually did. He seemed tentative, not his usual fearless self. Where was his confidence?

Kai dropped his hand. If Griff was struggling he wasn't going to hide from the sight. He'd be right there with him, rooting him on with every cell of his being.

The redheaded waitress appeared. "Jake, you should hear this."

"Little busy right now, Serena."

"I know, but this is important."

Kai tuned them out, completely focused on the race. The camera tracked the riders zooming past. The shot switched to another camera, which showed Griffin coming straight toward it. Behind his helmet, his face wasn't really visible, but Kai saw his intense focus.

He also noticed the tension in his shoulders. They weren't loose and easy, like usual. And why did he keep checking over his left shoulder? He'd never seen Griff do that before.

Jake and Serena were still talking, but it wasn't until he heard Nicole's name that Kai switched his attention back to them. "What was that?"

"Serena says that woman at the bar is here because of Nicole."

"Why?"

Serena shifted her grip on her tray of drinks. "She snagged

me and asked me a bunch of questions about the Rockwells. Her name is Felicity and apparently Nicole works for her."

Kai frowned. "You mean, used to work for her?"

"No, works for her *now*. Like she's at Rocky Peak Lodge because this woman Felicity sent her there. She only told me all this because she's buzzed and I told her I'm new here."

Kai forgot all about the race and looked over at the strange woman. She was gripping the edge of the bar and swaying back and forth. Every time she looked up at the TV with the bikes racing past, she looked closer to throwing up.

"Look, she's pretty wasted, so I don't know if she's just talking trash. But from what I've been able to piece together, she works for a real estate investment company that buys underperforming properties, fixes them up and resells them. I just thought you should know."

Kai wondered if he'd had too many Rolling Rocks, because his brain wasn't putting things together. "But Nicole is a nurse."

Serena shrugged. "I don't know. It sounds nuts to me. Nicole is one of the nicest people I've met since I got here. Want me to try to find out more? I can't give her any more liquor, though. I'm trying to get her to eat some crackers, but she keeps asking if they're gluten-free."

"Does she know that Jake is a Rockwell?" Kai asked.

"I didn't tell her anything."

"Thanks, Serena," said Jake. "You get all my tips tonight."

They looked over at Felicity again. She was busy with her phone, apparently trying to text something. It wasn't going well. She dropped her phone into her almost empty cosmo glass, then fished it out, dripping, and grabbed a handful of bar napkins to blot it.

Kai and Jake shared a long, worried glance. "Some people probably shouldn't drink," Kai said.

"Yeah, and it would be good if those people were clearly labelled. I don't like serving alcohol to people who can't handle it.

She probably has no idea she just gave away her so-called secret mission. What should we do?"

"You should make sure she doesn't get into that Jag."

"Goes without saying. But about Nicole?"

Kai set his jaw. A cold sense of calm came over him. If what the woman said was true, then Nicole had been lying ever since she'd arrived at the lodge. She was a liar. A deceiver. If she was working for a real estate investment company, was she even really a nurse?

Stop. Of course she was a nurse. A nurse aide, to be exact, certified and everything. He'd seen her in action, he'd called the references on her resumé. But she wasn't *just* a nurse, apparently. She didn't care about the lodge. She didn't care about Max. She didn't care about *him.* She was doing a job, end of story.

No wonder she didn't want to "get involved." No wonder she didn't want to partner with him to run the lodge. She must have laughed her ass off when he made that offer.

A cheer went up throughout the pub. Amazingly, despite everything, Griffin had won the race.

Kai glanced at the TV screen just as Griff was unbuckling his helmet. Normally he'd be grinning like a fool after a hard-fought victory like that. But now the expression on his lean face was one of relief.

And maybe a touch of fear.

Jake was already on the phone leaving a message of congratulations for Griffin. Kai gestured to him. "Throw in a fist bump from me. Tell him I'll call him soon."

Then he pulled out his own phone and dialed the number of the woman he should never, ever have gotten involved with.

26

NICOLE HAD NEVER WATCHED A MOTOCROSS RACE BEFORE. HER EYES glazed over as she watched the motorcycles zip past the camera. It required more acrobatic skill than she'd thought, and also the apparent ability to defy gravity. She couldn't tell which one was Griffin, but somehow Max could. His body leaned from side to side as he tracked his second son's movements.

Even though Griffin was in the lead—according to Max's yells —his father wasn't happy with how the race was going. "Don't hold back," he kept shouting. "Attack the course! Attack! What's wrong with you, boy?"

Nicole bit her lip to hold back her smile. Would Max ever be completely happy with anything his children did?

At any rate, she was just biding her time until the race ended and she could do the thing she'd been putting off for so long. She had to tell Max the truth. Even if it meant she'd have to leave Rocky Peak, even if he cast her out in a fury— the way he had with Kai— she owed him the truth.

This was the perfect time, she'd decided. Both Gracie and Kai had gone into town to watch the race at the Last Chance. There would be no chance of being interrupted. Max deserved to hear this before anyone else because he'd hired her. He was her patient.

She'd already texted Felicity about her intentions, just to give her a heads-up. Then she'd ignored the stream of responses that came back. Nothing was going to change her mind at this point.

Finally the race was through. The crowd on the TV was going crazy, and there was Griffin taking off his helmet. He had the Rockwell looks, smoldering deep jade eyes and charm to spare. His hair was a darker than Kai's, nearly black. His face was leaner and more molded, not to mention very photogenic. She knew that he got lots of attention from women; Kai had told her that random women showed up at his hotel after every race.

But to her, Kai would always be more compelling in every way. He did something to her on a primal level—and had ever since the first moment she'd seen him.

And now she had to throw a big huge monkey wrench into that amazing connection between them.

"Max," she said. "I need to talk to you about something important."

Focused on the sportscaster sticking a microphone in Griffin's face, Max waved her off impatiently. "Ask him why he hesitated at the turn, moron," he muttered at the screen. "Ask him why he rode like an amateur."

She tried again. "Max—" Her cell phone buzzed.

Saved by the bell. She whooshed out a breath. This wasn't the right time for this conversation after all. She'd try again later, after the excitement over Griffin's victory had died down.

"Hey Kai," she answered, so filled with relief that she sounded extra happy. "Great race, huh?"

"You can cut the crap, Nurse Nicole." The cold anger in his voice sent a chill through her entire body.

"Excuse me?"

"The part where you care about my family, you can drop that."

She froze. "What—"

"There's someone you know here at the Last Chance."

"I know hardly anyone in Rocky Peak. I really haven't spent much time—" What was she even talking about? Her ears were buzzing, her stomach clenching.

"She's not from here. She's from Seattle. Here to check up on you, apparently. Looks like you been getting the job done, whatever the job is. It wasn't what we thought, that's for sure."

Felicity was here? But she hated the mountains. And she'd promised not to interfere.

The phone felt slippery. She clutched at it as if it were an anchor. But it wasn't—it was more like a bomb exploding in her hand. "Listen, Kai, I can explain everything."

"Oh, I'm looking forward to it. But first, put Max on the phone."

She walked away from Max, who was still yelling at the TV, and stepped into the hallway.

"No. I'm going to tell him myself. I was just about to, actually, when you called and—"

"Would you please stop lying? I don't need your bullshit. I want the truth. And I want to make sure my dad is safe."

"Of course he's safe!" Nicole felt tears spring to her eyes. She reached the reception area, with its vintage ski photos and "Welcome to Rocky Peak" sign over the desk. "He's watching all the interviews and grumbling at the questions. Why wouldn't he be safe?"

"Why would a nurse be working for an investment group?" That hard edge in his voice felt like a stab right through her heart; but it also brought out her fighting spirit.

"Do you know how much nurse aides get paid? Do you have any idea how screwed up our health care system is?"

"So it's all about the money."

"How dare you! You have all this...family around you, this incredible place, this history. I have no one except...never mind."

She closed her eyes, feeling everything shift under her, as if she were walking through quicksand, every step sinking her deeper. "Kai, I know how this sounds. But if you could just try to understand."

"So it really is true, then? I thought maybe your friend had it wrong. Or that she was talking about someone else. But it's all true."

Oh God, she could deal with his anger, but the hurt in his voice just about killed her.

In the background, she heard the sound of a door opening and the din of excited voices. Footfalls passed Kai, and someone said, "Helluva race, Rockwell."

"Thanks for watching, man," Kai answered. The door swung shut again and the background noise disappeared.

"Kai, are you still at the Last Chance? I'm going to drive down right now and tell you everything. I'll explain from the very beginning."

"You should explain it to Max first. He's the one you've been deceiving since day one."

"I've been *taking care* of Max, you jerk!" she cried. " Jesus, Kai, do you really think I want to hurt him? Or any of you?"

"I don't even know who you fucking are, Nicole. How should I know?"

"I'm the *same person*. Exactly the same person. There's just a few blank spaces I need to fill in, that's all. I'm heading into town right now." She ran toward the mudroom to grab her jacket.

"Why should I believe you? You've been deceiving me this whole time. Was I part of the plan too? Sleeping with me?"

"Kai!" His name came out as a sob. "Stop that. You know that's not true!"

She was in the mudroom now, pulling on her jacket. Her keys jingled in her pocket. "I'm getting in my car right now. Just stay where you are. I'll see you at the Last Chance."

Hands shaking, she ended the call. She had to get to the Last

Chance, not just to see Kai, but to intercept Felicity before she did any more damage.

But what about Max? Crap. She'd almost forgotten about him.

She ran back into the media room and discovered that Max had dozed off in front of the TV, as he sometimes did. He hated being woken up from a nap and had given her strict instructions never to do so.

Gently, she tucked a blanket around him and scrawled a quick note on a stray Rocky Peak brochure. *Zipped into town, be right back. Nicole.*

Once she was inside her Jetta, she took a few moments for some deep breathing to calm herself. It wasn't smart to drive upset. *One step at a time. Find Kai. Explain as best I can. Then take it from there.*

Her cell phone buzzed with a text. Felicity.

Surprise! I'm here. We should talk asap. There's a hottie bartender here. Know his name? Enquiring minds...

Nicole gritted her teeth. She couldn't deal with Felicity now. *That would be Jake Rockwell,* she texted back. *Well done.*

A string of emojis followed. Not the right moment to try to decipher tiny icons on a tiny screen. Felicity would have to wait.

Nicole shut off her phone and hit the road toward town. Coming from the city, the idea of driving down a road with no streetlights had stressed her out from the start. Add in the winding nature of the Rocky Peak road, and the way the thickly wooded forests seemed to crowd in from both sides, and she could understand why Max never wanted to drive into town. Especially at night. Especially on a moonless night like this one.

She switched to the high beams, which cast light farther ahead, so she could see where she was going. With the new angle of the headlights, she saw that a light mist hung in the air. It almost looked like snow. She shivered with anticipation. Would she get a taste of a Rocky Peak snowfall before she got booted back to Seattle?

Of course not. She'd be booted out of here in no time once they all knew the truth. What would become of her in Seattle? When she got back, she'd face exactly the same problems as before—and worse. Birdie had no roommate. Nicole would have no job. What if the Rockwells decided to get the word out that "Nurse Nicole" wasn't exactly what she seemed? Would she be able to get another home health aide job? One that paid enough to keep Birdie where she was?

Her stupid decision to come to Rocky Peak had made things a million times worse.

"Idiot." She hit the dashboard with her fist. "Sorry, car. It's not you, it's me. This is all my fault."

If only she'd thought this through a little better. That was her problem. She jumped into things without factoring everything in. She should have known she'd get attached to the Rockwells. She should have known it would feel terrible to deceive someone. And the fact that she was doing it for Birdie was no excuse. Birdie wouldn't want her to go against her principles like that. Birdie wouldn't want her to live with this kind of guilt.

Well, maybe she would if it meant she could stay with her friends. Birdie didn't think "big picture." She thought only of the present moment.

But that was why Nicole had to do the thinking for both of them. And she was doing such a terrible job at it, she ought to be fired.

She smiled at the thought of Birdie firing her. That was the thing about a sister like Birdie. Birdie would never stop loving her. She could screw up to the extent of making them both homeless—with Nicole pushing her wheelchair down Pike Street—and Birdie would still love her completely and unconditionally.

Which was why she'd do anything in the world for her. Even sell out her morals and work for a sleazy real estate company.

But she couldn't expect Kai to understand that. She'd potentially hurt *his* family to protect her own. He had every right to hate her.

She'd brought this on herself, and this pain in her heart...this horrible shattered ache...was the price she had to pay. Because even if Kai hated her now, she still loved him. Every tempestuous, challenging, fascinating, exciting inch of him.

Another car came toward her and she switched to the low beams out of courtesy. Was it Kai, racing up the mountain to confront her? She peered at the car as it passed. It was a Camry-like vehicle, definitely not Kai.

As soon as it passed, she put the high beams back on—just in time, too. She'd nearly missed the next curve coming up. She adjusted quickly, yanking the wheel back to the right. Her tires slid sideways on the road, and she realized too late that the mist had turned to a frozen sleet-rain that was coating the road.

She swung the wheel back to compensate, realized she was going too fast, and automatically touched her foot to the brakes. *No. Wrong move.* She knew it a split second after she did it, and yanked her foot off the brake. But it was too late and now the car was skidding across the slippery road, like a bucking bronco with a mind of its own.

She tried to turn the wheel but nothing she did had any effect on the direction of the car. Her Jetta was going wherever it wanted to go. And that was right off the side of the road toward a gap between two trees.

The car sideswiped one tree, then bounced off the other, like some kind of demented pinball game. Nicole knew this was bad —she was going off the road! That was bad!—but she didn't feel fear. Instead it felt as if some force much bigger than her was taking charge. It was taking her on a wild ride, worse than any rollercoaster, and all she could do was hang on.

Then everything came to a sudden, jarring stop. The car

jolted to one side and she was flung forward. The seat belt cut into her ribs and her head hit the door frame of her little Jetta.

Ow, she wanted to cry. *That hurt.* But she was saying it into the void, to nothing and no one, because the entire world was engulfed in silence and darkness.

27

GOD, HE WAS A DUMBASS. NICOLE HAD SOUNDED GENUINELY UPSET —even anguished—on the phone. And he'd believed her. He'd *wanted* to believe her. So where was she?

Alone at the bar of the Last Chance, Kai checked his phone for the hundredth time in the past hour. He didn't want to send her a text while she was driving, but maybe there was a reasonable explanation for why she wasn't here yet.

Unless—something else was going on. Now that she was busted, maybe she'd taken the opportunity to slip away. Maybe that whole spiel about wanting to explain in person was designed to throw him off.

Because she *knew* how much he still wanted to believe in her. That was what people like Nicole did. They played with their victims' emotions. Like this alternating fury and hurt that kept rampaging through his heart.

And then the occasional whisper...had he been too hard on her? Had he reacted too harshly?

"Planning on spending the night?" Jake asked. He'd left Kai in charge of the pub while he escorted Felicity back to her hotel— the most expensive in town, naturally. Now he was back, wiping off the bar that Kai had already cleaned—but apparently not to Jake's satisfaction.

"Just wondering why I'm such a fuckhead."

"Hey. That's my big brother you're insulting there." Jake reached over the bar and squeezed his shoulder. "Falling for someone doesn't make you a fuckhead."

"Falling for a con woman sure does. I never should have bought that sweet and innocent act."

"Shouldn't you wait and hear what she has to say?"

"That's what I'm doing. That's what I *thought* I was doing. Apparently I'm just hanging out like a fuckhead while she gets the hell out of dodge."

"What?" Jake took a tray of beer bottles to the sink to rinse them out. "You think Nicole's skipping town? I don't believe it."

"Why not?"

"Because...I just don't." He shrugged. Kai generally trusted Jake's intuition about people. Either it came from being a bartender or it helped him be a great bartender—or both. "She wouldn't just disappear without a word. Would she, Gracie?"

"Who?" Gracie slid onto the stool next to Kai and leaned her head on his shoulder with a yawn. "Why are dates so exhausting?"

"Because romance is dead," said Kai gloomily. "If it ever existed."

"Gracie, what do you think? You've known Nicole the longest. Would she disappear without saying goodbye?"

"Of course not. She would at the very least say goodbye to *me*. She still has one of my sketchbooks. That's a sacred trust, everyone knows that." She tilted her head up to look at Kai. "Did you make her mad again? I hate to say this, but you have a way of making people mad even if you didn't intend to."

An uneasy thought occurred to Kai. "How many times has Nicole driven the mountain road?"

"She runs errands for Max all the time," said Gracie, a worried frown pulling her eyebrows together. "Why?"

"What about at night? She never goes out at night, does she?"

"She doesn't come here, I can tell you that. And this is the best pub in town," Jake added modestly.

"Why are you asking all this?" Gracie asked.

Suddenly it all went terribly clear, like the lights coming on at closing time. "I have to go."

His siblings followed him out the door, Jake leaving a mess behind—something he never did. Jake insisted on driving his rig, which had more powerful headlights than Kai's truck, as well as a tow hitch, chains and other tools that might be handy. As a volunteer firefighter, he had all the necessary gear.

Gracie slid into the backseat. "Remember how Mom used to call me 'bright eyes' because I was the best at finding lost things? You need me."

Kai didn't bother to say he didn't need them. Having taken part in hundreds of rescues, he knew how much teamwork helped. Usually the teams consisted of other trained paramedics or firefighters, but Jake was solid and he knew better than to count Gracie out. She had skills that could surprise you.

They drove up the Rocky Peak road in a silence so complete they could hear the freezing mist needling the truck. Such a dark night—why had he allowed Nicole to drive in? Why had he come down so hard on her? Why hadn't he simply driven home and confronted her there? He'd driven that road a million times, sometimes more buzzed than was smart. But he *knew* the road, every curve, every tree. Nicole didn't. And it was dark. And she was probably upset.

Unless she wasn't, and she actually *had* skipped town without telling anyone. In which case he was dragging his brother and sister up the mountain on a wild goose chase.

"Mom wanted to leave Dad," he said abruptly as they rolled up the dark road. "I was trying to stop her the night she died."

Jake glanced at him only briefly, then went back to scanning the woods for signs of a car. "She left him once before. Remember when she went to her 'high school reunion?' Yeah. Not a reunion."

"*What?*"

"Izzy and I figured it out. We played detective and called the hotel where it was being held and they said there was no reunion going on."

Kai drew in a deep breath. "Holy shit. So you knew they had problems?"

"Yeah. But we didn't tell anyone because she came back. I guess things got rough again. Sorry, man. That sucks that you were in the middle of it that night."

From the back seat, Gracie put her hand on his shoulder. "Geez. Poor Mom. Poor Dad. Poor Kai. Why didn't you ever tell us?"

"What was the point? She was dead. I wanted you all to have happy memories of Mom. She was—" He broke off. "She was Mom. Always ready to laugh, always up for something fun."

"Of course she was Mom! This doesn't change anything," Gracie cried. Something in Kai's chest loosened, a tight band of worry that he hadn't realized he'd been holding. He'd loved his mother so much, and didn't want anyone thinking badly of her.

"Did Dad know?" Jake asked as he peered at the dark road ahead.

"He did. He was afraid it was even worse, maybe suicide."

"Jeepers." Gracie went quiet.

"I'm sorry. Maybe I shouldn't have told you even now." Kai dragged a hand through his hair.

"No, man. She's our mother too. You don't have to protect us," said Jake softly. "I'm not even surprised, like I said. They were so different, like...earth and air."

"I totally agree." Gracie rested her hand on his shoulder again with a gentle touch. "I want to know everything about her, even the sad stuff. Sometimes she doesn't seem real in my mind. Like a forest fairy. Do you know I used to build fairy houses in the woods hoping she'd come to visit?"

Her wistful tone made Kai's throat close up. At least he had sixteen years' worth of memories of his mother. All kinds of memories—enough to know she was a real person, flaws and all.

He stared out the window, seeing silent trees standing guard along the road, but no little red Jetta.

"She told me she would have left years ago if not for us. Especially you, Gracie, because you were so young. I kept saying that you needed her, that we all did, but she didn't want to hear that. I tried everything I could think of to make her stay, but none of it worked. Maybe if you'd been there, Jake. You always know what to say to people."

"Fuck that, Kai." Jake's forceful tone felt like a slap on the jaw. "Stop blaming yourself. Mom wanted to leave. That's not your fault."

"You definitely shouldn't blame yourself," said Gracie softly. "Mom wouldn't want that, would she?"

"I shouldn't have argued with her. I got her even more upset. And then she lost control—"

"*Kai. It wasn't your fucking fault.*" Kai and Gracie both startled. Jake was usually so soft-spoken, so easygoing. Hearing him swear was a shock.

"What are you talking about?"

"Remember how I told you me and Izzy liked to play detective? We did it after the accident too, after Dad kicked you out. We remembered how you said you saw someone in the road. Well, we found out there was a crew of frat boys staying at the Majestic playing this fucked-up game where they stepped into the road to scare drivers."

"*What?*"

"It was some kind of initiation rite for their fraternity. The police never arrested anyone, but they got reports about it. It's not really proof of anything, but it's a theory."

Rage seared through Kai, and suddenly everything outside the car window looked red, even the frozen mist. "Fuckers," he ground out. "Mom died because of some stupid game?"

"Maybe. I don't know. I'm just saying, stop blaming yourself..."

Jake's voice faded away as those last moments in the car with Mom came back to him in a rush.

Tears on her cheeks, hands clenched around the steering wheel.

"Do you know why I'm not worried about you kids? Because you love each other. You look out for each other. And that, Kai, that is my greatest legacy." And then, "Who is that?"

And then the world spun and the trees came at them like an avenging army.

Back to here and now. Trees. Red. *He'd seen red.*

"Stop the truck, Jake. Now!"

Jake screeched his truck to a halt and Kai jumped out to the scent of rubber burning on the asphalt. He sprinted back down the road, the surface slick under his boots. Even with his thick treads, he nearly skidded a few times. Nicole had no experience driving in these kinds of conditions. She should never have been on the road. He should have—

Stop blaming yourself.

The words came crystal clear into his head, but not spoken in Jake's voice, the way they had been a few moments ago. They were spoken in Mom's voice.

Gracie was right. Mom would never want him to torment himself the way he had been. She would want him to have a life —a good life. A life he could be happy with, the way she struggled to do.

Red. Right there, in the gully past the shoulder. He ran that direction, playing his flashlight over the trees and moss-covered stumps and rocks. Yes, there it was. A red car. Nicole's Jetta, on its side, wedged between two tall spruce trees that seemed to be holding it tight, keeping it from harm.

"Found her!" he called back to Jake and Gracie. Jake was slowly backing his rig down the road. Kai saw his own footsteps in the thickening layer of sleet, but no tire tracks. They'd already been completely covered. If he hadn't spotted that flash of red...

No time to think about that. He switched into rescue mode—calm, controlled, logical.

With the flashlight gripped between his teeth, he thrashed his way through the underbrush, cutting a path to the downward side of the Jetta. Until he knew how unstable its position was, he didn't want anyone else coming close.

Headlights slashed through the darkness. Jake—parking the truck so he could light up the area.

"Stay back for now," he called to Jake and Gracie, who were getting out of the truck. "Let me check it out first. But go ahead and call the fire department."

Holding his breath, heart racing, he peered into the Jetta. Of all the rescues he'd performed, none had involved someone he loved. He had to stay focused. Take note of the details of the situation. Assess her condition as if he weren't dying inside at the thought of her being hurt.

Still strapped into the driver's seat, she sat slumped on her side. Eyes closed—that wasn't good. Getting knocked unconscious could mean brain damage, concussion, bleeding...

Stop that. He played the flashlight over the interior, saw broken glass, the contents of Nicole's purse spilled everywhere. *Check the gas line.* If the tank or the fuel line had been damaged, the car could explode. He ran around to the undercarriage and searched for signs of moisture leaking. Sniffed for gas. Maybe smelled some, maybe didn't. Hard to tell. If there was a leak, it was small, but any leak could spell danger.

He had to get Nicole out of there. *Now.*

28

A VOICE WAS CALLING HER NAME IN THE DARKNESS. A VOICE SHE loved, even though she couldn't pin down who it belonged to, or even what it was saying. She didn't recognize the name it was calling, but she knew it was hers.

And she knew she wanted to follow that voice.

It was warm and male, filled with worry, resonant with hope, vibrant with urgency.

"*Nicole.* Can you hear me?"

Everything snapped into focus. The voice belonged to Kai. She was in her car, which she'd driven off the road. And she *hurt.*

"Kai," she said weakly. "Hey you."

"Hey yourself." His voice softened. "We need to get you out of here. Can you move your fingers and toes?"

She frowned. "What does that matter?" Everything was so strange. Her head was sideways, or tilted or something. It was so confusing. She could hear Kai but couldn't tell where he was. A light kept shining in her eyes.

"Just humor me. Try."

She wiggled her toes, feeling them brush against the inside of her shoes. Then her fingers. The knuckles of her right hand felt as if she'd tried to punch out a brick wall. "Hurts, but they wiggle."

"Good." She heard relief in his voice, and realized things must be really bad. Ridiculous that it took so long to understand that. Her brain was moving so sluggishly. One minute she'd been rehearsing what she wanted to say to Kai, the next she'd been swerving and sliding and...

She started to cry. "I'm sorry, Kai. I'm so sorry. I didn't want to hurt anyone. I just wanted to take care of Birdie."

"Shhhh. We'll talk about that later, love. Can you unbuckle your seat belt?"

He'd called her "love."

"You called me 'love.'"

"That's right. You heard me. Did you also hear the part about unbuckling your seat belt?"

"Oh. Right." With her right hand, she reached for the latch. Her left arm seemed to be pinned beneath her. The buckle sprang open easily, which made her feel much better. Powerful. "Got it."

"Okay good. Now I want you to cover your face with your arm. I have to finish breaking this windshield, though you already made a good start of that. It's tempered glass, so it shouldn't shatter. But just in case, keep your face completely covered. Got it, love?"

"You said it again," she said from behind the crook of her elbow.

"Keep covered." In the darkness, she heard a series of weird sounds—glass breaking, a thud, a curse. A blast of chilly air rushed into the car.

Then Kai was back. "Okay, I got an escape route for you. I just need you to lean toward me and I'll do the rest."

She leaned forward, toward Kai, toward that voice that she loved with all her heart. His hands came through the window, along with part of his torso, squeezing past the metal frame and shards of glass. And then his hands were under her arms. With a strength that took her breath away, he lifted her free.

After that, everything became a jumble of disconnected images, like a crazy film reel that had gotten scrambled up. One of her legs wasn't working right and that scared the crap out of her. How was she going to survive? How was she going to take care of Birdie? Maybe the two of them would be in wheelchairs for the rest of their lives. That could be fun, like bumper cars ....

Don't laugh. It hurts. Hold on to Kai. Why is Kai here? Isn't he mad?

Jake and Gracie scrambled down the ravine to help Kai carry her up. Did they know how she'd betrayed them? She had to tell them, right now.

"Something...tell you..."

"Shhh." Kai shushed her in a firm voice no sane rescue victim would disobey. "Save your energy."

"But—"

"Just this once, sweetheart. Please." Now his voice softened to a tenderness that no woman in love could deny. She fell quiet and let him take charge.

She heard his labored breathing as he carried her through the underbrush. Jake and Gracie helped as much as they could by sweeping away all obstructions and supporting him up the steepest parts. All this effort—shouldn't they know the truth?

But it probably didn't matter. Jake was a volunteer fireman and Gracie was such a kind soul. Birdie would love both of them...too bad she'd never get to meet them...

She imagined Birdie pushing her in a wheelchair around the lodge, through the rose garden, down the trails. Cruising into the kitchen to steal a snack from Renata...scolding Max when he got too rude... Wait, that was backwards. She was the one who pushed Birdie, not the other way around...

She snapped back to attention when they reached the road and found a group of firemen and two yellow fire engines with their lights flashing. "Is there a fire?" she asked, completely confused.

"They're here for you, honey," Kai said in her ear. The rumble of his voice held amusement, but also worry. "You were in an accident, remember?"

"I'll take her," said another firm voice. "She probably has a concussion."

"Her leg is bothering her too," said Kai. "Possible fracture. Disoriented, confused, rapid pulse."

"We'll airlift her to Regional."

Regional. That was a hospital. She'd heard people mention it. Everything was moving so fast, and no one was thinking about Birdie. And the pain was swamping her. It felt huge and relentless, like a dragon opening its vast jaws.

She grabbed Kai's arm. "Not Regional. Seattle. Birdie."

"What, sweetie?"

Oh no! He hadn't heard her, she had to try again. She opened her mouth but this time she couldn't get any sound to come out at all. The dragon had arrived and was consuming her whole.

WHEN SHE WOKE UP, Birdie was staring at her from her wheelchair like a cat waiting to pounce.

"Nico!" She clapped her hands together when their eyes met. "You woke up!"

"Birdie." She feasted her eyes on her sister for a moment. Birdie liked to wear as many hair clips as possible; today about ten of them were scattered throughout her fine cornsilk hair. She wore her favorite sweatshirt—red with a cardinal perched on a baseball bat. She loved it for the bird; the bat meant nothing to her.

Nicole glanced around the unfamiliar hospital room. The

usual monitors, antiseptic smell, and bland color palette. "How did you get here?"

"Kai brought me," she said proudly. "He asked if I wanted to, and I said yes."

She stared at her sister in astonishment. "*Kai*? Do you...how do you know Kai?"

"He came to me, to my room. My own room. Lulu's gone. She won't talk to me."

"I'm sorry, sweetie."

Birdie shrugged cheerfully. "It's okay. I saw a pigeon out the window."

"Wow, that's so cool." Gently, she steered the conversation back to Kai. "But what about Kai?"

"Kai." She lit up again. "He's so nice. A lot nicer than stupid Roger. He said you got in a car accident. He got spe-special permission for me to come here. We got in a car and drove all the way here."

Her brain was still operating at maybe half its usual speed, but still, it raced to the obvious conclusion. "Is Kai here?"

"No. He went home."

The disappointment felt like a punch in the stomach. "Where are we, Birdie? Is this Seattle?"

Birdie's feather-light eyebrows drew together. "I love Seattle."

"I know you do." Nicole smiled tenderly at her sister. "I'm really happy you came here to see me."

"Kai says I can see where he lives sometime."

"Really?" Nicole's heart lifted again. Did that mean she and Kai might see each other again? Was that possible?

"Oh, whoops. Here." Birdie reached into the pocket of her jacket and pulled out an envelope. "It's from Kai. He trusted me to remember and I did," she said proudly.

"That's really great." Wincing, Nicole leaned forward to take the envelope from her. It had her name written on the front in Kai's bold swooping handwriting. "I'll read it later."

Just in case it made her cry.

She tucked it under her pillow. "If Kai left, who's going to take you home, Birdie?"

"That would be me." Felicity strolled into the room, dark sunglasses on top of her head, cup of coffee in hand.

"What are you—" Nicole struggled to sit up, then surrendered at the first stab of pain.

"Bruised spleen," Felicity explained as she came closer. "Also, fractured tibia. You'll be on crutches for a while, but they're just going to let the spleen heal on its own."

"You went to Rocky Peak. You—"

"I drank too much and let the cat out of the bag. I think it was my guilty conscience talking."

Nicole looked over at Birdie, who had wheeled her chair over to the window to watch the pigeon. "I didn't think you had one anymore."

"I didn't either. But I'll tell you something. Visiting Birdie twice a week made me slow down and think about things. And then this happened." Felicity sat down on the foot of the hospital bed and gestured at Nicole's cast.

Her cast.

Finally it sank in that she was seriously injured. She felt tears gather at the back of her eyes. Kai had saved her life even though she'd deceived him. He'd taken her to this hospital, located Birdie and brought her here. Then left. He must despise her.

"I'm sorry for everything, Nico." Felicity had dark shadows under her eyes and wore no makeup. Quite honestly, she looked terrible. "I pushed it too far. I got carried away with the whole partnership dream and it blew up in my face."

"What happened?"

"It's over. I went to see Max after your accident. I presented our proposal. He blew his top at first, threw a few things. Broke some kind of vintage snowshoe. Then he told me to get off his property."

Nicole cringed, easily imagining his fury. "He must hate me so much now. I was about to tell him everything, you know."

"He doesn't hate you. He's worried about you. He said—and I quote—" She flipped through the notes on her phone. "I actually wrote it down so I could get it exactly right." She read aloud. "Nicole's got a good heart. Besides, ain't none of us angels. Me especially. Tell her to get her skinny butt back here asap."

Her eyes filled with tears. "Oh Max. He's such a big grouch, but then he says something amazing."

"Yeah well, not to me. No sale. I lost my potential partnership. So I quit. I'll find another firm, I'm not worried. Oh, and I sold my Jaguar."

"Oh no! Sorry, Felicity. That sucks." She probably sounded insincere, because her first thought was that maybe the old Felicity would come back now.

Her friend was shaking her head. "I sold it for you, Nico. For you and Birdie. It's partly my fault you're in this situation."

"You mean, unemployed, injured and unable to work?"

Cringing, Felicity nodded.

"Yeah, it kind of is. You manipulated me. You know that Birdie is my soft spot and you totally took advantage of that."

"I know." Felicity screwed up her face in abject apology. "I'm sorry."

"No job is worth doing that to someone, especially a friend."

"You're right. A hundred percent right. Wait, you said 'friend.' Does that mean we're still friends? I did sell my Jag—"

Nicole flung up her hand. "*However,* I made that choice, so you're right, it's only *partly* your fault. And I will never, ever do that again. Want to know why?" Her tone made it crystal clear that Felicity had no choice but to listen.

"Why?"

"Because hurting someone else to get what you want sucks."

"Sucks!" Birdie echoed gleefully as she wheeled herself back over to them. "It sucks!"

Nicole laughed at her sister's fondness for strong words. "Besides, in some ways I have to thank you, Felicity. I now know that I'm an epically crappy spy, a pretty good home health aide, and an outstanding idea person. I'll figure out something for me and Birdie. Right, Birdie?"

"Right!"

"Amen to that." Felicity leaned forward to give them both a high-five. "I'm a hundred percent behind you both." She adjusted the sunglasses on her head, which had flopped forward. "And at least you won't starve. That Jag was practically brand new. It's a big chunk of change for you guys."

"Thank you, that's...really nice," Nicole said. She wished she could say no to that offer, but she had to be realistic.

She yawned so widely her eyes teared up. "I should sleep."

"Yeah. I'll take Birdie back to the hotel." Felicity got up and took hold of Birdie's wheelchair.

"The hotel? Where are we?" She looked out the window, but could only see an overcast sky.

"Mount Vernon. Skagit Valley Hospital. Birdie and I are staying at the hotel next door until they release you."

Her jaw dropped. "You drove with Kai all the way from Seattle, Birdie?"

"Yes! Road trips are so fun!"

Dumbfounded, Nicole looked over at Felicity.

"I helped, but it was his idea," her friend explained. "After they Medevaced you here, he came and got me at that sweet little Inn in Rocky Peak. He told me what happened, and how worried you were about Birdie. I was all hungover, God, I felt like crap. But we both flew to Seattle and worked it out with Sunny Grove. Birdie liked Kai right away and wanted to come see you. So I flew back here and Kai and Birdie drove."

Wow. This was all so...earthshaking she could barely grasp it. Kai and Birdie on a road trip. Kai's incredible thoughtfulness. Felicity's turnaround.

"Kai waited as long as he could, by the way." Felicity steered the chair toward the exit. "Good guy, and super-hot, for a mountain man. He said the lodge needed him and he had to get back."

"Yeah. It's okay." The lodge *did* need him. She was one hundred percent sure of that. With him in charge, maybe Rocky Peak had a chance of getting back on its feet.

From the doorway, Birdie looked back and gave her an incandescent smile. "Get better, Nico! I love you!"

"I love you too, Birdie. See you soon."

As soon as they left, she allowed the tears to stream down her face. She wasn't completely sure where they came from. Trauma from the accident. Release of the tension from months of deception. Missing Kai.

Loving Kai.

She pulled the envelope from under her pillow and opened it.

DEAR NICOLE,

I'm sorry I wasn't here when you woke up. I had to get back home. There's so much to say, I'm not sure where to start. The moment I met Birdie, I understood why you did what you did. I hold no hard feelings over it. I wish you'd told me, but then I wish a lot of things. Mostly, I wish we could start again. I wish we were back in that hunter's lodge together. Back in that "box" you made for us. But that's not how things work, is it?

I want to say more, so much more, but the most important thing is for you to heal. Please focus on that. We'll talk soon.

Love, Kai.

THERE IT WAS. That word again, love. She remembered that he'd called her that while he was extracting her from the car. But it didn't mean anything, did it? Because he'd left her with nothing but a letter.

He has a lodge to save, she told herself. *His hands are full. And I'm not there to help.*

Feeling lower than she ever had in her life, she tucked the letter back in its envelope. Even if Max forgave her, even if Kai held no hard feelings, she hadn't forgiven herself yet.

There was only one way she could accomplish that.

29

KAI CALLED A FAMILY MEETING A FEW DAYS AFTER HE GOT BACK TO Rocky Peak. Griffin and Isabelle participated via Skype, while the rest of them sat around the round glass-topped table in the solarium, Mom's favorite spot.

They'd stopped using it after her death, but now, it felt right.

"An offer is on the table from the Summit Group," Kai told them. "They want to purchase the lodge and all the surrounding land. It's a substantial offer. Max and I have talked about it, and decided everyone should get a chance to chime in before we give a final answer."

"I thought Max rejected the offer," said Gracie. "It was that woman from the bar who made it, right? Felicity Chin?"

"He did reject it. But then he thought about it again."

"I'll be dead, so it won't matter much to me," Max rumbled. "You kids'll be the one stuck with it. I decided you all should have your say. I'm keeping my opinion to myself, for once."

"Wow, Dad, how's that working out for you? Tough to pull off?" Isabelle teased. In the video feed from the desert, she looked tan and windblown.

"Hell yes. It's unnatural."

"He screams into a pillow at night. I hear him." Kai put a hand on his father's shoulder and squeezed affectionately.

The two of them had bonded even more lately because they both missed Nicole. Without her, the place felt empty. No wildflowers in the guest rooms. No one easing the way for new arrivals. No one helping Renata in the kitchen. No one keeping Max's spirits up. No one smiling brightly over the coffee urn, or showing up at his door in nothing but a parka.

Okay, that last one was just on Kai's end. Max probably had his own memories.

"So, anyone have any thoughts about this offer? Have you looked at the email I sent? It's very generous, to say the least. We'd all be rich, unless Dad keeps it all to himself." Kai slanted a grin at his father.

"I take what I need, divide up the rest," Max said. "I already decided."

Isabelle spoke up. "Do we have any idea what they want to do with the lodge?"

"Nope. They won't say. They're an investment company, so they could turn around and resell it, or tear it down and build something else. There's no way to know."

"What about the wildlife and so forth? Protecting the land?" Griffin was Skyping by way of his phone, and he appeared to be flat on his back on a hammock somewhere. Kai still hadn't had a chance to talk to him about the race, and whether something was wrong. He looked fine now, sipping from a large tumbler as he rocked in the hammock. Occasionally a bikini-clad woman flitted in and out of the background.

"They won't make any commitments other than to follow all laws and local ordinances." Kai tried to keep his voice as neutral as possible so as not to affect the others' opinion. But that part really set him on edge. Did the Summit Group have something in mind that they weren't revealing, or were they just leaving their options open?

"And who are these people? Do we know anything about them?" Griffin asked.

"Jake got to know Felicity a little bit. She was the driving force behind the offer."

"She doesn't work there anymore," Jake corrected. "But based on what I've seen and picked up, it's a very competitive and cutthroat company. Speaking as a Rocky Peak business owner, probably not the best neighbors."

"So you're a 'no'?" Kai asked him.

"I want to see what everyone else says first," said Jake. "But I'm leaning toward no."

"But what would we do with it if we don't sell it?" Isabelle asked. "Who's going to run it? How's it going to make money? Aren't we practically broke?"

Kai cleared his throat. "For what it's worth, I'm going to stay and do what I can. I have some savings. I'll sell my place in Colorado. That should be enough to keep us afloat through the winter."

"*What?*" Gracie, who'd been quiet up until now, jumped to her feet. "Why didn't you say that earlier?"

"Because I don't want it to affect your opinion. You might want a big chunk of cash to go explore the world or something. That's perfectly fair. Just because I'm willing to stay here and give it a shot doesn't mean *you* have to. We can all decide right now to let it go. We need to be real about this."

The seriousness of his tone made everyone fall quiet. Then Griffin said softly, "I have money. Too much money. You can have that too. And maybe...yeah, maybe I'll come back for a while. Just to give you a hand, Kai."

Max made a choking sound that might have been joy. Or crabbiness. Hard to tell. He banged his cane on the floor. "Is that a 'no sale' from you, Griffin?"

"Yeah, I guess it is. I don't really need the money. If any of you wants to sell, I can buy out your share. I'd rather lose money than lose our legacy."

Kai's eyebrows lifted in amazement. Griffin really had that much money? He sure kept that fact under wraps. "Okay, let's hear it. Who wants to sell?"

They were all quiet.

"Who wants to see if we can make this lodge profitable again?"

"But how would we do that, Kai?" On the screen, Isabelle held her hair back from her face as a desert wind whipped at her. "Do you have some brilliant idea to turn things around?"

He grinned. "Have you ever heard of raindrop therapy?"

ALL JOKING ASIDE, the first order of business was getting ready for winter. The roof of the fire station outpost needed repairing or it might collapse under the snow load. Kai used his own funds for that.

A colony of squirrels had built an entire community in the insulation of one of their best guesthouses. That took another chunk of his savings.

The more he worked over the next week or so, the more problems he encountered. If only he'd focused on the lodge structure itself when he first got back, instead of working on the trails. He'd done it that way so he and Max didn't blow up at each other too soon.

They should have just gotten it out of the way and moved on. Now time was running out fast.

Funny how time worked. He'd known Nicole for barely two months. In that time, everything had changed. He was home where he belonged. He was back on good terms with his father. Back in his beloved Rocky Peak.

But now there was a big hole in his life where Nicole used

to be.

He called her several times, but gotten no answer. She must be busy with physical therapy or hanging out with Birdie.

Or trying to find a new job.

Felicity had explained everything to him on their flight to LA. Nicole's "spy mission." How she'd talked Nicole into it by dangling a huge "bonus for Birdie" before her. It all made sense. But a residue of hurt still lingered as he'd written that letter to her.

Had he screwed up that letter? Was that why Nicole didn't answer his calls? He should have poured out his heart instead. *I love you. I don't care about the silly spy mission. Please come back. I need you.*

But getting up at dawn and working until late at night left him no chance to track her down. As he worked, he rewrote that stupid letter a thousand times in his head.

I'm sorry I thought the worst. I'm sorry I didn't give you a chance to clear things up. I'm sorry I let you drive that road while you were upset. I'm sorry I didn't tell you that I love you as soon as I figured it out.

Two weeks after the accident, he called another family meeting with Max and Gracie. They gathered around the big stone fireplace in the lounge, where he'd built a crackling fire to take the chill off. It made him think of Nicole, and the first time he'd seen her.

Then again, most things made him think of Nicole.

"I don't want to call in the others yet," he told them. "We have some big financial decisions to make, and I know Griffin will just want to hand over all his money. Jake's swamped at the bar right now and Izzy's traveling."

Max tapped his cane against the stone hearth. "What's on your mind, son?"

"I've been replacing the insulation in one of the suites. I found three layers of moldy wallpaper and the sheetrock was soaked through. I decided to check a few other suites, and it's bad."

"How bad? Health department bad?" asked Max.

"I never liked that cheesy wallpaper," said Gracie. "I think we should redo all of it."

"That's exactly what I'm wondering. We've been limping along at such a low occupancy rate. Maybe we ought to shut down for the winter and do some major renovations."

"Major," repeated Max. "How major?"

"Is that code for unbelievably expensive?" Gracie asked.

"Probably. I haven't looked into it yet. But yeah, we can count on a hefty bill."

Max shook ashes off the tip of his cane. "Well. I leave it to you, Kai. What do you think?"

"Me?"

"Yeah, you. You got the big picture. You'll make the right call." He sat back as if his part was done.

Kai glanced at Gracie, who shot him an irrepressible smile. "Big responsibility, huh? Are you up for it?" she teased.

"You know I've saved dozens of people from certain death, right?"

She made a talking gesture with her hand. "Blah blah blah. What's rescue work compared to renovations?"

He laughed wryly. "You might have a point there." He wiped his hands on his thighs. Maybe he was a little nervous about making a decision like this. "Okay then. I think we should go forward with a major overhaul. I think we have to. It's long overdue and this is the perfect time to do it, when we have so few guests. I'll get some quotes right away. We'll probably have to take out a line of credit on the lodge, or lean on Griff, or some combination."

"There's no need for that."

Kai's head jerked up at the sound of Nicole's voice. She stood in the doorway, exactly where he'd first laid eyes on her, except now she was on crutches. She beamed a wide smile at the three of them.

He lurched to his feet. "What are you doing here? How'd you get here? Did you drive? Are you crazy? You shouldn't be driving yet. You're supposed to be resting and rehabbing and—" He was already at her side, wrapping an arm around her. He hadn't known he could move that fast. "You should sit down. What the hell were you thinking, Nicole?"

"I was thinking that I had a brilliant idea that I needed to share with you all immediately. And that I missed you. And that I wanted to apologize in person." Her glance landed on Max. "Especially to you, Max."

"Pffft." He waved her off. "We all make mistakes. This one ain't fatal, so let's be happy about that. Welcome back, kid."

She crutched across the room to Max and dropped a kiss on his cheek. Which was more than she'd given Kai, he noticed.

Still propped on her crutches, Nicole beckoned to him. Her eyes were shining with excitement. She looked different—her hair was shorter, framing her heart-shaped face in pretty waves.

There was something else, and it took a moment for him to pinpoint it. She looked carefree. No longer wary and cautious, but free.

"Are you guys ready for my idea?"

Gracie held up her iPhone to record the moment. "Totally ready."

Feeling as grumpy as the old Max, Kai folded his arms across his chest. "Is this another of your wacko treatments? Snowflake therapy or some shit like that? Because we have some basic infrastructure needs that come first."

"I get it. Believe me, I know all the problems, all the soft spots. That was my job, remember?" She twisted her face in apology. "I figured I might as well use all that knowledge I gained for good. I can help you, Kai. We can fix everything that needs it, and more. Because..." She drew in a long breath. "I found an investor."

30

No one said anything, which sent Nicole into a fit of nerves. *Keep talking.*

"When I was in the hospital, I started thinking about how I could make up for my really poor decision-making and then it came to me. A silent investor who loves the wilderness! And then I remembered someone I met through my ex-fiancé who fit that description exactly. He's a wilderness fanatic and a billionaire. I met with him and told him all about the lodge. He agrees that between the fire station and all the wilderness maintenance we do here, that the best thing is for the lodge to stay in Rockwell hands. He wants to be a silent partner, nothing more. He won't interfere, except maybe to visit now and then and ski the black diamond run. Well, what do you think?"

Nicole hoped all of her words had come out in the right order, but she really couldn't be sure. Just getting here had taken so much effort and planning, not to mention the work that had gone into securing an investor. And now she was face to face with the combined charisma of the Rockwells, especially the one she was madly in love with.

She held her breath as she looked around at this family that had come to mean so much to her. Would they accept this "apology"? She felt a little like a cat who had captured a mouse and was laying it at their feet. *Will you accept this investor who I worked so hard to bring on board?*

Stealing a glance at Kai, she wondered what he was thinking right now. They hadn't spoken since he'd rescued her from her car. His letter was so vague. She didn't really know what it meant. But she did know that she was a grown woman who'd made the choice to come here under false pretenses. Now all she wanted was to make up for that.

Kai cleared his throat. "You said 'we.'"

"Excuse me?"

"You said 'all the maintenance we do here.' We."

"Oh. Right." She turned pink at that slip of the tongue. Probably not a good idea to broadcast her attachment to the lodge like that. "I misspoke. I meant 'you,' of course. You Rockwells."

"Well, I think it's a perfectly fine way to put it," Gracie declared. "You found an investor, you should stay here and help us. He probably expects you to be part of it, right?"

Nicole shook her head. "No, no, I made clear that it's your family, your lodge. I've done enough damage already."

"What damage?" Max snorted, then blew his nose in his big handkerchief. "The only damage you did is to poor Kai here. He hasn't been the same since you left. Moping around here like a teenager."

Kai shook his head at his father. "Give it up, Dad. When are you going to stop trying to get under my skin?"

"Next lifetime, maybe. If you're lucky."

He gave a wry laugh and stepped toward Nicole. "Can I talk to you for a minute in private?"

Unable to read his expression, she nodded. A lump formed in her throat. She'd read his letter a hundred times. She'd listened to the messages he'd left. She'd almost called him back a few times, but hung up before completing the calls. What was there to say until she'd fixed this?

Since then she'd been completely focused on righting the wrong she'd committed.

Well, that, and trying to figure out her next move. The money from Roger's ring was almost gone. Rumor had it one of the nurse practitioners at Sunny Grove was leaving. Nicole had already submitted her resumé. On the plus side, she'd see a lot of Birdie. On the down side, the pay was barely enough to cover expenses.

Kai put a hand on her lower back as she crutched her way out of the lounge. All the deer heads were gone, she noticed. In the three weeks that she'd been away, the temperature had dropped about twenty degrees. Kai wore a thick black sweater and thick fleece workout pants and looked as drop-dead sexy as ever.

"You never called me back," he said as they reached the reception area. "Why?"

She wetted her lips. "I...had a lot to figure out. I'm sorry."

He shook his head impatiently, shoving his hands in his pockets. "Enough with the sorry's. This is you and me. Tell me the truth, Nicole. I came back here to deal with Dad, thinking I'd talk to you soon. Then, poof."

"I'm here now. With the *best* news, at least I think it is."

He leaned one hip against the front desk, brushing against a bobblehead bear which immediately began jiggling away. "You didn't want to get involved when you were here. Is that the problem? Regrets? Second thoughts?"

"No! Nothing like that. I just...Kai, I was embarrassed. I came here as a real estate spy before. I couldn't come back until I fixed it."

"That's what the investor is all about? Fixing it?"

"Yes. You should accept his offer. He's a good person and we can make sure the contract completely protects you."

"This isn't about some contract." His jaw flexed, his eyes smoldered deep green. His muscles tightened under his black sweater. Every cell of her body wanted to sway toward him.

"What do you mean?"

"Jesus, Nicole. That's business. I don't want to talk about business. Give me a chance here!"

"A chance to what?" She blinked at him in confusion.

"A chance to..." He scrubbed a hand through his hair. "Shit. To tell you—" he burst out. "Damn it, Nicole. I left you that letter. You never answered."

"I thought you still hated me. It was so..." She couldn't come up with the right word. "Restrained? Like you were trying not to be mad?"

"Ah, shit. Forget the letter. I wasn't mad, except at myself for being such an ass to you that night. I know you, I know your heart, I know how much you care about Max and how kind you are and that you must have had a damn good reason for everything. But instead I had to go off like a jackass and—"

Stunning her to her core, he dropped to one knee on the floor in front of her. "Nicole, I love you. I want to be with you. I want to take care of you, I want to stand by you, I want to be your partner in every possible way. I want to do wild and crazy things with you. I want to hear every quirky idea you ever had about anything. I want to marry you, if you'll have me."

A funny sound came from her mouth. She was pretty sure it was a sob. "You do?"

"I do. All of that. And more."

Her head was spinning. Kai was always unpredictable, but this? "Please stand up. I can't follow you down there because my leg's in a cast. It's not fair."

Cautiously, he rose to his feet. "I recognize that look. What's wrong, love?"

"I can't," she burst out. "I can't leave Birdie."

He leaned toward her and cupped her face in his hands, the love burning in his gaze enough to make her faint.

"Of course not. You don't have to leave Birdie. I have a whole master plan here. I got to know her pretty well on our road trip. I know she likes the place where she's living, but I think Rocky Peak can win her over. First we'll bring her here for a visit. We show her the snow in winter. Set her up with a wheelchair-friendly toboggan, if she wants."

"She's never even seen snow."

"I bet she'd love a good snowball fight."

Nicole drew in a long breath. She'd never really allowed herself to dream about bringing Birdie here. She imagined her zipping up and down the rabbit warren of corridors, laughing with joy. "She would," she whispered. "She really would. But are you sure you want that? Roger—Roger couldn't handle her living with us."

"Roger didn't deserve either of you. And hey, if the snow isn't enough to convince her, there's always art therapy."

Another sob escaped her. "Kai, be serious about this. You really want us to be part of your family after...after everything?"

"Yes." His firm answer left no room for doubt.

"People will think you're crazy."

"You know me. Always the rebel." He smiled down at her and tilted her chin toward him. "I want you. I love you. Every wonderful, imaginative, occasionally imperfect inch." Tears stung her eyes. "The thing is, you fit perfectly with *my* imperfect inches."

That made her laugh. "I hate to break this to you, but your inches are nothing but perfection."

"Then how can you say no?"

Still, she hesitated. This was such a huge change, it felt as if she were careening down the highway with no guardrails and only a blurry glimpse of the road ahead. If she made the wrong move, took the wrong path, she wouldn't be the only one affected. Birdie would be too.

"Oh, I almost forgot," Kai said. He shifted so he could dig into his pocket. "I found this the other day, when I was going through Mom's things. I've been carrying it around ever since." He opened his palm, revealing a lovely, delicate filigree ring with an aquamarine stone the color of a sunlit sea. "She always loved this. It made her think of the ocean."

"The ocean. You mean, 'Kai,'" she said softly, touching the ring with wonder. It was so beautiful. The most beautiful jewel she'd ever seen. "It made her think of 'kai.'"

"I want you to have it, so you'll think of me. Hopefully in an engaged kind of way, but we can sort out the details later. I'm not going anywhere." He slid the ring onto her middle finger. The one right next to the ring finger, which somehow felt about right.

Almost engaged. When-she-was-ready-for-it engaged. Once-she'd-gotten-used-to-the-idea engaged. Her heart swelled at his thoughtfulness. Kai was a rebel in so many ways, but this was one of the best. He was absolutely willing to defer to her feelings.

"I love you, Kai," she said softly. "I love you so much. I have for so long, but I thought we didn't have a chance. I kept thinking that I could cure myself from it, but it just never happened."

His gaze intensified, those soul-deep green eyes capturing hers. "Good. Some things don't need a cure, Nurse Nicole. Some things are meant to be." He dipped his head to hers, kissing her with such depth and passion that the room spun around her.

A shudder of desire passed through her. Now that she was out of the hospital and off painkillers, she'd started to miss him physically. After all those glorious nights in his bed, her body yearned for him.

"I don't think I can make it all the way to my old room," she managed through the kisses he was peppering onto her neck.

"And my guesthouse is too damn far away."

"Plus you're supposed to be in a family meeting right now."

"I am. You're my family." That simple statement sent a river of joy coursing through her. He reached the base of her neck and drew her collar away with his teeth. "Besides, you just changed everything. A silent investor, that's big. I predict that before long every single one of us Rockwells will be back home, trying to pull this thing out."

"Pull what thing out?" she teased, sliding her hand along his upper thigh. The hard muscles tensed and flexed under her palm. "This thing, maybe?"

"Don't tempt me. Shit, Nicole. Anyone could walk in here. Guest, family member, staff."

"You said 'staff.'" She gave him her sassy face.

He groaned at her terrible double-entendre. "Wait, I have an idea. First, you need to stop looking at me like that for the next two minutes, until I can get us somewhere private."

He pushed her crutches out of the way and bent down to scoop her into his arms. She clung to his shoulders as he strode out of the reception area and down a crooked hallway she'd never explored. "Where are we going?"

"The only place I can think of that's guaranteed to be private." When he reached a door labelled "storeroom," he lowered her down so she could turn the knob. Then he whisked her inside.

For one astonished moment, she gazed at the room in silence. Then she burst out laughing, while Kai cursed under his breath. "I forgot we put these in here," he muttered as the two of them surveyed the collection of plastic deer heads stuffed into the room, jumbled every which way.

"I can't kiss you with Bambi staring at me," she said.

"Not Bambi. Benji." Kai put her down next to an antique desk to give her something to hold on to. Then he grabbed an old patchwork quilt and draped it over the deer. "Better?"

She contemplated it for a moment. "I'm still going to know they're there, but they are plastic, so I guess it's like kissing in front of...lawn ornaments or something."

"Exactly." He picked her up again and made his way through the jumble of vintage lodge detritus—a magnificent antique grandfather clock, old ice cream signs, broken ski goggles, antique apple boxes, so many intriguing items she couldn't wait to sort through. In the corner sat an old daybed covered with a crocheted blanket. He gently set her onto the bed. "How's your leg feeling?"

"My leg is feeling turned on, just like the rest of me."

"That's what I was hoping." He grinned and sat next to her, wrapping an arm around her.

She nestled against his side. "My leg also wants you to take your shirt off."

"Really? You speak fluent leg?"

"No, but it's a safe assumption."

He sat up and tugged his sweater over his back. She touched his warm skin, his rippling stomach, with a feeling like coming home. "In case you're still waiting for an answer, it's a yes. I would love to be married to you, Kai. I'd stopped thinking about a husband, you know. I was always too caught up with what to do about Birdie."

"And now?" He eased her back so he could brace himself over her and slid a warm hand under her shirt.

"Now I know *you*. And you make me do crazy things like make love in storerooms with plastic deer spying on us. Getting married seems sane compared to that."

His leg nudged between hers, offering gentle pressure through her clothes. She sighed and stretched sensuously as her nerve endings sizzled.

"I can't promise sane," he said. "It's not really my thing. But I can promise that I'll give you everything I have. All my heart, all my love, my body, my soul. My family. Everything I am and everything I will be."

The intensity of those words brought tears to her eyes. "Oh Kai. I promise that too," she whispered. "Everything I am, everything I will be."

The moment felt almost sacred as they sealed that promise with a kiss she felt all the way to her soul.

"With these plastic deer as our witnesses, so be it," Kai murmured against her lips.

And there they went, laughing again, until passion took over and they sealed things once and for all, body and soul.

31

AFTER MUCH DISCUSSION AND ARGUING AND JOKES ABOUT THE NEW investor being the only silent person connected to the lodge, the Rockwells said 'yes' to the offer.

Birdie said 'yes' to a visit—actually, she more or less shrieked it. Kai was completely confident that eventually she would want to move to Rocky Peak.

Since Nicole had already said 'yes' to everything—the lodge, Kai, the Rockwell family—he was happier than he'd imagined possible just a few months ago.

After all the "yesses" had been established, Kai drove Nicole down to the spot where she'd driven off the road. She examined the tire tracks she'd left, the trampled spot in the brush, the tall trees that she had somehow, incredibly, managed to miss.

"This isn't close to where you and your mother crashed, is it?" she asked softly. The treetops swayed and she tightened her jacket against the bite of the wind. It held the taste of autumn, which made him think about nights cuddled with Nicole in a cozy bed while the snow piled up in the forests and valleys. It had been too long since he'd experienced a Rocky Peak winter, and he loved the idea of showing her how magical it could be.

"No, not really. That happened further up the mountain. They installed a guardrail at that curve. No one thought this one would be a problem." He lifted an eyebrow at her.

"Yeah, well, that's me, making trouble wherever I go." She gave him that impish smile that he loved so much.

"Not that kind of trouble, not ever again," he said firmly. "I'm going to make sure of it."

"How are you going to do that?"

"I know a professional who volunteered to teach you in his spare time."

She swung around to stare at him. "*Griffin*?"

"Griffin." He nodded in satisfaction. "He's coming home. He'll be back any day now. The man can drive anything with wheels. He grew up driving this road and I trust him with my life." He pulled her close so she leaned against him, giving her a chance to rest from the crutches. "Which is what you are now. You're my life. I hope you're okay with that."

Her eyes sparkled like starlight. "You say the sweetest things, Kai Rockwell. How do you manage it, when you look so rough and wild?"

"I'm a man in love, that's how."

He held her hand as she leaned against him. A feeling of extreme satisfaction settled through him, something he hadn't felt since Mom died. As if things were finally in their right alignment. He was home, in all senses of the word. That restlessness that had nipped at his heels all this time was gone.

Peace. That was the feeling.

The peace wasn't only for him...it was also for his mother. *She* was at peace, he could feel it. Maybe now her spirit could fly away toward what it longed for the most, the ocean, the home of her heart.

"Ready to go?" he asked Nicole.

She nodded and rested her head against his shoulder. With

one last lingering look at the forest that had nearly claimed her, he took her crutches and tossed them into the car. Gently, he helped her into the passenger seat.

Together, so filled with happiness that they needed no more words, they drove back up the mountain, home to Rocky Peak.

EPILOGUE

GRIFFIN

"Excuse me. Hi. Hello?" The husky female voice brought Griffin to immediate attention. How long had the waitress been talking to him? And how had he missed her, with that dark red hair and tiny diamond in her nose? Unusual look for a casual pub like the Last Chance in a tiny town like Rocky Peak.

"Sorry. I'll have a beer."

"I think you maybe want to narrow it down a little?" She swept her hand to indicate the wide array of options lined up on the shelf behind the bar. It was his brother's bar, but Jake was in the back, apparently, and this unhappy waitress was stuck with him instead.

"Whatever has the highest profit margin," he told her.

She gave him a look that had him scratching his head. Something was missing from that look. What was it? Oh yeah. *Interest*. He'd been semi-famous enough, for long enough, that he saw it in most women he met.

Not this one.

"Do I look like an accountant? I mean, I could be. I'm great at math, which is why I know that you've been taking up a stool for at least eight dollars worth of drinking time, if it was beer, and fifteen if it was the hard stuff. But I'm not an accountant. I'm just a waitress, standing in front of a customer, asking what kind of beer he wants."

Cute. A *Notting Hill* reference. Come to think of it, he did get a bit of a Julia Roberts vibe from her. Not from the *Pretty Woman* era, but more like *Erin Brockovich*, with that attitude.

"I really don't care. In fact, screw the beer. Just bring me a glass of water."

"Care to know the profit margin of water?" she asked dryly as she stuck a pencil behind her ear.

He pulled out a fifty dollar bill and set it on the counter. "Make it nice and cold. Good old Rocky Peak well water, if you can manage it." He flashed his dimple at her, the one that always did the trick when his almost-celebrity didn't.

Not with her.

"Fifty dollars for a glass of water?" She sniffed in disapproval. "You're either trying to show off, or you're really bad at managing your money."

"I thought you weren't an accountant," he shot back.

Finally, finally, he got an unwilling smile from her—just enough to make him want to see the real deal. "Alrighty then. One glass of our finest Rocky Peak well water, drawn from the depths of a mountain aquifer, half a degree warmer than a glacier, coming up. We keep the good stuff in the back. You don't want it running through the soda fountain. Be right back."

He watched her go, appreciating everything about her—full figure, sassy walk, that red hair. What was a bombshell like her doing in a tiny mountain town like this? Had she been here all along? Nah, that was impossible. He would have noticed someone like her working in his brother's bar.

"Griff. Griff!"

Damn, it had happened again. It kept happening. Sounds, missing. That was why he needed to be here, not on a race course. "Jakey."

He stood up and hugged his brother hard. He saw Jake pretty often, but this was different. He was home and he was planning to stay, at least for a while.

"Great to see you, man," said his younger brother. "You were on my TV the last time I saw you. Nice race."

"Thanks." That race was nothing but a nightmare memory to him. "Any chance Kai's around? I gotta meet this girl of his."

"He's up at the lodge, but she's more than just his girl, dude. They're planning a damn wedding."

"Shit. That was quick."

"Not really. Not when you see them. They're about as perfect as it gets. What can I get you?"

"Oh, the waitress—"

"Nope. Anything but her."

"What?"

His brother's eyes had gone hard with warning. "Just saying. None of your usual roguish charm around Serena."

"Serena? That's her name?" He didn't pick up much "serenity" from her, to be honest.

"So she says."

Okay, this was definitely getting interesting. Was there more to the waitress's story? He shook it off, since sassy redheads weren't part of his agenda here.

"I'm not here to scam on your waitresses, Jake. Don't you worry your pretty head." He ruffled his brother's hair, which he could get away with—barely—since he'd been doing it all his life. At thirty, he was two years older than the twins, Jake and Isabelle. He'd always envied them their closeness, even though Isabelle was flitting around the world about as fast he rode around a race course.

Jake let out a tired sigh and sat down on the stool next to him. It was past closing, at least two in the morning, and he realized he was an ass for keeping that poor waitress up so long. He'd never had a good sense of time, except for the micro-seconds measured around a course.

"Why are you back, Griff? You just won a big-time race. Shouldn't you be out there racking up more wins?"

Griffin hesitated. He'd planned to tell everyone at once. But of all the members of his family, Jake was the best when it came to listening. So maybe this was the perfect moment to drop his bombshell. "I'm quitting."

"Quitting what?"

"Racing."

"*What*?"

Jake was so shocked that he reared back on the stool, not realizing that Serena had stepped next to him with a tumbler filled with water. Everything happened in slow motion after that, the way it did sometimes during a sweet ride. The glass arced through the air. Water cascaded onto Serena's white blouse. Griffin reached out one casual hand and snagged the tumbler out of the air. He even managed to catch some of the water inside it.

As the other two stared, he took a sip. "Ah, now that's what I'm talking about. Sweet Rocky Peak nectar of the gods."

Serena looked at Jake in utter confusion as she brushed water off her blouse. "Serena, this is my brother Griffin," he said. "He, uh, has very quick reflexes."

From her suddenly wary expression, she'd heard all about Griffin Rockwell, playboy motocross racer. And wanted nothing to do with him. "Here's your change," she said, handing him back the fifty.

He took it and left it on the bar. "For your dry cleaning."

"We don't have a dry cleaners in Rocky Peak."

"Then this will cover the gas to get to a dry cleaners. Jesus, is she always like this?" He turned to Jake, who was getting that "stay away from my waitress" look again.

"She's right here," said Serena, "and she can confirm that yes, she's always like this. Keep your money, big spender. It's a glass of

water." She glanced at Jake. "Am I done, boss? I need to change."
She shivered as she unstuck the wet fabric from her skin.

"Yup, I got it from here. Sorry to drench you like that."

She turned on her heel without so much as another frown in
Griffin's direction. His fifty dollar bill sat on the counter, and
suddenly he was acutely embarrassed by it. She was right; he had
been showing off.

"You know, things went much better with the ladies back
when I was a pro racer," he said lightly.

"I've heard the stories. I'm sure Serena has too. Don't worry,
you'll have no trouble. You're the biggest almost-celeb we have
around here. The girls will be ten thick at the bar. So are you
going to tell me what's going on or what?"

Griffin nodded slowly, his thoughts still with Serena the waitress and how very unimpressed she was with him. "Yeah, but let's
wait until everyone's together. You coming up to the lodge in the
next couple of days?"

"Wasn't planning on it, but now I will. I want to see Kai's face
when he sees you. Did he know you were coming?"

"*I* didn't even know. I got the itch and hit the road."

"Same old Griff, huh?"

Griffin didn't say anything, because the answer to that was a
big fat "no." He wasn't the same old Griff, and he never would
be again.

Out of the corner of his eye, he caught a glimpse of Serena,
now in jeans and a thick red wool jacket, slipping out the front
door into a swirl of early snow.

He definitely wasn't the same old Griff, because that guy
would have already moved on. But this guy—the Griffin Rockwell
of right now, wounded, retired, and scared shitless—wasn't going
anywhere.

He needed to be home. He knew that much. What he didn't
know was if "home" could handle his return—and everything
that was about to come with it.

He shrugged on his jacket, waved goodbye to Jake, and headed into the night.

THE ROCKWELL LEGACY continues with THE ROGUE, coming this fall.

THANK you so much for reading! Want to be the first to hear about new books, sales, and exclusive giveaways? Join Jennifer's mailing list and receive a free story as a welcome gift.

ABOUT THE AUTHOR

Jennifer Bernard is a *USA Today* bestselling author of contemporary romance. Her books have been called "an irresistible reading experience" full of "quick wit and sizzling love scenes." A graduate of Harvard and former news promo producer, she left big city life in Los Angeles for true love in Alaska, where she now lives with her husband and stepdaughters. She still hasn't adjusted to the cold, so most often she can be found cuddling with her laptop and a cup of tea. No stranger to book success, she also writes erotic novellas under a naughty secret name that she's happy to share with the curious. You can learn more about Jennifer and her books at JenniferBernard.net. Make sure to sign up for her newsletter for new releases, fresh exclusive content, sales alerts and giveaways.

Connect with Jennifer online:
JenniferBernard.net
Jen@JenniferBernard.net

ALSO BY JENNIFER BERNARD

Jupiter Point ~ Firefighters

Set the Night on Fire ~ Book 1

Burn So Bright ~ Book 2

Into the Flames ~ Book 3

Setting Off Sparks ~ Book 4

Jupiter Point ~ The Knight Brothers

Hot Pursuit ~ Book 5

Coming In Hot ~ Book 6

Hot and Bothered ~ Book 7

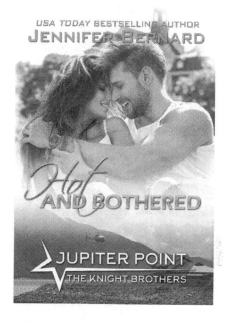

Too Hot to Handle ~ Book 8

One Hot Night ~ Book 9

Seeing Stars ~ Series Prequel

The Bachelor Firemen of San Gabriel

The Fireman Who Loved Me

Hot for Fireman

Sex and the Single Fireman

How to Tame a Wild Fireman

Four Weddings and a Fireman

The Night Belongs to Fireman

Novellas

One Fine Fireman

Desperately Seeking Fireman

It's a Wonderful Fireman

Love Between the Bases

All of Me

Caught By You

Getting Wound Up (crossover with Sapphire Falls)

Drive You Wild

Crushing It

Double Play

Novellas

Finding Chris Evans

Forgetting Jack Cooper